The Malevolent

by

P.F. Roquelaure

The Malevolent

Cover Art by *Teddi Black*

The Wild Rose Press, Inc.
PO Box 708
Adams Basin, NY 14410-0708
Visit us at www.thewildrosepress.com

Publishing History
First Edition, 2025
Trade Paperback ISBN 978-1-5092-6156-7
Digital ISBN 978-1-5092-6157-4

Previously Published 2021 LuLu.com
Published in the United States of America

Dedication

To all the masters of modern horror I watched on television as a wee lad often from behind a chair or couch.

Prologue

Antioch
June 22, 1919

A lightning bolt illuminates the sky, followed by the rumbling of distant thunder. It casts a momentary brightness over the stone pavement that borders the back porch of a great Victorian mansion. The storm is passing. A furious rain pelts the uneven flagstones, forming rivulets that flow into shallow puddles. The rain dilutes a larger pool of red, washing it away in thin streams between the stones. The red liquid spills from torn pale white flesh. Pinkish matter oozes from the fissure, revealing gleaming cracked bone. The grotesque display of anatomy is the crushed forehead of a human being. The being's longish blond hair is draped across the deep jagged laceration and the undamaged left half of the forehead and face. The bluish white eyes stare at nothing, bulging above prominent cheekbones. Blood trickles from the corners of pale, thin lips. The nose is long and thin, blood seeps out of the left nostril. The face is beautiful, without any visible wrinkles. The long pale neck is at an unnatural angle with the rest of the body.

The person is naked, lying on its right side with the left arm crossing its chest and lying on the stone pavement. The fingers are curled into the flagstone. The rain bounces off the flesh of the well-muscled, flat abdomen in small eruptions. The pale gray phallus lying flaccid against the pelvis and blond pubic hair indicates the deceased is male. His long muscular thighs and legs are folded together, his knees symmetrically bent. A long gash protrudes from his knee to the ankle, blood no longer pouring from the wound. His feet rest on the pavement and the toes of his left foot curl into the flagstones like the fingers. His body is becoming more rigid as rigor mortis sets in. Lightning flashes provide glimpses of the naked, broken, beautiful man who was strikingly handsome when he was alive. An angelic-looking creature that has fallen to the earth from the sky.

When will he be discovered?

Or has he been discovered, and the authorities are on their way to investigate what has happened?

Or has he been discovered and…?

Chapter 1

Antioch
Spring 1983

The first time I saw Antioch was in the spring of 1983. My mother, Mary Griffin Meade, purchased Antioch in an auction at Sotheby's in Boston in April. My mother restores old houses as a job or hobby, depending on which way you look at it. She has a degree in art restoration/history from an Ivy (by the way, I don't name drop, but suffice it to say, it is thoroughly "Preppy") and she produces coffee table books from her projects.

But first, before I go any further, let me introduce myself: my name is Griffin Andrew Meade. Her job as a restoration specialist requires thorough research in order to restore the buildings to the original state they were built; every cornice, wallpaper choice, or lighting fixture is exact (either an original or replica) or it isn't complete. She prefers the Victorian and Gothic era of architecture and furnishings, and that is why Antioch was an obvious choice for her.

Antioch is the ancestral home of the Bartholomew family in the town of Bartholomew Bay, Maine, located 50 miles north of Portland on the Maine coastline. The title Antioch refers to the ancient Greek city that is considered "the cradle of Christianity," and the term

"Christian" first emerged in Antioch.

The Victorian-style mansion was built in the late 1800s and sits on a hill that overlooks the coastal town. The house was built with many Victorian architectural features, including pitched and gabled rooflines, turrets on either side of the main structure, balconies, and a prominent widow's walk on the third floor with the most magnificent view of the bay and the ocean. The widow's walk was especially relevant to the Bartholomew family as they controlled the shipping industry in the bay from the mid-1800s to the 1940s, around the time that the United States sent the Navy to fight in WWII.

Chapter 2

Griffin Andrew Meade and family
June 1, 1983

Most people call me "Griff." I know, it sounds like a stock character in a John Hughes teen rom-com, but I'm sure my parents had no clue that using last names used as first names would be so trendy in the '80s.

I'm the first-born son of Mary Griffin Meade and Jackson Meade, and I have a younger brother, Jackson Jr. (Jack). My father is a professor of anatomy at the local university medical school. Although most people call me Griff, my mother calls me Andy, as her maiden name was Griffin, and she has always felt strange calling me by her former last name. She had to name me Griffin because of a family tradition. She often refers to me as G. Andy Meade for social engagements involving the Griffin family.

My mother was born to the Griffin (Gryphon, the original English spelling) family, an independently wealthy family that's a legitimate member of the New England aristocracy. Specifically, we can trace our roots to the first citizens of Salem and Boston. Had she become one of the society matrons of the Boston upper crust, she never would have had to work a day in her life, but my mother has more mettle than that.

I'm currently eighteen. I'm just over six feet tall

and have what is referred to as a "swimmer's build," long legs and arms, and a V-shaped torso which suits me because I swim competitively. I've been told that I fill out a Speedo nicely. I also have large/long feet that my mother calls my flippers, a natural advantage that helps with my specialty, the backstroke.

A group of pink plaid-wearing girls in Boston called me *Griffer*, a combination of *Griff* and *Surfer* because I have that Southern California look, which is ironic, as I've never been on the left coast. I have sandy blond hair that I like to wear just above my shoulders, which can be pulled back into a decent tail when it's hot.

My eyebrows are a light brown, and my beard is reddish blond. I was told that the blond hair and the dark eyebrows are genetic traits that can be traced back to Scandinavian/Northern European origins, and the red beard is indicative of Celtic/Scottish origin. A make-up artist once told me during a musical that my natural color combination would never be believable if it was done on purpose for a show. I'm interested in pursuing theater in college if that wasn't obvious. I have light cornflower blue eyes. Despite my Nordic origins, my skin retains a light tan shade all year long but darkens to a light brown during the summer months. I've been told that I look like a more rugged Shaun Cassidy—I guess it's the hair. My mom says that I look like Tab Hunter, a dude who did a lot of surfer and war movies in the 1950s.

On the surface, I look and act like a typical American kid. But I have a secret. I like dudes. I'm a dude who likes dudes. Ever since I can remember, I've liked boys more than girls. Girls make great friends.

But when you stare at the handsome fit dude in a Hawaiian Tropic commercial, ignoring the banging chick in a bikini next to him slathering lotion over her breasts, you know something is up! I've never told anyone and only acted upon my sexual orientation once.

Last fall, I messed around with another guy who had one of the leads in the musical *South Pacific* at my school in Boston. We were at a cast party at his house, drunk and stoned, and started to mess around in the hot tub when everyone left. I liked it, but it also freaked me out, and haven't done anything with another guy since that night. By the way, he's the one who said that I look good in a Speedo.

It's also not the greatest time for a young guy to be gay, because of Human Immuno-Deficiency virus (HIV) and Acquired Immune Deficiency Syndrome (AIDS). I met some gay guys in Boston who said that it was spreading fast in the gay community, especially in big cities. It's basically a death sentence if you catch the virus. They say rubbers will prevent you from catching it, but they're not 100% effective at keeping girls from getting pregnant, so how can that be true? HIV and AIDS are the only reasons why I'm glad that we moved from Boston. There'll be no temptation to go to a gay bar or cruise, fucking around in public parks, or have sex with an infected guy. What are the chances of catching it in a small town like Bartholomew Bay, Maine?

We moved to this bum fuck town in my senior year. Bart's Bay, that is what the locals call it, is an all right little town, a "charming hamlet" as the tourist board describes it, but uprooting me from my friends and school in the last year of high school was pretty lame. I was given the chance to stay in Boston with other Griffins, but I chose to come here with my family. I like my family. Weird for a guy my age to say that, but it's true. They're chill. Especially, my mom. Let me tell you about Mary and the rest of my family.

Mary Griffin Meade is tall for a woman, five foot eleven inches; and it is from the Griffin side of the family that I get my height. She has long auburn hair, with feathered bangs that frame her oval-shaped face. She has high cheekbones, a strong jawline, and a small dimple in her chin. She has almond-shaped light blue eyes, and full reddish-brown eyelashes and eyebrows. Her nose is long and thin, a regal nose as it was described in one of her book reviews, and her lips are full, especially the lower one. She's smart, "wicked smot" as they say up here. She's also generous with her time and resources to her family, to her profession, and to her causes. She's especially concerned about the environment: greenhouse gases and the pollution from fossil fuels' effect on the ozone layer—one of her main causes. We have been participating in protests about the environment since I was a kid. Which you can imagine goes over so well with the business-oriented Griffins. In her words, restoration of old historical structures not only preserves history but also recycles parts of history so that they don't wind up being destroyed or in a landfill. Sustainability is a word that she uses that I've never heard anyone else use before. My mother's a very special person.

My dad, Jackson Robert Meade, is shorter than my mom and has a stocky build like a football player, which he played through college. He's a handsome man: a full head of blond hair, which he keeps short, a square jaw, light blue eyes, and masculine facial features.

He met Mom in college. He had an academic scholarship to that Ivy, as they don't give athletic scholarships, but the Ivy's football coach knew he was a gifted player in high school. He pursued a Ph.D. at another Ivy in medically related research, and now teaches Gross Anatomy, which means "total anatomy" and not "nasty anatomy" (although cutting up dead people can be nasty), and Neuroscience and conducts research on Parkinson's Disease.

As I stated earlier, Jackson was on scholarship. The Meade family is your typical middle-class WASP family from the mid-Atlantic region of the United States, and by no means had the same kind of money or privileges that the Griffins enjoyed. They're hard-working, intelligent people who tend to be in service-oriented lines of work, like teachers and civil servants.

Jackson Robert Meade Jr., or Jack, is one year younger than me and looks a lot like my dad. In fact, relatives and friends have referred to Jack as a miniature version of Jackson Sr. He isn't that small anymore as he has inherited my mom's height and my dad's build. He likes contact sports like my dad; he has already contacted Bart's Bay high school about football tryouts in August. He'll be a junior this year, but I'm sure he'll make the varsity team as he hits like a Mack truck like Dad did when he played on the defensive line in high school and college.

He's also interested in science, Human Biology, in particular. He works in Dad's lab with his research during the summer. I'm sure he will pursue some type of medically related field of study when he goes to college.

Obviously, we're very different, but we get along. I think it's our differences that keep us from being too competitive with each other. He comes to my plays, even the musicals, and swim meets, and I never miss one of my baby brother's football games. We have a similar bizarre sense of humor that our parents don't understand but accept. We can get really goofy with each other when we're confined in spaces for a long time, like a long car trip. We also listen to the same kind of music. We like New Wave bands, especially those coming from England.

So that is the Meade family in a nutshell.

Life will be different living in the *Munster's* house in Bart's Bay. A far cry from Boston. We'll just have to see how different.

Chapter 3

Antioch: Moving Day
June 1, 1983

The movers are not particularly buff dudes. Rather, your average middle-aged guys with middle-aged bods, so I didn't pay much attention to them as they carried our stuff from the moving truck. I grab a box labeled "Andy" off the truck and proceed through the massive front door of the house.

The open foyer of Antioch is one of the most impressive features of the mansion—three stories tall, encompassing the wide wooden grand staircase to the second floor situated on the left wall of the foyer. The foyer floor is covered in white marble tile with gray streaks that was imported from Rome. The foyer extends to the massive living room to the right, the library/sitting room on the left, and the dining room and kitchen in the rear of the house. There's also a small bathroom tucked underneath the stairwell of the first floor.

The staircase from the first floor dominates the entrance to the mansion. The intricate wooden banister to the right of the stairs blends into the railing in between the landing of the second floor and the rise of the stairwell to the third floor. The railing of the second-floor stairwell, situated to the right of the stairs

11

as well, makes a sharp right turn into the hallway that leads to the bedrooms and attic on the third floor. At the end of this hallway is another narrow staircase that leads to the roof and the widow's walk. These stairs rise to a single door that opens to a small rectangular-shaped balcony, which is surrounded by an iron guard rail with spikes at the end, that are about two feet high. Traditionally, the widow's walk is a place where the wife of a seaman would walk each evening at dusk and look out to the sea for her husband's ship. If the ship never came back, presumably, it had sunk, and all died aboard. The balcony then belonged to a widow, thus the name widow's walk.

Mom said I could have a room on any floor. Being a senior in high school, I thought that a bedroom on the first floor would make it much easier to get in late at night if I had to climb through a window, if the front door locked after curfew, or at least minimize the noise when I stumbled home. The bedroom with a connecting bathroom on the first floor is much smaller than the bedrooms on the second or third floors. It was most likely the servant's quarter, so I opt for a bedroom on the upper floors.

Climbing the massive staircase to the second floor with my box in hand, I search the possibilities. The hallway on the second floor is long with three sets of doors on each side, with each door framed inside the thick wood paneling that covers the walls of the hallway.

At the end of the hallway, there's a large window made of three vertical panels. Walking down the hallway to the window, I scrutinize the view of the backyard, which is spectacular. Tall grasses wave in the wind, stretching to the coastline and the bay beyond.

Standing there, admiring the view, the distinct sound of creaking wood echoes in the hallway. Reflexively, I turn my head toward the sound to investigate. The last door on the left, closest to where I'm standing, is slightly ajar. Realizing there's no one else on the second floor, I cautiously walk over to the door, push it inward using my foot, and enter the room. It is rather large, with the same thick wood paneling as the hallway, except it's only chair rail height.

A massive four-poster bed with curtains sits against the far wall, with a large dresser and a desk on either side. The ornate style of the bed matches the dresser, whereas the desk is much simpler in style. There's also a large wardrobe with two mirrored, beveled doors against the inside wall to the right of the bedroom door. I remember from Mom's past projects that most older houses didn't have built-in closets, so people relied on huge, free-standing wardrobes that came apart in several pieces for transport because when assembled they were too large to get through a typical bedroom door.

On the right side of the room, there is a set of French doors with sheer white curtains concealing glass panels illuminated by the bright morning sun. I put my box down on the bed and walk over to the French doors. Turning the iron handles of the doors with both hands, I pull them inward to reveal a balcony. The balcony is about six feet deep and twenty feet long, basically the width of the whole bedroom. A solid wall about four feet high with a white wooden railing surrounds the balcony. Looking out from the balcony, it is the same magnificent view that I saw at the window in the hallway.

Looking to the right, I can see the windowsill of the hallway window. Glancing down, I see the driveway and the garage to the left, and on the right, the left corner of the back porch. In between the edge of the porch and the garage is a pavement made of large, gray flagstone. While surveying this view, something suddenly touches me on the shoulder, and I quickly whip around. It's Mom.

"Whoa, did you get lost in the view? Amazing, isn't it?" she states as she lightly places her hand on my right shoulder, hugging me gently to her.

"Yeah, it's amazing. Can I have this room?" I ask hopefully.

"Really? It's the only bedroom on this floor that doesn't have a connecting bathroom. But it does have this…" she says as she quickly extends her hand toward the magnificent view. "Our room is the other bedroom with a balcony on this floor, facing the ocean and bay, so we would be across the hall. I'll check with your father to see if he had any plans for this room, but if he doesn't, then I don't see why not." She walks back into the bedroom from the balcony. "I'll ask the movers to move this stuff out of here and get your bedroom furniture."

"Oh, I'm actually okay with it. It's a bit over the top, but I kinda like it. It just needs to be dusted. The bed looks like the one in the Rocky Horror Picture Show, you know that scene—"

Mom interrupts. "Yes, I know what scene. I've seen it before! I'm not that square. You want curtains around your bed?" she says with an incredulous expression on her face, pulling the threadbare curtain hanging from the bed frame.

"No, that's where I draw the line…besides, they look like they're about to fall apart," I say, sitting on the bed and examining the curtains that hang from the sides and the roof of the footboard.

"All right, I'll leave you to your cleaning and your…Victorian bedroom. Only my son…" she mumbles, shaking her head back and forth, as she leaves the room.

I unpack my box: personal souvenirs, pictures of my family and friends, my alarm clock, and my sheets. From downstairs, I retrieve some cleaning supplies: a vacuum, furniture polish, window cleaner, paper towels and rags. First, I vacuum the floor. Then, I pull the protective cover off, and vacuum the top of the mattress. Finding the other side fine, I flip it back.

I'm about to polish the headboard when I notice the curtains again. Thinking I should remove them before dusting, I examine them to see their attachment. They are held in place by curtain rings looped around wooden rods inside the perimeter of the bed's frame. While studying how the curtain rings can come apart, I tug on the curtain of the footboard, and surprisingly, the fabric disintegrates, and the curtain easily rips from its rings. Noticing this much dry rot, I pull and rip all of them from their rings. They tumble to the floor in a cloud of dust.

As I gather the crumpled curtains from the floor, I notice that the one on the left side has slipped behind the massive ornate headboard. But the curtain isn't resting on the dusty floor but draped over something. Tossing it to the side, I reach into the space to see what was suspending the curtain. My hand touches a wooden, square shape that feels like a picture frame. Grasping it with my fingers, I pull the frame out from between the bed and the wall. The glass in the frame is so dusty that I can't see the image clearly. It's a picture, not a photograph, of a figure lying down, but that's all I can see. I spray the glass with the window cleaner and wipe it with a paper towel, which makes a noticeable difference.

The picture is a charcoal drawing of a young shirtless man, lying on a large rock with the Bartholomew Bay lighthouse and point in the background. I spray the plate glass again and the details of the portrait materialize. I study the young man. He has shoulder-length hair, as the charcoal pencil outlines the shape of his hair falling to his neck; but it isn't shaded, so I deduce he was blond. His head is turned toward the bay. His nose is long and thin, regal, and his chin is round with a strong jawline. He has high cheekbones, almond-shaped eyes, and a short forehead. His neck is long, attached to a strong set of shoulders. His chest is broad and well-developed, as are his arms, especially his biceps and delts. The deltoid muscle on his right side is accentuated, with his right arm propped up on another rock and bent at the elbow. Interestingly, the nipples and areola were drawn with detail, something that is often neglected in male figure drawings or paintings.

His abdomen is flat with the faint outline of musculature beneath a thin trail of hair that extends from his naval to the top of his trousers. There's also a faint line drawn from the top of his hip toward his groin, separating his thigh from his abdomen. I call these lines "the Davids," in reference to Michelangelo's sculpture of "David" in Florence, Italy. As for his lower extremity, he's wearing shorts cut below his knees, and his legs are folded together and lying along the smooth surface of the rock. His feet, bare and exposed. The background is composed of other large boulders to the right, and the coastline, the lighthouse, and the point to the left. He's incredibly handsome, stunningly handsome some would say, with an equally magnificent body that reminds me of the classical statues of the Greek gods.

"Hello, handsome," I utter aloud.

Suddenly, I hear exhaling air in my right ear. Reflexively, I turn my head, but nothing is there. Looking around the room to see if there's anything that could have made the strange sound, nothing is apparent. Nothing is there.

I look down at the charcoal drawing again. This time I notice the initials L.B. in the lower right corner of the picture. The artist's initials. Picking up the framed drawing, I place it on the dresser, leaning it against the wall.

After cleaning my new bedroom, polishing my new bedroom furniture, unpacking the rest of my treasures, and putting clean new sheets on the bed, I've worked up quite a sweat. Pulling off my V-neck t-shirt, I wipe the sweat off my face, neck, shoulders, and chest. As I lift my arms, I catch a whiff of my body odor. I definitely stink.

Mom's shouting from the first-floor stairwell, "Andy, we're ordering pizza from the village, and then Dad and Jack are going to pick it up. Do you want your usual: grilled chicken and mushroom? Do you want to go with them?"

"Yeah, that sounds great. But I'm going to take a shower, I stink."

"Thanks for the update," she responds sarcastically, her voice trailing as she walks away from the foyer toward the kitchen.

With that reprieve from going into town, I unbutton my khaki shorts and drop them to the floor. Grabbing a towel from one of my boxes, I tie it around my waist. Picking up the toiletries I had set out earlier, I head into the hallway, turn right, and step into the bathroom that Jack and I'll share. The bathroom is large and dominated by black and white tile on the floor and along the wall to chair rail height. The top of which is lined with solid black rectangular-shaped tile. A large white porcelain pedestal sink with silver taps and a silver faucet sits beneath a large mirror attached to the wall.

Water slowly trickles all over the sink once the tap is on. The immense white porcelain bathtub with its ball and claw feet dominates the room. Pulling the white opaque shower curtain back, I see a showerhead surrounded by the tiled wall, unusual for older houses as most strictly relied on bathtubs for bathing. I turn the handles and adjust the water to an acceptable water temperature.

Letting the towel fall to the floor, I place my shampoo and soap on the built-in shelf and peel off my boxers. Stepping over the high rim of the bathtub, I stand in the tub, then pull the shower curtain closed. The water remains cold, even after adjusting the hot water handle. I will make the best of it. With my back to the shower, I shampoo/condition my hair first, and then turn around to scrub my face, arms, and shoulders.

While rinsing, I rub the soap across my chest, lightly grazing my nipples with the soap. Rubbing the soap against them felt good. I lather them again, circling the areolae with the edge of the soap, I softly moan. My nipples are sensitive, one of my "erogenous zones." A friend of mine from Boston once called them "erroneous zones," when he repeated the term when he was high.

Looking down, my penis has come to attention. As good as my nipples felt, I rarely jack off in the shower—and won't now—as it stings when the soap gets into the opening of my penis. Only when I'm in a situation where I don't have my own bedroom, like on vacation, and it is my only resort for whacking off. I'm an 18-year-old guy! I would save that fun for later.

Propping my right foot on the rim of the tub, I turn toward the showerhead to get better access to my "nether" regions. A chill sweeps across my back. I turn around to investigate where the breeze is coming from and discover the shower curtain has been pulled back. Curious. I pull it back and forth. There is no malfunction, and the curtain is not sliding on its own. Chilled, I quickly turn the tepid water off, and grab the towel. Finding no air coming from a grate, I chalk it up to old houses having mysterious drafts.

****

Mary is not a stickler about much, but one thing that she's adamant about is that we have at least one meal together every day. No matter how busy our schedules, she insists that we eat together daily to discuss the day's events. That meal is usually dinner, but there have been times when it was a quick breakfast. Today's meal is dinner. In anticipation of our meal, I bring the framed drawing I found in my room to the dinner table to discuss. After eating and discussing the various trials and tribulations of moving into Antioch, I pull the picture out.

"Look at what I found in my new bedroom. A charcoal drawing of a young guy, local probably…Bartholomew Bay lighthouse and the point are in the background. He might have lived in this house. Mom, have any idea who it might be?" I inquire as I hand the framed picture to her.

"No, he doesn't look familiar. He's very handsome though. Judging by the type of breeches he's wearing; I would say early 20th century. Probably a member of the Bartholomew family," she answers as she continues to study the drawing. "Huh? He's posing in an interesting position, lying down with his legs folded next to each other, arm propped; this is not a typical position that a man would pose in during this time. Too feminine. Young women during that time might have posed like this, which is ironic, as it is a classic pose, often seen in statues of fallen Greek and Roman heroes."

She then rose from the dinner table, went into the living room, and came back with her camera. "Let me take a picture of it in case I discover another likeness of this young man during my research on Antioch. I'm almost sure he has to be a member of the Bartholomew family."

After dinner, it's already late, so I retreat to my room. It has been a long day, and I'm tired. I put on my typical sleepwear: mesh basketball shorts, and I slip in between the sheets. I was beat and it doesn't take long for me to fall asleep. As I drift off into a deep sleep, the dream begins…

I hover above my body, looking at myself sleeping on my back in my bed. I study my face and neck, scanning down to look at my chest and my abdomen. Abruptly, the sheets pull back, as if lifted by an invisible hand, and my lower body is visible. The examination continues as the view focuses on my thighs, legs, and feet. I rise higher to see my entire body lying on the bed.

Unexpectedly, the view changes, and I'm moving toward the French doors of the balcony. I fly right through the closed doors and sail out into the daylight. Soaring past the backyard, I'm above the coastline, moving toward the lighthouse in the distance. As I approach, I quickly drop down into a rocky area with a small strip of grassland. There are two figures on the rocks below, the same area where the portrait of the young man had been drawn.

As I fly closer, I literally enter the mind of a blond young man lying on the rock. Now, I see everything through his eyes. I'm looking at the seascape as I turn my head to look at my broad and well-developed chest. My skin is pale white. Perfectly formed pink areolae and nipples crown each half of my chest. Then I briefly glimpse my pale abdomen and the fine trail of blond hair descending from my naval.

I look to see what is directly in front of me—there is another young man sitting on the rocks. With a sketchpad propped on his knee, held by his left hand while his right hand is moving back and forth behind the pad; he's presumably sketching. The young man sketching has dark brown hair and a dark tan complexion. His brown eyes flash at me as he draws me, his full mouth smiling slightly. He opens his mouth to laugh, but there's no sound in this dream.

Quickly, the scene shifts to a different view of the young artist: he's standing in front of me, nude, wet, looking at me as he exits an outdoor shower with a towel in his hand. The artist's body is magnificent. I'm now closer to his face. The damp tendrils of hair lay across the high cheekbones of his face and forehead. His soulful eyes are surrounded by lustrous black lashes and topped by thick dark eyebrows. His thin nose slopes into his thick lips, slightly parted as the water drips off them sensuously.

I zoom out to scan the rest of his body, the sunlight illuminating half his torso. His chest, perfectly sculpted with dark brown areolae and nipples, is dusted with fine black hair. His v-shaped torso reveals a flat, smooth abdomen that is well-muscled. A thin trail of dark brown hair grows from the naval to a mass of curly dark brown pubic hair, his pelvis bordered on each side by his "Davids." Hanging between his legs is his thick, golden brown perfectly shaped penis, and tight scrotum. His well-muscled thighs frame his cock, a shadow of which is cast against his right thigh. His thighs blend seamlessly into his kneecaps and well-proportioned legs. His feet are muscular with perfectly shaped toes as he stands on the rough stones below.

The view changes again. I'm soaring high once more, getting closer to the sun when suddenly, day turns to night, and I'm back in my bedroom. I'm now looking up at the frame of the four-poster bed and there's a face above mine. The face of the artist that I had just admired in the shower. His mouth comes closer to mine, and I kiss those full lips. But it isn't me. I'm there in the body of the blond man, as I recognize the pale skin of his arms when I hold the artist closer.

Our lips meet, and I part mine slightly as our tongues gently explore and dance together. It feels amazing, and I'm becoming aroused.

The artist's face then moves to kiss the right side of the neck of the pale being, starting below the ear. He forms a trail of kisses along the neck muscles to the chest, flicking the right nipple with his tongue. The being I inhabit is overwhelmed by ecstasy, yet remains silent. The pale young man is breathing rapidly. My erection is rock-hard now. When the artist moves his mouth to the left nipple, I look down and see the blond man's hand grasp the shaft, moving his hand up and down. The artist then moves his mouth from the left nipple to the middle of the chest, kissing the flesh in between the well-defined pectoral muscles. Gradually moving down to the abdomen, he kisses and licks the skin, tracing the blond trail of hair that leads to the patch of blond pubic hair. The artist then lifts his head and buries his face in between the blond man's legs. His mouth is giving him/me the most exquisite pleasure. Still no sounds. He's getting closer and closer...breathing rapidly, almost suffocating from the short gasps of air...he's about to explode...

I wake up to hear myself whimpering and moaning in a semi-wakeful state. Looking down at my crotch, there is a large wet spot on my shorts. My penis throbs beneath the mesh fabric of my basketball shorts, spurting out the last of my semen. I'm breathing heavily, gasping for air. With sweat pouring down my face and into my eyes, I can taste the salt on my lips. There is a thin layer of sweat glistening across my chest, arms, and abdomen. I realize that the sheets are no longer covering me and are instead lying in a pile at my feet, just above the footboard of the bed.

I question myself: How did that happen? Did I kick them off during this dream?

The room feels cold, and my sweaty body is quickly chilled as the warmth from my orgasm fades. Removing and compressing my stained shorts into a ball, I wipe off my softening erection and abdomen. It's been a long time since I've had a wet dream, or "nocturnal emission" as my Boy Scout handbook so boldly called it. During puberty, I quickly learned I could control this embarrassing act by regular masturbation. Trying to justify what happened, I conclude it's been a long time since I last masturbated, and I *did* have that erection in the shower. Pulling the sheets up, I cover my sweaty, cold, naked body. I unfold a quilt at the base of the footboard and drape it over myself before drifting back to sleep.

Just before I drift fully off to sleep, I become aware of a glowing presence in the room, its light seeping through my closed eyelids. I open them and look toward the balcony where the glow is emanating. A white translucent figure materializes next to the bed. It is the handsome blond man from my dream and the portrait: pale, soaking wet, his hair is matted against his head, and he is naked. His arms stretch out to me. Then his beautiful mouth opens.

A blood-curdling scream explodes from the being's lips, reverberating around me as phosphorescent blood starts to pour from a grotesque gash on the right side of his forehead, forming a circular pool of blood next to his head, as if it were collecting against a flat surface, suspended in the air. His face begins to collapse as more blood pours from the enlarging crease in his face, soft tissue oozing out of the ever-widening crevice of crushed bone. He continues to scream as the right side of his face contorts into a gruesome heap of splintering skull and facial bones, luminescent blood spurting all over what remains of his beautiful face and neck. His neck then mechanically bends into an unnatural angle, so severe is the displacement that I thought his neck would snap apart from his shoulders when…

He changes back into the undamaged young man; the anatomy is assembled into its normal form. No more gaping wounds, not a blemish on the perfect white skin of his face. The cheekbones fully repaired. The skull no longer caved in. He is also not wet his dry hair hangs to his shoulders. He's now the image of the handsome man of the portrait. Smiling at me with those thin, pale lips, a menacing smile, perhaps, and then…

He's gone in a flash. But this time, jarred as I was by what I had seen, I was not sweating or breathing heavily as before. I think to myself as I contemplate the grotesque transformation that I have just witnessed.

Was that another dream?

Chapter 4

Antioch
June 2, 1983

The morning after my dream(s), I'm still shaken by the experience. As I lie in my bed thinking, I'm not sure what had happened in my bedroom last night. What is clear is that I had a vivid dream about the young man in the portrait, and it was sexual, and I ejaculated in my shorts as a result. My abdomen still has patches of dried semen. What isn't clear—was the image of the young man slowly developing a fatal head wound a dream? Or was it…an apparition…a spirit…a ghost?

After thinking about it for a while and not coming up with any answers, I decide to get up and get on with the day. That day would be more of the same as yesterday: unpacking boxes, cleaning, and organizing my space. First task, cleaning out the large double door wardrobe of dust, debris, and spider webs so that I can hang my nice clothes inside on my wooden hangers. Second task, once the drawers of the dresser that match the bed are wiped down inside, the rest of my folded clothes can be placed in the drawers. Third task, complete some forms for school registration. I was going to Bartholomew Bay High School tomorrow to take placement tests to see what courses I would need to register for to graduate in 1984, as well as what level of math, science, and composition/grammar I would be placed. I'm coming from a private school, so it isn't as easy to matriculate as if I had come from a public school. Jack would have to do the same, as he's entering as a junior, and he too went to a private school.

Why were we going to public school, when we clearly had the means to go to any private school? First, the closest private high school is about an hour drive; not that it is so far, but the windy, twisting roads along Maine's coastline make every endeavor more time consuming. I think that's one of the main attractions of living here: the slower pace of living in general. Second, the public schools in Bart's Bay have an excellent reputation for academics and extra-curricular activities. It seems that the Bartholomew family set up a trust that provides plenty of resources to the public schools, so the schools don't have to rely completely on tax revenue and, therefore, they can afford to hire the best teachers and fund new and old initiatives. Third, I wanted to try public school. There wasn't much diversity in my private school. All the students, for the most part, were from wealthy families and had the same boring and trite issues. The scholarship students at my former academy could be chill, but they also had to concentrate on keeping their grades in the A range to keep their scholarships. I was ready for a bit of diversity, to learn with and about kids from all walks of life. What better training for a budding actor?

Chapter 5

Bartholomew Bay High School
June 3, 1983

The energy is high in our household this morning. My alarm didn't go off, and I overslept. I knew I set it correctly, as I tested it before I went to sleep. Maybe it was damaged in the move. I couldn't contemplate it for very long as I was going to be late for my appointment at 9:00 am with the principal and a guidance counselor. Not a great first impression! As I'm scrambling to get myself ready, taking the quickest of showers to clean those areas that would most offend, I manage to get showered and dressed in ten minutes. Running down the stairwell with my registration papers in hand and with my toothbrush in my mouth (probably not that smart in retrospect if I had fallen with said toothbrush) I dash into the kitchen, "I'm late; why didn't you wake me up?" I ask as I spat out my toothpaste, set my toothbrush on the sink, and proceed to make some sort of breakfast sandwich out of toast, peanut butter and banana.

"Andy, you're 18 years old. You're not a kid anymore," my mother replies like a mother. "Your brother didn't seem to have any problem this morning. As you can see, he's patiently waiting for you at the kitchen table so that you can drive him to his first day as well," she says smugly. Mary could be like that.

"It's not our first day…well, not our first day of classes," I respond as I wolf down my sandwich. "Come on Jack, get into the car," I shout as I grab the car keys and bound out the side door of the kitchen into the mudroom. The mudroom connects to the porch, but the main entrance to the porch is through the living room, the largest room in the house. Running across the porch, onto the flagstone patio, I reach the driveway.

We're taking my car, a 1983 Jeep Wrangler. I got it for my birthday. It's painted black with a black soft top. It has a V6 engine, manual gearshift, and it runs like clockwork. Perfect for riding up challenging inclines, like the hilly topography of the Maine coastline. Jeeps are built to accelerate on more vertical roadways as they seem to increase in speed when you near the top of a hill. They are also great for "gravity riding," taking the car out of gear and coasting down a steep incline. The top was already down. I jump into the driver seat, buckle my seatbelt, and not seeing Jack, blow the horn a couple of short blasts. He appears at the side of the porch, running toward me as I rev the engine, and confesses, "Sorry, I had to take a wicked piss!"

"Wicked piss? Jack, you refrained from using that expression when we lived in Boston. Next thing you'll be saying is that weird form of yes they use up here— Ayuh."

Once he was in the car and strapped in with his seat belt, I put the car in reverse, roll around to the side of the garage, shift into gear, and speed down the long driveway. Stopping at the large stone gates that flank either side of the driveway, I look both ways for traffic, and then turn left onto the coastal road. Antioch is about three miles from the main part of town. Bart's Bay high school is situated on the south side of town. I decide to drive down Main Street, risking traffic from tourists, but it's the most direct route to the high school, and we're late. Bart's Bay is your typical coastal town in Maine, a combination of large and modest houses in mostly Federal, Victorian, Greek Revival and Colonial architecture. The storefronts and municipal buildings are all simple in design: square or rectangular, two or three stories tall, made of either white-washed brick or limestone and wood, with discrete white wood finishes like Corinthian columns or ornate cornices. There's a main square located between Main Street and Bay Street, where the town hall is located, as well as a well-manicured park with a statue of Angelus Bartholomew. He was not the founder of the town, but he was the member of the Bartholomew family who through his business ingenuity made this sleepy little town into the thriving port that it has become. The docks and the bay's coastline are east of Bay Street. The best taverns and restaurants are located on Bay Street, with spectacular views of the rocky coastline along Bart's Bay and the Atlantic Ocean. I arrive in the parking lot of the high school with minutes to spare. The high school is a large two story, stone, and brick rectangular structure. The many multi-paned windows are flanked by white shudders. The main entrance to the school is a set of heavy, thick double doors made of dark wood and framed in massive wooden beams painted white.

I quickly find a parking space in the visitor's section, park the car as I undo my seat belt, and jump out of the Wrangler with my completed registration papers. Jack follows my lead, also with his papers in hand. We both run across the road in front of the school entrance where buses unload the students, open the massive doors, and then we both instinctively slow our pace walking into the lobby. We both see the sign indicating Principal Snowe's office and walk through the entrance to the office suite. We approach the secretary at the counter in the office, stating that we have an appointment, and she instructs us to sit in the waiting area. Ten minutes later, we are called into the office. Upon entering the principal's office, a large, friendly-looking man walks from behind his desk, extends his hand to shake our hands, and introduces himself. "Hello, I am Principal Henry Snowe. You must be Griffin and you must be Jack."

I shake his hand first and then Jack copies the gesture. During our initial conversation, we discuss our interests. Principal Snowe seems especially pleased that I'm interested in the drama club and that Jack wants to try out for the football team.

We discuss our academic records, and he makes a surprising suggestion to me, "Griffin, normally we would wait until the fall for student orientation, but because you are a rising senior, I thought it would be a good idea if you went to some classes with a student from your graduating class, after your math placement test. I assume you're looking at colleges and will be busy with preparing your applications, so you don't need the extra stress of learning how this place works in the fall. I've taken the liberty of looking at your co-curricular transcript from your previous school and contacted another student with similar interests.

"Jack, I've arranged a meeting with the football coach, Coach Matthews, after your math placement test.

He's going to give you a tour of the facilities and a day in the workout room so that you can meet some of the other players trying out in August. You will come back here tomorrow, to take your Science and English tests and have a similar schedule. How does that sound, boys?"

We both agree that the schedule looks fine. Standing from behind his desk, Principal Snowe smiles and shakes our hands again and then leads us to the guidance office. We meet the guidance counselor who would proctor our placement tests in a common room in the guidance suite.

My test was not difficult, but it was thorough with problems that ranged from simple word problems involving arithmetic, algebra, and geometrical proofs to more challenging problems involving calculus, and trigonometry. We had two hours to take the test. We both finish around 11:30 am and then are escorted to the lunchroom.

It is a standard cafeteria with long wooden and metal tables and the buffet line offers the usual school lunch selections, with more emphasis on seafood, including lobster rolls. The food tastes as good if not better than the food Jack and I had at private school. Jack and I are sitting together with our trays at a table discussing the questions on the test, when an interesting looking dude comes over and stands next to our table.

He is shorter than me, but he's stocky, well-built, with massive biceps straining under a tight short sleeve black t-shirt with a silk-screened logo of the synth band Depeche Mode. Looking up to see the head that belongs to these arms, I see a pleasant-looking face smiling back at me. His long strawberry blond hair flops over to the right side of his face and tapers toward his nape, streaked with platinum white stripes. It looks like a psychedelic lion's mane. His face is wide, but he has high cheekbones, which produce hollow cheeks. His round eyes have deep blue irises, and are surrounded by black eyelashes, a trait which doesn't match the rest of his coloring. Then I realize he's wearing subtle mascara and eyeliner, or "guyliner," as we called it in Boston. He's wearing faded blue denim cut-off shorts held up by a large black belt, paired with black military-style boots laced all the way to the top to finish his look.

The handsome stranger extends his large right hand toward me, "Hello, you must be Griffin Meade. I'm Christian Gutmann. You are coming with me to some of my classes today."

I grasp his large hand and give it a firm shake. My grandfather on the Meade side told me that the best way to make a good first impression is to make sure you give another man a firm, strong handshake.

"You can call me Griff. This is my brother, Jack," I say, placing my hand on Jack's shoulder.

"Nice to meet you," he states as he shakes Jack's hand. "So, I was told we have a lot in common, which doesn't happen to me very often, as you can probably guess, I'm not your typical Bart's Bay resident. What kind of music do you listen to?"

Gesturing with my hand toward the brand on his shirt, I respond, "I like Depeche Mode...and a lot of the synth bands coming out of the U.K. like the Eurythmics, Tears for Fears, Psychedelic Furs, and Duran Duran, but I also like the punkier bands like the Cure, Siouxsie and the Banshees, and The Clash. Are you in a band? You definitely have the look and the guns of someone who plays guitar."

"I am, but I don't play guitar, I play keyboards. My band is called the Wilde Boys, Wilde like Oscar Wilde. We play occasionally at the Bay Street Bistro. The 'guns' come from lifting weights; I also throw shot put, discus and javelin."

"No way, I also throw discus. I also swim competitively, but the school doesn't have a team, so I guess that will be my sport. Do you like theater, I mean do you act or sing in the school shows? Principal Snowe said we had a lot in common," I inquire.

"Yeah, depends on the show, but I have been known to 'tread the boards,' as they say," the hot boy states as he finally sits down next to me, his knee grazing my naked thigh, momentarily. When I don't pull it away, he continues to rest his knee against me. I didn't want to overthink it, but there was definitely a chemistry between us that I couldn't ignore.

"So, we have about five minutes before biology starts. I am the student lab assistant. Have you ever dissected anything? We are dissecting fetal pigs today. You will be helping me unless you are a vegetarian or a conscientious objector."

"No, I've no issue with it. Our dad is an anatomist at a medical school. He dissects people for a living. I probably will wind up in some type of medical field if I decide not to do the acting thing," I state as I finish the last of my lobster roll.

"Four for four," Christian says as he looks into my eyes.

"You want to be doctor?" I say incredulously as I pick up my tray and rise from the table, purposefully rubbing my thigh against Christian's thigh.

Christian smiles at me. I wasn't sure if it was the question or the gesture.

By this time, a man wearing athletic gear approaches our table. He introduces himself as Coach Matthews with the customary handshakes, and then guides Jack out of the cafeteria to their next destination, leaving Christian and I alone with each other.

Christian and I spent the rest of the day together: dissecting pigs, making fun of the math teacher's strange inflections, and surviving a grueling lesson on how to diagram a sentence. We also found out that we are both 18 years old, unusual for guys entering their senior year, but we learned that our parents held us back because of medical conditions we didn't elaborate upon. We end the day in the parking lot next to my car, waiting for Jack.

"So, I guess I'll see you again tomorrow. I hope Bart's Bay High didn't disappoint compared to the schools in Boston," Christian states as he looks down at the ground. "I had fun hanging with you." He lifts his head and stares into my eyes.

Bobbing my head away from his stare and then back, I respond, "I did too. You're a cool dude. I think I'll like it here."

As Jack walks toward the car, I escape the somewhat awkward moment by opening the door on the driver's side, sitting down, and closing the car door. In a counter move, Christian moves closer and leans on the car door. I'm looking up at him like I did when we first met in the cafeteria. For reasons I can't quite pinpoint, a wave of nerves washes over me.

"I'll meet you for lunch at eleven-thirty, after my tests are finished," I state somewhat nervously to break the tension. By this time, Jack has settled himself into the car.

Christian, looking at me, makes his closing statement, "I'll meet you in the guidance office so that we can walk to the cafeteria together…just to make sure you guys don't get lost."

He then offers a big toothy smile that reveals a silver-capped tooth I hadn't seen before. It's official: he's adorable, and he's flirting with me. I smile back and start the car. Driving off, I peer into my rear-view mirror to study this strange new creature.

****

As we make our way along the lengthy driveway of Antioch, I spy a large shape perched on a branch in one of the bigger trees bordering the path. As the car gets closer, the creature's identity becomes clearer. A massive bald eagle is sitting there, surveying the property with its quick head movements, its' dangerous flesh-tearing talons wrapped around the branch of the tree. The enormous black feathered body stands motionless as the white head peers down at us as we pass by, its golden yellow eyes tracking us as we park the car and walk to the porch.

As we walk, I notice that it's completely silent: there are no birds chirping and the squirrels are not running about. Prompted by this visitor, I recall the traits of bald eagles I learned in biology class: the eagle is a keystone predator, with no natural enemies except man; they only eat live prey they capture or animals suffering an injury that prevents them from being able to defend themselves; and they are the kings of the sky. Then two thoughts pop into my head. I wonder if bald eagles are common in this area, and if so, do they occupy trees this close to the ground?

What I didn't know was that the eagle had just begun its residence at Antioch.

Chapter 6

Bartholomew Bay High School
June 4, 1983

For the second day of placement testing, Jack and I didn't have to be at the high school until 9:30 am. An extra 30 minutes can mean a lot when you are trying to organize two teenage boys. This morning, I'm feeling excited at the prospect of seeing Christian again. There was an undeniable chemistry between us, and I sensed he was equally interested in me. The few gay guys I met in Boston called it "gaydar," a play on the word radar to sense when someone was gay.

After breakfast, we walk out the front door of Antioch, round the corner of the house, and look up into the large tree on the opposite side of the driveway; there is no sign of the bald eagle anywhere. I'm disappointed. I don't know why. It was menacing...but it was also beautiful. The power and strength of its massive body and talons were attractive but also worrisome for the violence they could inflict. Standing on the edge of the driveway, I detect the sounds of birds chirping in the trees; that is the definitive proof it had moved on. For now.

We pile into the Wrangler, secure our seat belts, and drive down the driveway at a reasonable speed until we reach the intersection with the coastal highway.

There is a significant hill immediately to the left after the turn onto the coastal road, which is bordered on the west side by a split rail fence and a vast pasture in which sheep and cows graze.

Reaching the precipice of the hill, I took the Wrangler out of gear and coast down the other side of the hill. Because I'm not in a hurry this morning, I want to see how far I can go using only the gravity of the car. This obviously takes more time, because once you reach the bottom and the momentum decreases, then you go slower. I like the speed I get when I'm just relying on gravity to propel the car; it also saves on gas. Jack hates it. He likes to go fast all the time.

In my little experiment this morning, the car keeps its same speed about a half mile further than the bottom of the hill until it starts to slow down. We are halfway to town. Cruising at this slow but steady rate allows us to peruse the homes on the outskirts of town. The first houses that you see when approaching the town limits of Bart's Bay is a row of architecturally identical small, one-floor rectangular houses with wood siding and large front porches that are the length of the house. Settled into small lots perched above the bay's coastline, the lot accommodates a driveway to the right side of the house and a small front yard The houses are either painted white or gray, or the wood has been stained and treated so that the wood changes color depending upon the season. A light brown shade in the warmer months, and a weathered gray color during the colder months. I follow the same route through town that I used yesterday to Bart's Bay High School.

As we head toward the Guidance Center office, I inform Jack that Christian is going to meet us after our tests to walk together to the cafeteria. He then tells me that some of the guys he met in the weight room yesterday said they wanted to join him. Hearing this, I made the following suggestion, "If you want to eat with them alone, discuss football stuff, that's fine with me. Of course, you are welcome to eat with me and Christian."

Jack looks at me, smiles, and answers nonchalantly, "Yeah, sure."

There is something about his smile that is different. It unnerves me for a few seconds. We walk into the Guidance Center office and into the testing room.

Two hours later, after our testing was complete, we wait outside the office door in the hallway for Christian. When I see Christian coming down the hallway, I almost don't recognize him as the same guy I met yesterday. His hair is pulled back into a tail, which reveals the right side of his buzzed head, dyed the same platinum white color that streaks his hair. This wasn't evident yesterday when his hair was parted to the right. He looks punkier and even more masculine with this asymmetrical haircut. He's wearing the same gear as the day before, but he has on a different shirt with a distinctive print: a white t-shirt with a row of cherubic-looking creatures leaning their chins on their left hands, floating on a thin cloud. It is the album cover for *Japanese Whispers,* the compilation album of The Cure's singles.

"Dude! That is one of my favorite albums ever!" I say as I giddily pull the shirttail down and away from his chest to get an unwrinkled view of the logo, not thinking about how forward this action is.

"I remembered that you said you liked The Cure,

and I couldn't get it out of my head," he comments as he looks down at the shirt while I'm still pulling on it. "Are you ready, I'm starving?"

Finally realizing what I'm doing, I let go of the shirt and regain my composure. "Yeah, oh, Jack is going to eat with some of the guys he met in the weight room yesterday, so it will just be us, unless you want someone else to join us," I explain.

"Most of my friends either have a different lunch time or they go off campus," he states as the three of us walk to the cafeteria.

Once inside the cafeteria, Jack, spies his football buddies, and after their jock-like hand slaps and handshakes, heads off to a table with other football players. Christian and I get our food, and sit at a table. As we eat, we talk about yesterday's events and current music getting to know each other better through the usual teenage guy banter. We have about five minutes left before we must leave for his American history class when Christian abruptly grabs my arm with his big paw.

"Oh, before I forget, my band is the opening act at the Bay Street Bistro this Friday night, and I would like to put you on the guest list. We usually have a few beers after our set. Can you come?"

"Yeah, that sounds great! What time?" I ask.

"Doors open at seven p.m. but we'll go on around eight after sound check. You're welcome to come at seven, but I'm wicked busy until we play our set. Also, we usually stay for the headliner, band etiquette…and you can get to know the rest of the 'Boys'," he elaborates as we pack our stuff to go.

I look over to Jack's posse, and once I have Jack's

attention, I shout to him, "Meet me at three-thirty at the car!"

We attend Christian's classes for the rest of the afternoon: American history, gym, and the same calculus class I visited yesterday, with the teacher who had the same goofy vocal inflections. It was in his gym class that I got the chance to see more of Christian's spectacular body, as he could no longer wear the baggy clothes he favors. At Bart's Bay HS, everyone wears the requisite gym uniform, which is form-fitting, to say the least. Christian's broad chest and big biceps look great in the grey, short sleeve t-shirt with "BBHS" printed across the chest, but it is the way his full round butt looks in his gray polyester mesh shorts that has gotten my attention. His globe-like glutes transition perfectly into his thick hairy (blond) thighs, normally covered by his long shorts. He looks very hot running around the track doing wind sprints.

Running back from the track, I tell him to meet me outside the locker room after he showers. I was not going to be that guy in the locker room that gets excited looking at him draped in a towel, and then must hide and or explain my boner. As we near my car, I decide to show off my physical prowess by jumping into the Wrangler using the roll bar and sliding through the open window without opening the car door.

"Very impressive, very James Bond of you," he says with a smirk, leaning against the car.

"I'm stoked that you're coming Friday night. I'd like to get to know you better," he says as he places his hand on my shoulder.

Perfectly platonic move. Then I feel him lightly rubbing my shoulder. Not so platonic. Jack suddenly appears and opens the door on the passenger side. Christian moves his hand away.

"Hey, Jack! Later!" he says, waving goodbye to the both of us. I watch him walk across the parking lot in the rearview mirror.

I'm strapping my seat belt across my chest when Jack says something that surprises me, "He likes you."

"Yeah, he's a cool dude," I nonchalantly respond.

"No, I mean he *likes* you," Jack states, correcting me.

Slowly turning my head to look at him, I say nothing as I try to read his facial expression. Quickly, I turn my head away and stare at the steering wheel. "What? What do you mean?" I'm still staring at the steering wheel, pretending not to know exactly what he meant.

"It's okay, I know. I know you like guys," Jack says with a sympathetic tone.

I quickly look at him. He's smiling at me with this big, goofy lop-sided grin. Turning my head back to the steering wheel, I can feel tears welling up in my eyes. I look at him again, and the tears start to move slowly down my face, "How long?"

"A long time."

"Am I…that obvious?"

"No, not at all. I just…knew. You're my big bro, I notice everything about you. I love you."

"I love you too," I say as I collapse into a crying mess.

Instinctively, I bend my neck forward, placing my head in my hands so no one can see me. Jack comforts me by patting my right shoulder. Quickly gaining my composure, I wipe the tears from my eyes with the palms of my hands and start the car. I then look over at Jack, still wearing that goofy smile, and I smile back. I put the car in reverse, and we drive home. It feels like a huge weight has been lifted off my shoulders, a weight that I didn't even know was there. We were both silent the whole way home.

As we drive up the driveway to Antioch, we both notice that the bald eagle has returned to the same branch on the same tree. I park the car and run into the house. A few minutes later, I came back out with my Polaroid Instamatic camera in hand. Walking over to the side of the driveway opposite the edge where the tree stood, I aim my Polaroid at the eagle and snap away, a brief flash of light, followed by the whirring sound the camera makes as it spits the picture out. I grab the edge of the photograph and shake it.

Then, without warning, the mighty bird screeches, looks right at me, spreads its wings, and flies out of the tree over my head. Once the eagle is out of sight, I look down at the photograph. Watching the picture develop, it is evident that the image of the eagle is not developing correctly. There is a black blurry mass where the eagle is in the frame, but it is impossible to distinguish that it is an eagle, much less a bird. I thought to myself, the film must be damaged, but then why are the branches of the tree surrounding the eagle in clear focus?

****

We had one of Mom's favorite meals for dinner tonight: cream of crab soup, homemade sourdough bread, and strawberry and almond salad. She makes the most delicious cream of crab soup. She only uses back fin crabmeat and makes a base from equal parts half-

and-half and real butter. I'm so spoiled by her recipe that every time I order the soup at a restaurant, I'm always disappointed, so I stopped ordering it. She also makes killer crab cakes and spectacular tarragon chicken salad as well. After dinner, I was thoroughly satiated and ready to retire to the living room to watch an old movie or summer re-runs.

I had just settled in, when unexpectedly, I hear Mary exclaim, "Oh, Andy, I almost forgot. I think I discovered the identity of your mystery man in the drawing." She then walks into the living room, where she has set up her office, and returns with a large white envelope.

"I developed that photograph of the drawing you showed me and then I compared the face with photographs of the Bartholomew family that I found in the archives in the town library," she explains with a tinge of excitement in her voice. She then produces a new photograph of a vintage photographic portrait of a young man in a tuxedo and hands it to me. "This is Angelus Bartholomew III, and I think this is who is in your drawing."

I look at the photograph and I cannot believe my eyes. It's him. The being that materialized in my room, except without the head wound and with clothes. The young man's hair is slicked back so it is difficult to discern if he has blond hair, but it is his face. He has a confident smile and bright eyes. He wore a finely tailored black tuxedo with thin satin lapels, a white shirt, and a satin black bow tie. One of his hands is tucked into the pocket of the jacket, and the other is lying at his side. He has long thin hands. I had not noticed this trait before. He looks like a vintage

Hollywood matinee idol, like the glamourous headshots photographers like George Hurrell took in Hollywood during the 1930s.

"According to what I have been able to dig up so far, he was the only son of Angus and Victoria Bartholomew. She died in 1912, when Angelus was eleven years old, from 'consumption,' which is what they called cancer. Angus was the last Bartholomew to live in Antioch." Mom then pauses, sighs, takes off her glasses, and continues, "Angelus Bartholomew III died in 1919; he was just eighteen years old. He committed suicide…he jumped from the widow's walk of this house." Mom is clearly distraught by what she has just told us.

I put the photograph down on the table. Suddenly, everything made sense. The crushed skull, the pooling of blood. I'm sure at this moment that I've seen a ghost. The ghost of Angelus Bartholomew III after he had fallen onto the stone pavement below the widow's walk. But why was he naked?

"Was it raining the night he jumped?" I ask.

"Oh, Andy, I don't know, the newspaper articles didn't have that much detail. Wha…that's an interesting question…why do you ask?" she questions with a perplexed look on her face.

I realize then that I just revealed something that I wasn't ready to discuss.

"I don't know. It just popped into my head." I lied.

"Well, it seems that our handsome mystery man had a very tragic life, short as it was. These kinds of stories always break my heart. People do not think the wealthy have hard lives because they have money and privilege. It doesn't matter how much money you have when you experience so much loss," she states with tremulation in her voice. Mom is a very sensitive person and doesn't have any problems expressing it. I admire her for that.

After learning the brief history of Angelus Bartholomew III, I'm feeling very emotional. I had been pensive during dinner, as I wasn't ready to discuss what happened between Jack and me today, even though it was very much on my mind. Contrary to Mary Meade, I wasn't good at expressing my emotions.

"Can I be excused?"

"Of course, honey. Did I upset you?" I clearly hear the concern in her voice.

"No, I just had a long day, and I'm beat. Thanks for the information. Good night." I kiss her on the cheek then go over to Dad and hug him goodnight.

"Good night sport," he says as he hugs me back.

Climbing the stairwell slowly, I think about all that has happened today. I came out to my brother, or rather, he guessed. Same difference. I might have the beginnings of my first same-sex romance. I realized that I had seen the ghost of a guy who killed himself in this house. Quite a day by any stretch of the imagination.

Reaching my room, I collapse on the bed and close my eyes. A few seconds later, I open them and stare toward the dresser where the portrait leans against the wall. I stand and pick up the framed drawing from the dresser. Lying back down on the bed, I prop the pillows behind my head and study the portrait. I now have a photograph to compare with the likeness of the young man in this drawing, an image that isn't as grotesque as the wounded soul I saw four nights ago. "So your name is Angelus. Fitting."

I then scan the drawing and notice the artist's initials in the lower right corner. Are these the initials of the handsome young artist with dark brown hair and tan complexion that I have seen in my dream?

"So, who is L.B.?" I say.

Immediately, I hear an exhalation of air in my right ear, the same breathy sound I had heard the first day I found the drawing of Angelus. It catches me off guard, even though I had anticipated a response. Reflexively, I turn my head to the right to see if the ghost materializes next to me. It does not. Suddenly, the room becomes very cold. So cold, I can see my breath. Then I notice that the glass panels of the French doors are fogging up. Something is being written in the condensation of the fogged panes by an invisible finger, but I cannot discern what is being written. Swinging my legs off the bed, I walk hesitantly over to the doors. I look at the glass panel with the letters.

One word is visible: Lazarus.

Chapter 7

Antioch
June 5, 1983

Lying in bed this morning with my hand down in my crotch under my basketball shorts, like most guys do when we think (something left over from holding ourselves when we were toddlers...?), I contemplate the previous night's event.
LAZARUS
The word or name that Angelus had written in the condensation of the glass pane of the door. By the way, I decided I would call my specter by his first name from now on. I wonder...is Lazarus the first name of the initials for L.B., the artist of the drawing of Angelus? Lazarus is a strange first name, but then again, with a name like Griffin, I don't have much room to talk. Was he referring to Lazarus, the man that Jesus brings back from the dead in the Bible? The act that put into motion the events that led to Jesus's trial and crucifixion? Was Angelus telling me that he was going to come back from the dead? I mean, as a ghost, he's sort of already back from the dead...or was he never completely dead? Mind-boggling. Is he planning a return to corporeal form? Possession? Me? I do not think he would tell me his plan if he was planning to possess me. Right?
As I continue to think about the endless

possibilities, I'm awakened from my daze by the sound of a buzz saw. Loud. Grating. Close. I get out of bed and walk into the hall to investigate. The sound of the electric saw is more muffled. As I walk back into my bedroom, the roar of the saw is louder. Walking over to the balcony doors, I open them, and the buzzing sound becomes louder. Looking around the left side of the yard and driveway, I find the source. There is a black pickup truck parked in the driveway next to two sawhorses with a piece of plywood lying on top. I cannot see who's doing the work. I put on a t-shirt and walk downstairs to the kitchen to investigate. Mom is preparing breakfast as per usual.

"Good morning. So, who's out in the driveway sawing wood? And why's he doing it so early?" I pour myself a cup of coffee.

"Good morning. His name is Anvil Millstone, and he's doing some carpentry work. During the house inspection, it was evident that there was some structural damage, luckily nothing serious that needed to be repaired while I did the restoration. He'll be doing basic carpentry; the intricate period woodwork will have to be done by a restoration specialist. Mostly, he'll be working in the basement and on the widow's walk," she explains as she moves the scrambled eggs around in the skillet so they don't burn. "As for the time of day, I appreciate someone who starts the day early. You never can tell what you're going to find when you tear down a wall."

Anvil Millstone? He sounded more like a medieval blacksmith than a carpenter from Bartholomew Bay, Maine. Jack then joined us a few minutes later, asking the same questions. Mom instructs me to fill him in, as she must get ready for an appointment. Proceeding to eat breakfast, I inform Jack who Anvil Millstone is and what he's doing, and then return upstairs to get ready to go back to Bart's Bay High. This morning, we are going to find out the results of our placement tests and which classes we'll be taking in the fall.

After showering and dressing, we walk to the driveway. The sawhorses with plywood are set up in the middle of the driveway behind the black pickup. I look at the truck more closely. It's covered with scratches, rough spots, and dents. There's white press-on lettering on the side of the door that spells "Millstone Construction." After surveying the situation, I conclude that it's not going to be easy to navigate the Wrangler around the sawhorses and plywood. No one is in sight. I call out for someone to move them. "Mr. Millstone? Are you around? We need to leave." No one answers. "Jack, help me move this over a couple of feet," I suggest as I place my hands on one end of the plywood.

As soon as we start to move the wood to the ground, a gruff voice calls out, "Hey! Don't move that. If you get hurt, you ain't on my insurance!"

His tone is angry, which accentuates his strong local dialect. I turn around to see a large, slovenly-looking, almost bald man with the remaining hair buzzed short. His unkempt, bushy eyebrows arch over his squinty eyes. He has a wide nose and heavy jowls that frame his thick-lipped mouth, which holds a cigar butt in the left corner. That filthy t-shirt does nothing to conceal his beer belly. His meaty arms are tight against the fraying short sleeves. His dark work pants are belted below his protruding abdomen. He wears black, paint spattered construction boots.

"Sorry. I called out, but nobody answered. I'm Griffin Meade, and this is my brother Jack," I say as I extend my hand for the customary handshake. He does not extend his hand, leaving mine suspended in the air.

"Anvil Millstone, I got dirt on my hands, I don't want to get you dirty," he says snidely.

Understanding that we need to clear a path for the cars, he begins to move the plywood and sawhorses. He says nothing else. I back up the Jeep next to the garage, turn it around in the driveway, and drive slowly toward where Mr. Millstone is standing.

"Thank you," I say as I pass him standing to the left of the car.

He looks at me with a sullen expression, cigar butt sticking out of the corner of his mouth, and says nothing. His eyes follow as we pass him, and when I look at his reflection in the rearview mirror, I see he's turned toward us, staring as we drive to the end of the driveway.

"Nice guy," I say sarcastically to Jack.

Jack's expression concurs with my impression. As we reach the bottom of the driveway, I also realize that the eagle did not return to its favorite tree. Looking briefly into the rearview mirror for any sign of the eagle, I make the left turn and drive off.

Jack and I met with separate guidance counselors to find the results of our placement tests. I scored very high in math and science but not as well on the English test. On the science test, I placed out of biology and chemistry, so I would be taking physics. I wondered if I would be in any of the same classes as Christian. I couldn't meet him for lunch today because he was on a field trip with the biology class. Jack also did well on his tests. He seemed to be pleased with his schedule.

I suggested we go into town and try one of the local restaurants for lunch. The guidance counselors suggested the Bay Street Bistro, or some place called Hank's Café. I was going to the bistro Friday night, so we opted for the café.

Hank's Cafe is a typical American grill with an emphasis on fresh seafood specials. The food is good, and the portions are big, something I always look for as I have a healthy appetite. After I pay the bill, I suggest we go for a walk and explore the town. The café is located next to the Main Square.

We walk by the docks to check out the waterfront. When we reach the bayside beach area, the tide is out. The contours of the empty bay are strewn about with small sailboats and watercraft stranded on the sandy bottom. It looks like a graveyard of rowboats, small motorboats and sailboats poking out from the dunes of the seafloor. In several hours, the tide would return, the watermark would rise, and the grounded boats would be floating above their anchors and moors. The drastic intertidal zone of the Maine coastline that affects the rivers, bays and creeks was something we had heard of but had never experienced. A whole industry is built upon this phenomenon of being able to trudge through the muddy intertidal areas and dig for clams and other bivalves that live most of their lives submerged in the water, but for several hours in the day, dig themselves into the soft bottom to rely upon the muddy camouflage to provide them protection and oxygen.

We walk a block west to the square and then into the park. It's a nicely kept park with lots of shade trees and benches and a fountain in the middle. That is where the statue of Angelus Bartholomew is erected. We walk over to get a closer look. I study his face. There is a slight resemblance of the Angelus that appears to me and this Angelus. The man in the statue is dressed in Victorian-era clothing and has a solid build. His right arm is extended and pointing his index finger, as though giving a speech or lecturing on something specific. I had heard that one of the churches in town was built by him, and that a trust he started is still providing the money the church needs to survive. Maybe he's preaching.

I was getting tired, so I suggested we go home so that I could take a nap. I like to nap. I can fall asleep anywhere if I'm tired enough. Which is good if you're lying on a couch or bed, but not so good if you're driving long distances or sitting through a boring lecture. My family hates that I can fall asleep so quickly. I enjoy naps more than I do sleeping at night. Someone once suggested that I may have narcolepsy, but I didn't have all the symptoms, like the weird paralysis and weakness in your arms and legs when you're awake. Hallucinations are also a symptom. Wait a minute. A new thought suddenly came into my head: Did I hallucinate seeing Angelus?

As we drive up the driveway of Antioch, I look at the tree branch hanging close to the driveway, but the eagle still has not returned to the tree it had inhabited for two days. As we come closer to the garage, the pickup truck that was present this morning is still there. We pull into the same space in front of the garage and unload. There is no sound of an electric saw. Rather, as we walk into the house through the back porch, we hear a banging sound coming from the basement entrance below the grand staircase.

Mom is not answering as I call out her name. This means that either she's walking the grounds, or she's in town with Jack Sr. Her green Volvo 240 GL is in the garage. It has been a few hours since lunch, so I decide to make my favorite snack, a banana and peanut butter sandwich. As I collect the parts of my snack, laying them on the cutting board for assembly, I hear a voice resonating from the basement. It's rough and gravelly. A man's voice involved in a conversation. I move closer to the basement door to hear it better.

"If jobs weren't so fuckin' hard to find, I wouldn't have taken this job. I hate this fuckin' place."

I hear the footfalls of two people coming up the stairs, so I move quietly and quickly back to the kitchen and continue to make my sandwich. The two men reach the top of the stairs. Then the sounds of their footsteps move away from the basement stairs and toward the direction of the foyer. I quietly move out of the kitchen and creep to the edge of the foyer. Peeking around the wall, I see Anvil and another worker walking through the front door. Then the door closes. I walk back to the kitchen to my sandwich. I think it is Anvil's voice that made the statements about the job and Antioch, but I couldn't be sure. It could've been the other worker. The low-pitched gurgling rumble of a tailpipe rocks the kitchen. Walking quickly through the mudroom into the porch, I watch as the pickup truck revs its engine, and then speeds into reverse.

I was left with the burden of whether to tell Mary about what I had heard or keep quiet. On the one hand, if an employee does not want to work in an environment, how much is going to be invested in the quality of the work? That could affect Mary's plans for the renovation and restoration of Antioch. On the other hand, Mom has vast experience in all types of construction, she has been doing this for a long time, and if it were below acceptable quality, she would be the first one to detect it. I can't be sure about who said it...Anvil or his hired hand? I decide not to tell her. I hope it's the right decision.

Chapter 8

Antioch
June 6, 1983

Bright and early, Anvil Millstone and his electric saw are busy repairing some structural defect in Antioch. This time, the buzzing sound is coming from inside the house and not from the balcony. Rolling out of bed, I walk to the bedroom door, open it, and the sound intensifies. It's coming from the second-floor stairwell.

As I'm walking down the hallway to go downstairs for breakfast, I hear a man's voice yelling from the third floor. Curious, I creep up the second-floor stairwell in my bare feet, wearing only my basketball shorts and a tank top, onto the third-floor landing. Following the brash voice, I tip-toe down the short hallway to the door to the stairs of the widow's walk. The cord to the electric saw is plugged into the wall of the hallway and the cord is wedged between the door and the doorframe. I cannot understand what the man is saying. I move closer to the stairwell door.

"God damn fucking piece of shit outlet! Why the fuck does she want to fix anything up here? This is where that little faggot did his lover's leap! Died too quickly, perverts should suffer!"

Peeking behind the door, I see that it is only Anvil

at the top of the narrow stairs with the saw in his hands and he's cursing to himself. I had heard enough. I softly tip-toe back down the hallway, down the stairs onto the second floor, where I can still hear him, and then down the staircase to the main floor, where that ingratiating voice can't be heard. Walking into the kitchen, I get a cup of coffee and head to the porch through the living room entrance.

I sit down in one of the large Adirondack chairs. They're my favorite kind of outdoor chair because of the high back and the scoop-like seat, which is comfortable for my frame. I'm alone on the porch, and I didn't see anyone when I walked to the kitchen. Where is everybody?

It's a beautiful morning despite the ugliness I had just listened to. The sun's slowly rising above the ocean. It's going to be a sunny, clear day. We had not had a lot of clear days since we moved to Bart's Bay.

Mesmerized by the flaming fireball of the sunrise, my solitude is abruptly interrupted by a blood-curdling scream coming from the rooftop. Jumping out of my chair, I run out of the porch onto the backyard to look up to the roof. I don't see anyone on the roof or widow's walk, and the screaming has stopped. I've a bad feeling about this. Running back into the porch, through the entrance into the living room, I bound into the foyer and up the grand staircase to the second floor.

I call out once I reach the second-floor landing, "Anvil! Anvil! Are you all right!"

No answer. As I run toward the second-floor stairwell, I detect a weird, low-intensity humming sound. The humming sound intensifies as I near the top of the stairs to the third floor, but it doesn't sound like an electric buzz saw would sound at this distance. I run down the hallway and stop in my tracks.

I was not prepared for what I was seeing. There lay Anvil motionless on the floor, blood spurting against the hallway walls. The strange humming sound I heard is a gurgling sound at this distance. As I slowly move closer, I can now see that the blood is shooting from Anvil's abdomen. The electric saw is gnawing through his internal organs in a huge pool of blood, rotating into what I only could imagine were his intestines, liver, and stomach. The saw continues to eat away at his viscera. His eyes are open, staring blankly at the ceiling. I reach for the cord and unplug the saw. The humming and gurgling sounds stop and the saw sinks into the hollowed-out abdomen.

Moving closer, I lift the cord, pulling the saw out of the bloody chasm in his torso. The electric saw makes a grotesque sucking sound as it emerges from the blood bath. I release the cord and drop the saw onto the floor. Suddenly feeling nauseous, I bend over at the waist, vomiting on the floor next to the body. Wiping my face with the back of my arm, I feel light-headed and unbalanced. My equilibrium is severely disturbed.

Trying to gain my composure, I stumble down the hallway, grasping the railing around the stairwell. I move around the landing and then down the stairs, gripping the railing to prevent myself from falling down the stairs. Reaching the landing of the second floor, I use the railing along the balcony to pull myself to the grand staircase and down the stairs. I fall to my knees on the foyer floor when I miss the last step of the grand staircase. Crawling across the marble floor of the foyer into the living room, and then across the Oriental rug on the living room floor, I finally reach the phone on an end table. I pull the phone off the table by the cord, and it comes crashing down to the floor, the receiver bouncing across the floor. Lying on the floor, I pull the receiver toward me using its cord and then slowly dial 9-1-1.

"This is 9-1-1, what is your emergency?" the voice says.

"There has been an acci...accident...electric saw...killed him. He's...dead," I say as I gasp for breath, my chest heaving rapidly.

"Sir, are you all right? What is your address?" the operator asks.

"I...live at An...Antioch, Ba...Bartholomew Bay, I...I don't know the a...address, I th...think I am ha...having a ha...heart attack," I say in between gasps.

"I have alerted Bartholomew Bay Fire and Rescue. They should be there in a few minutes, hang on!" the 911 operator states.

I then fall onto my back, and I go limp.

****

I woke on the living room floor with something pressing against my face. It surrounds my mouth, and I can feel the air pushing against my lips. My lips feel dry and cracked. I lick them to give them moisture. I then realize that it is an oxygen mask that is surrounding my mouth. Looking up, I see the image of two people, they're both blurry, but I can see they're wearing dark-colored shirts. One of the figures is closer to me, hovering above my chest, moving his hand toward my chest. I now feel the sensation of something cold resting on the left side of my chest. The other figure is resting his fingers against the wrist of my left hand.

Then I hear a voice. "Sir, how do you feel? Are you getting enough air?" I direct my gaze toward the voice and shake my head up and down.

"Heart rate has decreased, he's not in v-tack... good breath sounds...good color in his cheeks," reports the closer figure.

"Pulse rate has decreased, just above normal, ready for blood pressure," the other figure says as I feel a padded sleeve around my upper arm inflate and press uncomfortably, choking the flesh of my arm. "BP is 125 over 90."

I pull the mask off my face and flex my neck muscles to pull my head off the ground. I attempt to sit up. Rolling onto my right side, I place my right hand on the carpeted floor, push against the floor to elevate my torso, and then rotate my butt into a sitting position. I'm a little dizzy, but it's not disabling. The blurry figures are now clear and solid—two men wearing dark blue shirts with emblems sewn into the sleeves that look like shields with the words "fire" and "rescue" embroidered against a red field. I also realize that I'm on the floor of the living room. The men helping me advise me not to get up quickly as I'm still recovering from my trauma (their words). One of the emergency technicians places a blanket around my naked shoulders; they had cut off my tank top to administer their aid. I nod my head to indicate that I understood. Then I hear a commotion of several people coming down the grand staircase.

Turning my head to look in the direction of the foyer, I see several men carrying a gurney with a sheet covering a body. A large red area has stained the sheet in the midsection of the body. As people in medical scrubs and white coats walk the body across the foyer and through the front door, I also notice that there are two serious-looking men in brown uniforms with wide-brimmed hats standing near the doorway and talking into walkie-talkies. Obviously, the local police are here to ask the only witness what has happened.

I place my legs into a position on the floor to try and stand up using my arms and knees. Lifting myself to standing, my wobbly legs give way and I drop down into one of the big Victorian-style chairs in the living room.

The taller man with graying hair at the temples approaches me. "Mr. Meade, I'm Sheriff Roberts, and this is Deputy Hill. Are you feeling well enough to answer some questions?"

"Yeah, I think so," I groggily answer as the men from Fire and Rescue remove the oxygen mask and the blood pressure cuff.

"Can you tell us what happened? What you saw? Heard?" Sheriff Roberts asks.

I tell them the story including all the gory details, but I do not tell them about the tirade that Anvil had on the widow's walk that preceded his mysterious death. Without warning, a chill comes over me during the interrogation. Did Angelus's spirit have anything to do with this grisly death? Did he somehow exact revenge on the man who cursed the "faggot that leapt from the widow's walk," the homophobe who blasphemed him? Was this just a coincidence, or did he have the power to cause this "accident?" Then I hear a deep voice talking in the background.

"Mr. Meade? Mr. Meade, did you hear me?" Sheriff Roberts asks me repeatedly.

I look at him with a blank expression, "What? Sorry, no I didn't."

"To the best of your knowledge, was anyone else in the house besides you and Mr. Millstone?"

"No, I didn't see anyone else in the house."

Chapter 9

Bay Street Bistro
June 7, 1983

Morning came like it did yesterday, but the world is a different place. I had seen my first dead body. Unlike most people, who usually see their first corpse in an open casket viewing or funeral, I had an up-close view of a fresh mutilation that was at best a horrible accident and at worst…murder. The image of Anvil's viscera and blood exploding out of his open abdomen is a memory I will never forget.

I was recovering this morning from what the medical officials characterized as a severe traumatic shock. My brain could not cope with what I was witnessing and went into panic mode which meant that I went into survival mode. As it was explained to me, after I saw what had happened to Anvil, my body prepared itself to defend against whatever had killed Anvil. My heart rate increased dramatically to send blood to all the tissues in my body that would need blood to operate at an extreme level, like my muscles, to physically fight off the murderer. My breathing rate also increased dramatically, to provide oxygen to the blood that was being pumped faster from my heart. My digestive organs decreased activity so the blood pumping from the heart doesn't have to go to these organs, which is the reason why I vomited.

I also started to sweat more to decrease the temperature generated by the fast-flowing blood, by evaporation, and this in turn, dehydrates the body quickly and lead to my dizziness and lack of balance. When the dangerous presence was removed, then my body returned to normal; but not until after my brain had closed off stimuli from the world, and I lost consciousness…fainted. I felt like I had been beaten up, without any visible bruises or cuts. Increasing my bodily functions had also depleted the natural resources I had stored, and I was fatigued.

I was also dealing with the fact that although I was not necessarily a suspect, I was a witness that the police would be investigating and watching. Oh, and my parents. When Mary received word of the fatal accident and that I had lost consciousness…well, you can just imagine what went through her head. This is a mother's worst nightmare: the prospect that their child may have been killed, or worse, murdered. After hearing the grisly details of Anvil's death and my physical reaction to discovering the body, she went into protective mother mode:

1—I needed to go to the hospital to be checked, even though my vitals were fine by the time she arrived, and I didn't sustain any physical injury.

2—Regarding my involvement in Anvil's death: of course, her son did not have anything to do with it! How could the police even think that and what would be the motive? He's not a serial killer!

3—I would have to see a therapist to help cope with the trauma I had endured.

All of this, and then later in the day, when I

announced that I still intended on going to the Bay Street Bistro to see Christian's band...

"Andy, you're still recovering from shock even if you feel fine. It's too soon to be in an over-stimulating environment!"

After a long, drawn-out argument, she finally acquiesced when I agreed to rest all day until the concert. She also understood that I needed to be away from this house for a few hours to get my mind off what had happened.

Dad was obviously concerned about my well-being as well, but he always has a much more hands-off approach to parenting. He always believed that everyone should make their own decisions and they accept the ramifications that come with those decisions. That's how you learn.

Jack Jr. was also concerned. He hugged me tightly when he heard what happened and then became a spectator listening to everyone discuss and argue their points about the incident. However, when I went to my room after dinner, or what small amount of food I was able to eat and keep down, he came to my room and asked if I was doing okay and if I needed him to do anything. No questions about the gory details that a boy his age might have been curious about, only that he was worried about my mental and physical health. Jack is thoughtful. Mom always said he was the more nurturing, paternal child of the two of us. I didn't disagree.

In addition to the grotesque imagery I would have to live with for the rest of my life, I was pondering whether Angelus's ghost might have had something to do with Anvil's violent death. I wasn't even sure it was possible, but after Angelus caused the temperature to drop in my bedroom to produce the condensation to be able to write the word "Lazarus" onto the glass pane with his invisible finger, it was not out of the realm of possibilities that he could have caused Anvil's horrible death.

I was surprised that he didn't try to contact me last night. I thought if he murdered Anvil, after the man had disparaged his name, he would tell me about it. I don't really know much about who Angelus Bartholomew III is, or was, but that seemed like something he would have communicated to me. But nothing. I also didn't feel up to it as well; to try to contact him. I was either too exhausted to try to have a conversation with a ghost or I didn't want to know the truth. Either way, when I went to bed, I was asleep the moment my head hit the pillow. Maybe Angelus knew I was exhausted and traumatized and left me alone to get my rest.

This is my life now: contemplating whether a ghost can have sympathy.

****

As agreed, I rested all day in my room before the concert tonight. By dinner time, I felt physically better, not exhausted. Dinner was a solemn occasion. Mary was not happy about my plans for the night, but she accepted them.

After my shower, I put a towel around my waist, and then walked to my closet to select the outfit for my…date? Opening the beveled mirrored glass doors to the wardrobe, I start to visualize the evening. My usual routine consists of deciding whether the attire for the evening is going to be influenced by the space or the entertainment, or both. I have not seen what the Bay

Street Bistro looks like inside, but I imagine it would be like most taverns that feature bands. So, the dress code is not going to be centered on the venue, it would be in accordance with the clientele who went to see these types of bands. However, that also presents an issue, because I'm not sure what kind of music Christian's band, The Wilde Boys, plays. They could be hard rock, bubble metal, or country-western for all I knew. Christian said he plays keyboards in the band, and that it is "his" band, so did that mean he sings and plays synthesizer(s) or just plays synthesizer? With all these unknowns, I finally decided that I would blend in with Christian's aesthetic: lots of black clothing, Goth rock eyeliner and mascara, high hair, and jewelry influenced by pop stars.

My ensemble for the evening consists of acid wash jeans, a black t-shirt with a white silk screen of the unmistakable eyes and lips of Siouxsie of Siouxsie and the Banshees, a thick black leather belt, and black lace-up combat boots with zippers on the side. I apply a thin line of black eyeliner, from my actor's supplies, under my bottom lashes, stack my hair higher than normal with spray and mousse, and then comb it into a "faux hawk." I put five round rubber bracelets on my right wrist, a leather wristband with a big silver buckle on the left wrist, and a silver ring with a silver skull and black glass eyes on my ring finger. To top it off, I pull on my black leather motorcycle jacket. I look sufficiently prepared for a range of musical tastes.

I walk downstairs so that the family can check out my look. Mary does not give me her usual response of a high-pitched "Woooo" before a compliment; rather, she looks at me, turns her head to her work, and says quietly, "You look nice." Dad didn't say anything, as usual, and Jack gave me a thumbs-up. He also has a big smile on his face. I'm sure that isn't because of my look, but that he knew I was getting dressed to impress Christian.

I leave Antioch at 7:15 pm and park on Bay Street a block from the address that Christian gave me. Walking down the street searching for the address, I come upon a huge dark gray limestone brick building with black wood finishes. I can see that there are large windows displaying clothing for women. When I get closer, I realize the entrance to the bistro is below the storefronts in the basement. There's a sandwich board sign with Bay Street Bistro in black lettering on a white background as a border at the top and a chalkboard below that has a list of bands performing and the dates they are performing, written in chalk. It states that tonight's show, June 7, is an "All-Ages Show." The Wilde Boys are the third band listed after two other bands that I've never heard of. A stone stairwell descends to a set of doors: painted black on the outside but red on the inside. Another small discrete sign hangs above the doors with Bay Street Bistro painted on it. There's someone at the door sitting on a stool smoking a cigarette.

I walk up to the door, and I'm promptly stopped by a rather thin, surly looking dude, "There's a ten dollar cover tonight."

"I think I'm on the comp list for the Wilde Boys. Griffin, Griff, Meade," I tell the bouncer.

He grabs his clipboard next to the stool and scans it for my name. He gives me a thumbs-up, "Have a good night."

The Bay Street Bistro's walls are made of limestone and painted white, but the paint is peeling in large patches to reveal the real surface of the rock, which gives the whole place a subterranean look. Antique oil torches with glass globes mounted on columns line up with the supporting beams of the ceiling, which create a very cool effect, but also interfere with the sight lines of the stage. There are several round tables with large columnar candles in round glass enclosures placed in the middle of each table. An antique bar made of darker wood on the left looks as if it could have been here since the earliest days of this town's sea-faring past.

The stage is a raised platform in the rear of the bistro that's the entire width of the building. Blood red velvet curtains hang on either side of the lip of the stage. A drum set, a synthesizer, a guitar stand, and three microphones sit in the middle of the stage. The stage is illuminated with aqua blue light that gives the club a mysterious marine like glow, fitting for a venue by the sea.

The club is packed, people standing and leaning against the columns. Denizens dressed appropriately in modern gear that reflects the bands that would play tonight: loads of black clothing, black leather jackets, boots, belts, wristbands, and t-shirts that honor various bands.

I venture to the bar and order the darkest beer they have on draft: Guinness Draught, a beer and a meal in one. I find the nearest column to the stage and lean on it like the other occupants. Looking down at my gear as it is juxtaposed against the peeling column and low light of the torch. It fit.

A young woman with black and purple hair, several piercings in her ears and nose, a black leather jacket and skirt, fishnet stockings with more than one obvious hole, and black stilettos walks on stage and stops at the center microphone, "Hello Bay Streeters! Are we ready to party with some great bands tonight?" she confidently yells into the audience. The crowd yells back. "Bay Street Bistro is proud to present one of our own to start the night. Please welcome local fave, The Wilde Boys!"

The band walks onto the stage with Christian stopping and standing behind the synthesizer. He looks every bit the rocker wearing his requisite black leather jacket, black shorts cut below the knee, and black leather combat boots. Tonight's t-shirt features a face secured behind a black leather mask that had no eye holes only a zipper where the mouth should be, with the word ANARCHY written below in primitive scratch-like lettering.

His faux hawk has extra blond streaks that blend with the aqua light making his head glow, as if he's standing at the bottom of the sea. Thick eyeliner accentuates his beautiful blue eyes.

A silver hoop in his right ear glistens in the aqua light. The right ear. Suddenly, I remembered what the guys at my previous school had warned me about if I was thinking of getting my ear pierced: "left is right, right is wrong." If you pierced your right ear, it meant you were a fag, queer, gay, whereas a pierced left ear was acceptable.

Christian certainly seems to have no qualms about stating who he is in this arena. This thought excites me. This is my definitive proof that he and I could be more than just friends.

The Wilde Boys are good. Besides Christian playing his Korg synthesizer, the rest of the band is composed of two other dudes playing drums and lead guitar, dressed similarly to Christian, and a petite pretty girl playing the bass and singing lead vocal. She is dressed not differently from the announcer.

I don't recognize any of them from Bart's Bay High, but then again, I was only there for two days. They played some original songs that were not horrible, but not memorable, and competent covers of current synth bands including Yaz/Yazoo, Soft Cell and Depeche Mode.

The female vocalist announces it is their last song for the night. It begins with Christian playing a distinctive synthesizer chord progression that makes the crowd go wild: Joy Division's "Love Will Tear Us Apart." Unlike the rest of the set, Christian is singing the lead vocal, capturing Ian Curtis's remorseful droning voice perfectly!

Ian Curtis's suicide pops into my head and I was sad for a moment that the world would never get to hear more songs from such a tortured genius. I also briefly think about Angelus.

Christian looks like he's in his element, closing his eyes as he sings the penitent chorus, playing the haunting synthesizer melody. I'm totally enamored. Members of the audience are dancing on the floor in front of the stage and in between the columns, crowding the club with slow melodic head swinging and arms swaying to the rhythm of Christian's playing. Instinctively, I join this mob, swaying to the beat and blending into the swirl of bodies.

When the Wilde Boys finish their last song, the crowd rewards the band with thunderous applause and catcalls. After their bows, Christian comes bounding from the stage over to me, with a huge grin on his face.

I immediately embrace him, hugging him closely and forcefully, my head resting against his neck for a brief period. He doesn't resist. I feel the curvature of his strong neck as my head blends into his shoulder. As my arms encircle the broadness of his back, my t-shirt-clad chest molds into his massive pecs, his hard nipples pushing into the thin fabric and depressing my flesh.

Our torsos are melding into each other. I can feel an unmistakable growing hardness in his groin, pushing against the crotch of his shorts and onto the tight denim surrounding my thigh. My developing erection is pushing with equal force against his thigh. I'm excited by his touch, the pressure against my body, but it is more than that. The trauma of the night before has left me vulnerable, and the feeling of a man's strong embrace makes me feel safe.

Christian knew it. When we finally release each other, we look at each other, smiling big dumb smiles that anyone could have recognized as something more than friendly grins.

"You guys were excellent! You sounded so great, especially the Joy Division song. You never told me you were a singer," I shout over the in-between-sets music, The Clash's "Should I Stay I or Should I Go."

"Mandy usually does most of the singing, but she couldn't quite capture the sound for that song, so I tried it one day and the band liked it, and we decided to keep it in our set," he humbly responds.

His humility makes me even more attracted to him.

"I have to stay for the next band. They are responsible for us getting this gig, but we can cut out of here after that if you want. Alternatively, we could stay for the headliner; they are hard-core, very Butthole Surfers. What do you want to do?" Christian shouts to me over the music and the low roar of the crowd as the next band is setting up.

"Whatever you want to do. I'm open. I'd like to have a few more beers and hang with you here, but maybe we could get some food, just the two of us later?" I hopefully request as I look into his eyes.

"Yeah, that sounds good. I didn't get any dinner. I was running late for the gig," he states as he orders his drink from the bar.

"Let me get that," I interrupt as he's fishing for some money from the black leather and silver studded wallet he has chained to his shorts. He obliges and lets me pay for his beer, a draft from a local brewery I had never heard of. I order another Guinness Extra Stout Draught, and raising my pint glass to shoulder level, I make the gesture for a toast to Christian. He holds his pint glass in the same position. "Here's to your band, to your singing…and to us," I boldly state.

Christian smiles at me with that beautiful toothy smile, gently tapping my glass, and we both drank. He introduced me to the other members of the band, and we had a few more beers with his crew. Chatting by the bar, we discuss current music, our residence at Antioch, Reagan's fucked-up administration, including his botched handling of the AIDS crisis, and the prospects for the Democratic Presidential nominee in 1984. We hung with them through the second band, smoked a bone made from the drummer's homegrown in the alley behind the bistro, and then left after Christian thanked the lead singer of the second band for the recommendation. He also collected his share of the $50.00 they made for the night.

After Christian divides the spoils with the rest of the band, he tells them we're going to get some food. They get the hint that he wants to be alone with me. I shake the guy's hands customarily and kiss Mandy on the cheek as we depart. Heading toward the Main Square, we arrive at Hank's Café, the only place open at 10 p.m. on a Friday night. The clientele is composed of other young people who had been at the show and grizzled-looking shore men. It is not an Edward Hopper crowd.

We order something called *poutine*—French fries covered in a special brown gravy and topped with cheese curds and onion rings with mayonnaise instead of ketchup—and we split a lobster roll. We eat our food slowly, talking about our families and our aspirations for college, and other plans. We do not talk about the incident with Anvil Millstone, although I sense that Christian wants to, to see how I'm handling the trauma.

It's midnight, and Hank's is closing. I cannot believe that two hours has passed. It went by so fast. We decide to go for a walk by the shore to walk off some of the food and beer. We make our way down Bay Street where the final band is just finishing at the bistro and we head toward the beach. Christian unexpectedly cups his right hand into my left hand and clasps his fingers around my hand. We are holding hands out in public, albeit at midnight in the moonlight of a small town, but in 1983 for two men to show this type of affection for one another openly is a risk.

Strolling to the end of the dock/boardwalk, we jump down onto the beach releasing our hands. But once we find our footing, we quickly clasp them together, fingers intertwined, and slowly make our way around the shore of the bay. As we walk, we cannot stop staring at and talking about the brilliance of the full moon and how brightly it is reflecting on the calmer water of the bay. Feeling the moment, I pause and swing Christian gently toward me so that we are face to face. The moonlight reflecting on the contours of his masculine face, I gaze into his eyes. Releasing my hand from his and using both of my hands, I cup his strong jawline so that my thumbs rest on either side of his mouth and place my lips softly against his. He responds to my kiss by placing his hands on my hips and pulling me closer so our bodies are nestled next to each other. I then open my mouth slightly to feel more of his lips on mine, and he does the same. Then I feel his tongue glide tenderly along my upper lip. Opening my mouth, my tongue softly massages his lips and tongue in return. It feels amazing. I release myself totally, allowing our kissing to get more intense, breathing faster through my nose.

Dropping my hands gradually from his face along his neck, I circle them to his broad shoulders, then to the back of his muscular arms and then to his shoulder blades. Rubbing each other's back, our hands explore each other's muscular frames until we both find the curvature of the lower back and then pull each other so that our groins are completely meshed. We groan into each other's mouths as we feel the hardness in our pants rubbing against each other. I can feel Christian's impressive girth. Grinding our hips against each other, torsos locked together, our hands begin to explore the lower part of each other's back simultaneously, feeling the fullness of our butts.

Christian moans as I forcefully cup his muscular cheeks. Our breathing starts to get more rapid and shallow, our breath escaping in between kisses. The pleasure from our erections rubbing against each other through our pants is indescribable. The heat in my erection intensifies. I explode in my boxer shorts, groaning loudly into Christian's mouth. Releasing my mouth from his, I gasp for breath as shocks of pleasure ran through my body, shaking me as I continued to hold him against me. My erection, enveloped in the wetness of my pelvis, slides against the spunk as Christian continues to grind his thick erection into my groin, both of us breathing heavily.

Suddenly, he gasps, a slight high-pitched cry escaping his lips. His face contorts in pain, eyes tightly closed. After groaning, his expression relaxes, gasping for air. His rapid breaths become more controlled, as he licks his lips and labors to inhale through his nose.

Looking at him as he continues to reel from the pleasure of his release, I kiss him passionately on the lips, circling my tongue and tracing every inch of his lips as I paint his mouth with my tongue. He does the same until our involuntary shocks disappear.

I pull slightly away from him, so that our torsos are not locked together, and look at him with a sense of wonder. I then kiss him lightly on the mouth and bend my neck toward him so that my forehead rests against his. I can hear the cessation of his breath as well. I then start to laugh quietly. Moving my head back, I look up to see him with a small grin on his face and detect a guttural chuckle coming from the back of his throat. Then we burst out laughing together. Embracing him tightly, I place my right hand on the back of his head and start to rub back and forth in the stiff hair messing up his finely coiffed faux hawk.

"Well, what do we do for an encore?" I quietly joke. We both snort at my strange statement.

Moving away from him slightly, I look down at my pants to see a rather large spot of darker-colored denim illuminated by the light of the full moon. Christian did the same, but I cannot see any trace of a darker area on his black shorts. I bend my knees and slowly lie down on the sand. Christian follows my lead and lies down next to me. Nuzzling next to me, he places his head in the gap between my left shoulder and neck and places his left thigh on top of mine. I part my thighs slightly so that his thigh could fit more easily between mine. My left arm is now around his back, and I start to stroke the back of his head.

We both look up, staring at the sky in silence. The moon, large and radiant, seems to be within our grasp. I start to feel drowsy and let sleep take over. Waking a few minutes later, I turn my head slightly to the left and see the most handsome face sleeping on my chest. I raise my hand and gently caress the outline of his jaw and cheekbones, glowing in the moonlight, with my fingertips. His face is magnificent. Christian begins to rouse from his sleep. He opens his eyes, those piercing blue eyes staring at me for a moment. He then moves his head so that his lips are heading toward my mouth. I meet his mouth with a light kiss, gently caressing his fine cheekbone.

"I wonder if it will always be this perfect,"

Christian asks me as he tucks his head closer into my neck.

I think about his question for a few moments as I stare into the sky. I then felt a sudden sense of dread. Moving my arm around his back, I pull him closer to me as if to meld our bodies together into one. I close my eyes.

****

I get home late. As I drive up the long driveway, I turn off the headlights of my Jeep so that the bright lights wouldn't alert the parental units that I was coming home way after my curfew. The moon is still brightly illuminating the contours of the driveway as I slowly creep along. I detect the movement of a large black shape in the trees in my left peripheral vision. Turning my head to focus on the shape in the trees, I see that it is the bald eagle. It has returned. As I drive next to the branch it is perched upon, the eagle cocks its head toward me, fixating its stare directly at me. In the pitch blackness, it is unnerving to say the least.

After parking the car, I quickly get out and approach the side of the house where the balcony to my room is located. Looking around to see if the house and grounds provide any possible way for me to climb into the balcony, I deduce that if I can get onto the roof of the porch, I can grasp the low railing of the balcony and hoist myself over it. The only problem is that there is a two-foot gap between the railing and the roofline, which means that I will have to jump to grab the railing, and it's a good 15 feet to the ground from the bottom of the balcony. I must try.

Stealthily, I use the railing on the ground floor and the column of the porch to shimmy onto the roof of the porch. Standing on the roof of the porch next to the balcony, after taking a deep breath, I jump to grasp the side of the railing with both hands. It's easier than I thought. Using my upper body strength, I slowly pull my torso up to the ledge of the railing. Swinging my right leg around, my right foot lands on the railing with a low-intensity thud. I rotate the rest of my body over the railing and roll onto the floor of the balcony with a louder thud. Instantly, I look over to the balcony of my parent's room to see if there is any movement, and seeing that there's no stirring of any kind, I quickly recover and quietly open the French doors to my bedroom. With light footfalls, I walk over to the bed and strip myself quickly. I take my stained boxers and wipe off my pelvis, stashing my boxers under the bed with my soiled jeans so that I can wash them by hand in the morning. I then slip on a pair of basketball shorts and get into bed.

As I lay in bed, I recap the events of the night, thinking about how hot Christian is and the amazing orgasm I had a few hours ago. As I envision our deep kissing and the feel of the curves of his muscular body, his erect nipples pushing into my chest, I start to get hard again. Flipping the sheet off my chest and abdomen, I put my right hand under the waist of my basketball shorts. Sliding my shorts down past my pelvis, I grab my erection with my right hand for a hot masturbation session thinking about Christian. Lightly stimulating my nipples with my thumbs, I visualize Christian's pecs rubbing against mine...unexpectedly, the room becomes very cold.

My chest, abdomen, and pelvis feel like they're being covered with a thin sheet of frost. My nipples are uncomfortably erect. The water vapor in my breath crystallizes as I exhale through my mouth. I grab the sheets and yank them up over me. Reaching for the quilt at the foot of the bed with both hands, I unfold it, snap it open in the air, and lay it across my shivering body. Crossing my arms under the sheet and quilt, I try to conserve my body heat and warm myself to calm the chill.

Shivering, watching my breath form in the air, I see a white filmy mist floating in the air next to the bed. The translucent mist quickly increases in size and intensity. As it starts to take shape, the opaque mass becomes more defined, lengthening into a human-sized form with arms, legs, and a head. The details of the misty being become sharper. It is developing into the shape of a naked man. Angelus. As frightened as I am, I cannot help but study this stunning apparition. He's perfect in every way, glowing with angelic resonance.

Angelus then approaches the bed. His figure becomes somewhat blurry as he moves, as if part of him must catch up with the rest of his being. When his ethereal parts are assembled next to the bed, he leans over me and looks me in the eyes. His face has a serious expression, but I don't feel as if he's going to do me any harm. Knowing I'm overwhelmed by his presence, his facial expression changes and becomes more sympathetic. He then slowly raises his ghostly hand and moves it closer to my face. Placing his spirit hand on my forehead, I feel a distinct chill, and then I lose all consciousness.

Visions flash rapidly in my brain during my dream state.

****

81

I'm in the body of a small person standing and peeking over a pew into the interior of a church. I see a flash of a bright stained-glass window of Jesus, the Virgin Mary, and angels. A statue of Mary and an angel stand next to the window, a sculpture of the Annunciation. I'm now looking down the aisle of the church at the figure of Jesus on the cross as it hangs above the pulpit. My view focuses on the body of Christ, the muscularity of his arms, his chest, his abdomen with the wound, the sinewy legs that cross over each other, and the long feet that are nailed together. Quickly, the scene changes, and I'm looking down at a crucifix that fits into my small hands. The cross itself is made of gold, but the figure of Christ is sculpted from silver. It is a lovely likeness of Jesus. I study the sculpture of the naked, muscular lean man in bondage on this smaller intimate cross. Suddenly, I hear a voice, a woman's voice:

"Now you have your own Jesus, Angelus. The Lord is here to protect you."

I now look toward the woman's voice, and I see her face. She's beautiful. Her strawberry blond hair is pulled back into a bun, with tendrils of hair framing her kind face. She has pale white skin and flashing blue eyes. She's smiling, the generous lips pulled back to the corners of her mouth to reveal perfect white teeth. The high collar of her white blouse is accentuated with a cameo, placed in the middle of the lace that adorns her collar. Her blouse has long sleeves that are puffed at the shoulder. I lean into her so that my head is resting on her arm, my face looking at her neck.

The vision changes again. The gold cross with the silver Jesus is now hanging above a small bed made of dark wood. I hear another voice as I admire the cross. It's a darker voice, a man's voice:

"Ayuh, Angelus, don't you rely too much on that hunk of metal to save you. There are two kinds of men that go to church, the penitent man who asks for God's forgiveness for his shortcomings in life and the hypocrite. I choose to be neither. Which will you be?"

A flash of bright light and another change of scenery. I'm in a bedchamber, looking at the woman who gave me the cross. She's lying in a bed and her beautiful face is withered-looking. She's wearing a white nightgown with a high collar and long sleeves, but it is unbuttoned around the neck. The sheets and coverlet of the bed are pulled up to her waist, her arms lie next to her motionless. She slowly turns her head toward me. She's still a young woman, but her cheeks are hollow, and her white skin is grayish around the sockets of her eyes.

There's another woman in a white Victorian-style dress with an apron and a white head covering that drapes behind her shoulders. I think she's a nurse. She's sitting next to the sick woman in bed, holding a large piece of white cloth in her hand stained with blood. There's a basin of water between the women. The sick woman is now coughing, and the nurse takes the cloth and places it over her mouth. I can see more blood on the cloth after her coughing fit. The nurse removes the cloth from the woman's mouth, places it in the bowl, wrings the bloody water from the cloth, and gently cleans the blood from the dying woman's lips and the corners of her mouth.

The sick woman turns her head to look at me, smiling weakly to reveal teeth darkened with blood, and speaks slowly to me in a low forced whisper, "Angelus, my angel, I will be with our Lord soon. I love you so much. I'm so sorry that I'm leaving you. You be a good boy for your father."

She then closes her mouth and there is silence. Her turned head then sinks further into the pillow as the tension in her neck disappears and she closes her eyes. The people in the room are crying and wailing. The being I'm possessing places his small hand into her hand. I can hear him sobbing as well. My point of view soars above the bed to look at the dead woman and the people crowded around her, and then I'm flying out of the window.

Another flash of bright light. I'm now inside a large building seeing blurry shapes of people in Victorian dress sitting in the dark in rows of seats ascending along a slope. The vision is hazy, and I'm looking at the people from the vantage point as if I'm lying down. I realize I'm lying down on a stage of a theater. I'm hearing a male voice, an actor presumably, speaking on stage and it is an old version of the English language. I recognize it as I hear more of the actor speaking; it's Shakespeare. Now my view is changing as my head is being lifted, turned, and settled onto a soft but firm surface. I'm now squinting at the actor, as my head has been lifted closer toward him. He's dressed in medieval clothing, peering down at me, speaking to me as he props my head. "Now cracks a noble heart. Good night, sweet prince. And flights of angels sing thee to thy rest!" I recognize it as Horatio's soliloquy in the final death scene in Hamlet.

A flash of bright light and I'm looking at a wooden floor. It's not the floor of the theater. There are small droplets of blood dripping on the floor coming from a place on my face close to my eyes. I see a pale hand coming toward my face and feel the exquisite pain once the hand slaps my face. I have a wound and I'm trying to stop the bleeding. I then look up to see a large gruff-looking man standing above me and he's holding his right fist in the palm of his left hand. He has short gray hair, small angry eyes, a handlebar mustache above a cruel-looking mouth, and a square jawline. He's dressed in a long-sleeved white shirt, rolled to his elbows, suspenders with silver clips buttoned to leather straps attached to dark trousers.

"When I tell you to do something, I don't want excuses!" he barks at me.

As he leans down toward me, his hands move in front of my eyes. I'm cowering from the man. His hand grasps my shirt and the pressure of the cloth tightens against my back, pulling me up from the floor. I see him pull back his fist and it is coming toward my face…

****

I wake up. A thin film of sweat covers my face, neck, chest, and arms. I'm breathing rapidly. The freezing temperature in the room has disappeared. I check the space between the bed and the balcony, but it's empty. Angelus is gone.

Lying in my bed, I try to understand what I have just experienced. I assume the visions were parts of Angelus's past. Why did Angelus reveal those deeply personal moments of his life to me?

More importantly, why now?

Chapter 10

Antioch
History of the Bartholomew Family
June 8, 1983

The next morning, I'm more intrigued than ever to find out more about Angelus Bartholomew III and the Bartholomew family. I have a gut feeling that Angelus showed me those flashbacks of his life to spark my curiosity and discover more about him. I quickly put on a t-shirt, and descend the grand staircase to get coffee. Mom is preparing for our traditional Saturday morning breakfast when I enter the kitchen,

"Good morning, honey, I'm making Belgian waffles today."

"Okay. Hey, how much research have you done so far on the Bartholomew family?" I inquire.

"I've completed my preliminary research. Why? Are you interested?" she responds, with an air of surprise in her voice.

"Yeah, I mean the town is named after them, not to mention every other building in town. If we're going to live here, I would like to know more about them." This wasn't completely a lie.

"Sure, it's on my desk in a blue folder," she says, pouring the batter into the griddle, "Hey! How was your concert last night?"

I shout my answer as I walk into the living room. "It was great! Christian's band had several original songs, and they played some great covers. Christian sang the lead on that Joy Division song I like."

I find the blue folder, walk back into the kitchen, and sit at the table. "We went to Hank's for some food after the second band. The third band was too hard-core, I wasn't up for that. Christian's a cool kid," I say nonchalantly as I skim the document, coffee in hand.

"I'm glad you're making friends."

As I continue to examine her research, I'm waiting for her to say something about my coming home after curfew, but she never says anything. I thought that was curious. Of course, I wasn't going to mention my late-night maneuvers on the porch and balcony. I guess she didn't hear me.

"Is it okay if I take this outside and read it on the porch while I eat my breakfast?"

"I would prefer you read it after you eat. It's my only copy," she answers as she places a waffle on my plate.

Preparing my waffle with copious amounts of butter and syrup, I quickly gobble it down. I then rinse my dish and place it in the sink. Once on the porch with my coffee, file in hand, I settle into one of the large Adirondack chairs and read her tome of the Bartholomew family.

Here is a synopsis of the research my mother conducted on the Bartholomew family:

The shipping company was named 153 Fishing Industries; apparently, the number 153 refers to the number of fish that the disciple Simon Peter caught when Jesus told him to throw his net over the right side of the boat in the Sea of Galilee. Angelus Bartholomew I, the wealthy, religious patriarch of the family that built the shipping empire and the mansion Antioch, gave the company the name. Angelus Bartholomew I touted himself as the epitome of the religious man in the Edwardian era, but he was a hypocrite. Although he pontificated about Christian values and built one of the churches in Bartholomew Bay, Bartholomew Bay Church of Christ, he cheated on his wife, Adelina Bartholomew, from the day they were married. A frequent visitor of the brothels in Boston and Manhattan (these were the main ports for his import/export business), he contracted syphilis from a prostitute and died at the age of 40 in 1893. Although the family stated that the cause of death was dementia, Angelus I died in an insane asylum; it was discovered post-mortem on the death certificate that he died from syphilitic plaques in the brain. This diagnosis was discovered by one of his sons, Angus Bartholomew, in 1895, when he was 15 years old.

Angelus I and Adelina had two sons, Angelus Bartholomew II, born in 1878 and Angus Bartholomew, born in 1880. The brothers were very close. Their father was absent most of their lives, and their mother, although kind and loving, was very religious and completely submissive to her husband, and had little to say about how their sons would be raised. The brothers had to rely on each other to navigate the challenges of their lives, specifically, those associated with their father's erratic behavior in the last years of his life. Angelus I had begun to show signs of his disease long before he was committed to an asylum, and unfortunately, he acted upon his delusions with his sons when he was in his worst state of dementia. Accusing the boys of being possessed by the devil for typical boyish behavior, then punishing or torturing them to drive the "demons" out. In addition to the physical abuse, he mentally and emotionally abused his wife and sons until he was committed.

Angelus II, named after his father, was killed in 1895. He was struck by lightning when he and Angus were caught in a sudden, violent, thunderstorm while they were walking along the cliffside on the grounds of Antioch. He was 17 years of age. Angus was devastated, as his big brother was the only real father figure he had growing up. Adelina Bartholomew literally died of a "broken heart" shortly after losing Angelus II. She was already fragile after her husband's death, but the shock of her son dying so young was too much for her delicate constitution. Angus was alone in the world at 16 years of age. Because of his father's religious hypocrisy, his mother's death, and Angelus II dying so young from a lightning strike, Angus abandoned the devout Christian beliefs his mother tried to instill in him. His father said there were two types of men that go to church: the penitent man and the hypocrite; and since he was neither, he didn't go to church. However, when Angus inherited the family business after Angelus II passed, he continued to provide for the church his father built in Bartholomew Bay. He knew that if the villagers were content with their religious needs, then there would be little animosity toward him for not being a "church going man."

It was under Angus' control, that 153 Fishing Industries became the most powerful company in the area. He had a keen business sense. He also suffered from alcoholism. The scars from his father's abuse had made him turn to the bottle early in his life. Angus married Victoria Carstairs Bartholomew in 1900, when he was 20 years old, and she was 18 years old. Victoria Carstairs, an extremely beautiful woman, came from a prominent family in Portland. Victoria was an avid supporter of the arts, responsible for sponsoring and bringing nationally recognized symphonies and theatrical productions to Bartholomew Bay. She was responsible for the construction of the Bartholomew Theater in town. Sadly, she passed away from consumption (cancer) in 1912, at the age of 30, before it was finished. They had one son in 1901, Angelus Bartholomew III, who was named after Angus' brother, and not his father, a fact that Angus repeated when anyone inquired. Angelus Bartholomew III inherited his mother's looks. A tall strapping young man with sharp features, strawberry blond hair, and pale white skin, he was an exceptionally handsome "angelic looking" young man. He was only 11 years old when his mother passed away. He watched her deteriorate from a beautiful young woman to an emaciated sickly creature. This early experience with death was something that changed Angelus III forever, never recovering emotionally from her death.

It was widely known in the town that Angus was a tyrannical father, but after Victoria died, he expected perfection from his son. When Angelus III did not live up to his father's expectations, Angus physically and emotionally abused him, especially when Angus had been drinking. Angus transformed into his father when he drank. Unfortunately, Angelus III committed suicide *by jumping from the widow's walk of Antioch in 1919, when he was just 18 years old. They found his nude, broken body on the stone pavement below the widow's walk. The obituary described him as an "artistic soul," a euphemism that was often used at the time to describe someone with a sensitivity uncommon for men in that era.*

Many blamed Angus' physical abuse during his alcoholic rages for his son's suicide, but some believed that it was his son's uncanny resemblance to Victoria that fueled Angus's anger toward Angelus III, and that is what caused Angelus III to take his life. The townsfolk were forbidden to talk about this tragedy for 20 years until Angus' death in 1939. He died from cirrhosis of the liver. The fact that Angelus III was found naked raised many questions, increasing the scandalous talk in the village. Many people of Bartholomew Bay suspected that it was not suicide that killed the beautiful Angelus III; that it was his father who pushed him from the widow's walk.

After Angus's death, it was the end of the Bartholomew family line. He never re-married nor had any more children. Without any heirs or will, the shipping business was taken over by the state of Maine and Antioch went up for auction. The many tragedies that happened to the Bartholomew family at Antioch, which had to be revealed by realtors, discouraged people from buying Antioch. Many who had worked in the house after Angelus the third's death claim that it is haunted by his vengeful ghost. Antioch lay abandoned and in ruin for 44 years. Until Mary Meade purchased it in 1983.

After reading about the history of the Bartholomew

family and learning more about Angelus III's life and tragic death, I felt more sympathetic to his visitations. He was a young man who seemed to be born into the perfect family: wealthy, charitable, and prestigious. However, he was tortured emotionally and physically by his alcoholic father and either committed suicide or was murdered in the prime of his life. The image of his head being crushed by the pavement, as Angelus had shown me that first night, confirmed that he had fallen from the widow's walk, but it did not tell me how or why he fell. Perhaps, he would reveal this to me. Perhaps, not.

****

Later that same day, Christian calls. Essentially checking in with me to make sure I had gotten home all right, which is sweet. He was also curious as to how I got in after curfew. I explain how I climbed on the porch roof and jumped to the balcony, hoisting myself over the railing. He's impressed. We're talking about what a great time we had together when I change the subject.

"Hey, Christian, what do you know about the guy that fell off the widow's walk at Antioch, Angelus…" I ask coyly.

"Ayuh, Angelus Bartholomew III. It was widely believed that his father pushed him off the widow's walk because he found him in bed with another man. One of the servants said he had heard a commotion on the porch the night Angelus III died, like someone jumping from the porch roof to the ground and saw a naked man running in the backyard. However, it was never reported or discussed at the time, not until after Angus Bartholomew's death. My grandpa told me that

Angus threatened the newspapers or anyone in town never to talk about his son's death. Everyone was to accept that he jumped, and never speak of it again. It is the biggest scandal that has ever rocked Bart's Bay. If the part about the naked man running away from the house is true, then Angelus III was probably pushed off the walk by his father for being gay. To me, that has always been the saddest part of the story."

A split second later, Christian interjects, "Have you ever seen what Angelus III looked like? He was hot!" I'm silent as I absorb Christian's tale of Angelus. "Hello, are you still there?"

"Yeah, sorry, I was just thinking about what you said. Man, what a tragic story. So, what are you up to today?" I say, changing the subject again.

"I have to help my dad with some stuff around the house, and then we're going to my aunt's house for dinner. Are you busy tomorrow?" Christian inquires.

"No, want to meet in town for breakfast or lunch?"

"Ayuh, let's meet for lunch after I get back from church. How about Hanks at twelve-thirty?" he responds.

"Sounds like a plan. And then we can decide what to do...afterward," I say with a bit of mystery in my voice.

"I'm sure we can think of something," he says demurely. "Hey, I've been meaning to ask you this ever since I found out that you live in Antioch. Have you seen any ghosts? I've always been told that that place is haunted."

I'm silent for a moment. "No, not yet, just creepy noises, it's an old house."

I'm not ready to talk about my encounters with

Angelus to anyone…yet.

****

I was beat from the previous night, so I go to bed early. It's the earliest I have gone to bed on a Saturday night in ages. I've the whole summer to stay up and party, with Christian, and hopefully, with other new friends. After taking a quick shower, I put on a pair of basketball shorts and slip into bed. I'm tired. It won't take long for me to fall asleep tonight.

Lying there on my back, my head resting on the pillow, hand on my crotch, I'm almost asleep when I feel the temperature in the room drop quickly. The cold permeates my exposed face, arms, chest, and my nipples become uncomfortably erect, again. I know what's coming next.

I open my eyes, and this time, Angelus is floating above me. His ghostly face hovering above mine is close enough to kiss me, if that's possible. I'm not afraid, but I don't move a muscle. My frosty breath dissolves when it comes close to his visage. He's smiling at me, looking like the stunning young man in the portrait and the photograph Mary had unearthed. His blond hair falling to his shoulders, not hanging down around his face like it would if it were a human in the same position. It's as if his body looks like it would if he was standing up, only inverted so that he's parallel to me. I tilt my head to look down at the rest of his naked ghostly body as it is suspended above mine; he had an amazing body when he was alive. I want to reach out and touch his ethereal presence, but I don't.

Angelus then raises his hand toward my face to touch my forehead. I knew he was going to share more of his life with me through a dream, as he had done before. The chill from his fingertips sends a shiver down my spine. I'm unconscious in seconds, rapidly propelled through a dark tunnel and then I hear a voice and see a light.

Chapter 11

Angelus and Lazarus
Re-acquaintance
June 13, 1919

The first time I saw Lazarus Benedictine was in the summer of 1919. We're both 18 years of age. My father asked me to deliver some shipping schedules to the lighthouse keeper, Erasmus Benedictine, at the Bartholomew Bay lighthouse, a few miles from Antioch. I ride my bicycle along the coastal road that hugs the rocky shoreline and the thick Maine forest until the northernmost point of the bay, where the Bartholomew Bay lighthouse stands.

The point is a steep rocky promontory that serves the shipping industry well in Bartholomew Bay which gradually slopes to the sea. The coastal road becomes a narrower path as it crosses into the rocky interior, approaching the small cottage and lighthouse made of white-washed stone with red roofs. I ride my bicycle along the path where it ends in front of the cottage and lean my bicycle against the wall next to the front door, also painted red but faded from the weathered peeling paint.

Securing the satchel with the papers around my neck, I give the door a series of swift knocks. I wait a minute or so but there's no answer. The peeling door receives another series of swift knocks, louder this time, and again, no answer from inside.

I walk from the cottage toward the lighthouse, looking up into the tower and call, "Hello."

The sun reflecting from the large glass plates that surround the light casts a brilliant haze, but the details of the balcony surrounding the light tower are discernable and nobody is present, nor does any being respond to my call. Walking around the lighthouse to investigate the grounds further, I spy a small shack made of gray weathered boards and a large barrel perched above the pitch of the roof. The sound of water splashing onto rocks emanates from the structure.

I surmise that this must be some sort of crude outdoor shower in which the water was collected by the barrel. As I move closer to the shack, I notice the barrel's metal spigot, a shower stall made from crude slat board, and a half door. I call out to the person operating the shower. No answer. I walk closer, down the steep path of rocks and grasses to the ram-shackled structure to indicate my presence when, suddenly, a young man steps into the path away from the archway of the shack. He is completely naked, facing the sea, with his back turned to me, toweling himself.

His skin is a golden brown, from the nape of his neck to the soles of his feet. There are no white patches of untanned skin like the sunburnt people I have known all my life. His hair is dark brown, curled only at the ends, and it hangs to the base of his head. From behind, the youth looked like Michelangelo's David, fallen off its pedestal and soaking up the dewy droplets left from the morning's sea mist.

His shoulders are broad and well-muscled,

blending into two strong arms that hold the towel as it brushes back and forth across the young man's sinewy backside. The smooth muscled flesh of his back forms a V as it progresses toward his waist. The arc in the small of the back slopes into two well-rounded buttocks, separated by a triangular mass of flesh and bone that keeps the orbs of muscle firmly in place. The smooth cheeks transition into two well-developed thighs, appendages that glisten in the morning sun. His lightly hairy thighs blend into solid calves, well-defined and sculpted. The perfect toes of naturally tanned feet bend with ease as he changes positions to towel the moisture off his well-proportioned legs.

He then places the towel onto his head to dry his dark brown locks, turning his back to the ocean, giving me a view of the front half of this Poseidon that had climbed out of the sea. With the towel over his head, he cannot see that I continue to admire his body.

His chest is perfectly shaped, each mound crowned by a quarter-sized, dark brown circle and nipple, brilliantly outlined by the sunlight when he rotates his body. The expanse of the chest is matted with fine, dark hair, increasing in density in the valley between each rectangle of flesh. The well-defined chest tapers into a belly, flat, smooth, and chiseled, intersecting lines of muscle forming six cubes of skin. The dimpled naval caps a trail of exquisitely delicate, dark brown hair that sprouts from his flesh and leads to a mass of curly dark brown pubic hair.

Further defining this area are two indentations on the outer edges of the cubes of abdominal flesh that separate the groin from the upper part of his thighs. Each of these gutter-like structures progresses toward the pad of dark, curly hair. Below this triangle of flesh, bone, and hair, his beautifully shaped cock sprung from his body, bouncing slightly as he moves his body. The length is the same shade of pigmentation that covers the rest of his body, but the perfect mushroom-shaped cap is a slightly lighter shade. The phallus is nestled next to a golden, brown sack of skin that conceals two round orbs. The sunlight illuminating his member casts a shadow on his right thigh. The view of well-built thighs, legs and feet is consistent and complements the previous view.

With the rocky cliff of the point and the ocean as the background to this beautiful scene, I'm reminded of a painting: Flandrin's *Nude Youth Sitting by the Sea.* Of course, this man isn't sitting on the rocky shore, but his bowing head, anatomical features, and coloring could have inspired Hippolyte Flandrin's masterpiece.

I soon realize that I've been observing this beautiful man for a considerable amount of time, and out of guilt and purpose, I finally make the gesture to communicate once again. "Hello?"

The young man, startled, quickly covers his mid-section with the towel, and angrily barks, "Who are you! How long have you been standing there?"

His oval-shaped face is framed with dark brown hair, the wet tendrils gently lying across the forehead, and prominent cheekbones. His soulful eyes are almond-shaped with chocolate brown centers, surrounded by lustrous black lashes. Thick eyebrows as dark as his hair arch perfectly above the deep, penetrating eyes. A thin nose that slopes into a button-like knob sits above lips, thick and curvaceous: the top lip arching triumphantly toward his delicate nose, while the bottom lip curves downward to form a shape that reminds me of an archer's bow. This magnificent face is completed with a slight indentation in the chin that accentuates his full bottom lip. His was a face that someone could fall in love with at first sight. And I did.

"I knocked on the front door several times and called out, but nobody answered. I walked around to see if there was anyone at home on the other side of the lighthouse, heard the water splashing and…here I am. I'm Angelus Bartholomew, and I'm here to get some papers signed for my father, Angus Bartholomew. Do you know who—"

"Yes, I know who your father is," the young man exclaims, cutting me off.

"Erasmus needs to sign these papers and I need him to sign for the receipt," I explain.

"My papa is not home," the young man responds.

"Oh, Erasmus is your father! Well, if you are a Benedictine, then you could sign them. As I said, I'm Angelus…and what is your name?" I ask as I extend my hand.

"Lazarus Benedictine," he states as he shakes my hand.

Tightening his towel to make it more secure, Lazarus grabs his clothes hanging over the shower stall, and proceeds to walk up the path toward the lighthouse in his bare feet. I follow Lazarus up the path, around the lighthouse and enter the cottage through the door I had knocked upon earlier. We enter a large room with white plastered walls, rafters made from unfinished lumber, a fireplace made from fieldstone, and a kitchen of sorts in the back. The room is furnished with the most basic furniture: a kitchen table with a few chairs, two large, cushioned chairs, and a couch in front of the fireplace.

"Why were you taking a shower outside?" I ask.

"Plumbing is old and it's easier in the summer to use the rain barrel shower than bathing in the tub like we have to do in the winter when we have to boil water on the stove and pour it into the tub," Lazarus humbly explains. I'm horrified by this notion, as we have running taps in Antioch.

Lazarus leaves the room through a door on the right side of the kitchen to change into his clothes. I assume he's going into the lighthouse as there is no more area in the cottage and the lighthouse is attached on the right side of the cottage.

Sitting down in one of the big chairs, I notice a sketchbook on the seat. Curious, I open it and flip through a series of charcoal drawings: immaculate seascapes of Bartholomew Bay, renderings of a park with people and tall buildings in the background, and rough figure drawings, most of them male and of the working class. Lazarus returns to the room wearing a simple white button-down shirt, and blue trousers. Walking briskly, he quickly grabs the sketchbook out of my hands.

Innocently, I smile at him. "You're good," I say, trying to distract him after invading his privacy.

Lazarus doesn't say anything. He gently lays the sketchbook on the table. His eyes are purposely averting mine. He's blushing.

"I've lived in Bartholomew Bay my whole life and I've never seen you, how is that?" I ask, trying to change the topic of conversation.

Looking at me with those beautiful sad brown eyes, he tells me his story: "I had been living in New York

City with my mother's family. My mother passed away when I was nine. She had a heart condition that was brought on by the stress of my birth. My father was not able to take care of a young boy, so he left me with my aunt and uncle. I came back here after my aunt died last year. My uncle died the year before. I had nowhere else to go."

I'm amazed that he reveals something so personal that quickly to a virtual stranger. I guess he wanted to tell someone about it for a long time but didn't have anyone to talk to. It was obvious that his father had abandoned him when he was a young boy, and he couldn't talk to him.

"Where are those papers you need me to sign?" he asks.

I retrieve them from my bag and lay them out on the kitchen table for him to sign. Lazarus had fetched a pen from the lighthouse to sign the papers. Sitting down at the kitchen table, he signs them and the receipt. He has an expressive signature, fitting for an artist.

Like a light bulb going off in my head, I suddenly remember the person, Lazarus Benedictine. I remember his name. I remember the boy who left my grammar school in the middle of the year, the beautiful boy with tan skin.

"Now, I remember you. I remember asking my mother what kind of name Lazarus was. She told me that it was the name of the friend that Jesus raised from the dead, and that act is what made Caiaphas mad enough to have Jesus arrested and crucified. I thought that you were so blessed to have the name of the man who led to Jesus dying for our sins. Of course, I later learned from my father that it was Pontious Pilate who was responsible for Jesus's crucifixion."

"I've had to contend with the significance of my name my whole life. I was named after my mother's grandfather," Lazarus confesses.

"Are you going to go to school in Bartholomew Bay in the fall?"

"My papa says that I can if I'm able to keep up with my work at the lighthouse. It wasn't possible during the winter." Pausing briefly, he looks at me again with those beautiful sad eyes, and states, "I have to get to work, so if there isn't anything else to sign. I need to go."

I got the message, "Oh, all right. I'm sure I'll see you in town this summer, it's a small town."

"Maybe."

I would see Lazarus much sooner than he thought.

****

The voices of the characters in my head became silent. During this silence, I'm transported away from the room in the cottage through the same dark tunnel as before, but this time there is no light at the end of the tunnel.

I wake from this dream state without the sweat and fatigue I had felt the night before. I look around my bedroom, but Angelus's ghost is gone, not floating above me, or standing next to me like in the past. The room isn't cold anymore. It's still nighttime.

Lying in bed, I think about this dream. This dream was different. It was a pleasurable dream. A happy dream. A sexy dream. It was also different because it was about one point in time, not like the dream the night before that was so erratic, jumping from one scene to another.

Angelus wants me to see how he met this man Lazarus for some reason. Lazarus. The same name that Angelus wrote on the frosty glass of the French doors a few nights ago. Lazarus Benedictine (I think that was his last name) was a beautiful man. It was obvious that Angelus was attracted to him. I've so many questions.

Did Angelus share this vision with me because he knew I was attracted to men also?

Is that why he was showing me this part of his life?

Was this the man that Christian had mentioned who was seen running from Antioch the night Angelus died?

Was this the reason Angelus introduced me to Lazarus Benedictine?

I turn over onto my stomach, adjust my head on the pillow, and close my eyes. I want to go back to sleep but one thought keeps creeping into my head…

…this is just the beginning of what Angelus wants me to know.

Chapter 12

Bartholomew Bay
June 9, 1983

I wake up much later than usual the next morning, which isn't a surprise, considering the journey that Angelus had taken me on. I'm not as exhausted after the dream about Lazarus as I had been with the other about Angelus as a child, but it still took a toll on my mind. Angelus had left me more to think about.

Rolling over, I get up and stand in front of the dresser. Picking up the portrait of Angelus, I examine his handsome facial features. With all that I've experienced, I half expect the mouth of the portrait to start to move and tell me more secrets. *What is your endgame?*

Looking at the initials in the right lower corner, L.B., Lazarus Benedictine. Some of the details of the dream were a bit fuzzy, like most dreams, but I knew this name. It was mentioned at the beginning of the dream and throughout the scenario at the lighthouse. Angelus made sure to repeat it often so that I would not forget. Suddenly, I remember the scene at the cottage when Angelus found Lazarus's sketchbook at the lighthouse. "So, Lazarus Benedictine is the mystery artist," I say aloud, proud of my detective work.

As if on cue, an exhalation of breath touches my

right ear. Instinctively, I turn my head to see if Angelus has materialized. He did not. I realize that if he had, this would have been the first time I would have seen his presence during the daylight hours.

I shower, dress, and dash downstairs to meet the rest of my family in the kitchen. "Good morning," I say to everyone as I enter the breakfast area making a beeline for the coffee pot.

"Good morning, honey. I'm making French toast and bacon. How many slices can you eat this morning?" Mary asks.

"A couple. I'm meeting Christian for lunch at twelve-thirty, so I don't want to fill up too much," I respond as I measure the sugar and milk for my coffee.

"Oh? You're seeing a lot of this young man," she comments, using an expression I think sounds oddly like something you would hear on a PBS show, like *Brideshead Revisited.*

I correct her. "Young man? He's a dude, Mom. We like hanging with each other."

"Oh, sure. Hey, maybe you can introduce him to Trista when she comes next weekend?' she adds.

"Yeah, sure."

Shit! I had completely forgotten that Trista Morten, a friend of mine (she thinks we are more) from Boston is coming on Friday and staying for the weekend. She attends a preparatory school for girls that is a companion school to my former all-boys prep school, a feeder school to Wellesley and some of the Ivys. Our families have known each other for generations, and Trista seems to think there will be an inevitable marriage in our future to "secure our families' legacy." She can be fun when she isn't being too much of a preppie.

"All right, I'm outta here," I say, bounding for the front door.

I leave earlier than the time it would take me to reach Hank's Café so that I can check out some of the buildings I had seen in town, namely the Bartholomew Theater near the Main Square. On the way to the garage, I spy the familiar black and white figure lurking in a tree, but this time, it is perched on a branch in a different tree nearer the house, next to the garage. I run back into the house to retrieve my Polaroid Instamatic.

Approaching the tree, looking through the viewfinder at the majestic bald eagle to determine how to frame him for the photograph, I notice it's staring directly at me, as is this eagle's routine. His head occasionally turns slightly to the right or left tracking my every move, but I'm never out of his view. Nevertheless, I do not feel threatened. It could have easily attacked one of us by now if that was its intention. Training my gaze on him, I snap the Instamatic. The flashbulb pops brightly and the white, shiny square expels from the camera. Shaking it to activate the chemicals with the air, the wait for the image to appear begins.

"Sonovabitch," I exclaim loudly.

The image of the eagle is blurred again, but the tree branches and the background are in focus like the previous photograph. I inspect the camera. There are no smudges on the lens or the viewfinder. I make a mental note to get new film while in town.

I park the Jeep in one of the many available parking spots on the Main Square. It's Sunday in a sleepy small town, after all. I walk about a block from the city hall on the main Square to the Bartholomew Theater. It's a fine example of the Gilded Age architecture that Vaudeville theaters were known for, something I had studied in my theater arts class in Boston.

In addition to hosting productions from the Bart's Bay Players, it's also used as a movie theater: a large retractable screen is installed in the ceiling, behind the side curtains on the stage that can be retracted when the stage is in use. Currently, a movie called *Wargames* starring a guy named Matthew Broderick is being advertised on the marquee.

There are flyers on the doors advertising auditions for the summer season of the Bart's Bay Players. The first audition is in two weeks, June 23-24, at 7 p.m. at the Bartholomew Bay community center for the Noel Coward comedy *"Blithe Spirit,"* a play about a vengeful ghost, Elvira, that comes back to kill her husband, Charles Condomine, so that he can be with her for eternity, but accidentally kills his new wife, Ruth. I read the play in school in Boston and was always interested in playing Charles. I grab one of the flyers on the vertical shelf mounted to the wall next to the door.

I then walk to the statue of Angelus Bartholomew I in the middle of the main square. I stare at it, studying his face. He doesn't look like a lunatic infested with syphilitic plaques. He does have the same eyes as Angelus III though: almond-shaped and expressive. Peering into his eyes, I contemplate the cycle of abuse among the Bartholomew men: the physical and emotional acts associated with the mental decay of Angelus I against his sons Angus and Angelus II and the suicide of Angelus III because of Angus's alcohol-infused violence. Glancing at my watch, it's time for me to meet Christian.

Walking into Hank's, the cafe is full, unlike the last two times I had eaten there. Christian is waiting in a booth and stands up when he sees me enter. l almost didn't recognize him. He's not wearing his requisite uniform of black shorts, t-shirt with a band emblazoned on it, and military boots. Rather, he's wearing a light blue button-down short-sleeve shirt, a black tie, khakis, and dark brown docksiders. However, it's his hair that really confuses me: there is no sign of a faux hawk. His strawberry blond hair lying closer to his head, the long bangs combed back behind his right ear to cover the buzz cut along his right temple. He looks sorta preppy, a look that surprisingly suits him. It's obvious that he has come here from church. I walk over to the booth.

"Wow, what a difference!" I say, hugging him. A short but thorough hug, strong enough to feel the iron-like muscles of his chest through the thin cotton shirt.

"Ayuh, I wanted to go home and change before I met you, but coffee hour lasted longer than usual because my parents were the greeters, so I had to wait," he explains in his usual masculine purr, flashing me those innocent but sexy ice blue eyes.

"I think it suits you, I mean, I like the combat rock look also, but you clean up well!" I sit, scooting along the padded bench in the booth. He blushes a little, which surprises me, as he sits down opposite of me.

As soon as he's settled, I place my right hand under the table, reaching over to his side to search for his hand. Touching his right thigh mistakenly during my search makes him jump briefly, with a look of surprise to match the gesture. Eventually, his left hand finds mine and he grasps it tightly, interlocking our fingers together. He flashes that sexy, schoolboy grin.

A waitress comes over to our table, gives us menus, and asks for our drink order. Christian reflexively tries to pull his hand back, but I wouldn't let him. Holding onto it, I rub my thumb over the base of his thumb while smiling at him. His expression of concern soon melts away.

"I'll have a fountain coke," Christian orders.

"Make that two, and can we have an order of onion rings to start?" I say, still holding tightly unto Christian's hand. The waitress nods and leaves our booth.

"Sorry I was so jumpy. I'm not used to holding anyone's hand in public, much less a guy," he apologizes.

"It's cool. I haven't held a guy's hand in public either...I just feel comfortable with you. I feel like I could do a lot with you that I wouldn't have dared a few months ago. I guess I'm just like...fuck it, life is short." Thinking to myself at what I just said, *Cursing on a Sunday? This is a new Griffin Meade.*

After a few minutes, the waitress comes back with our cokes and rings. "Okay, boys, what'll it be?"

"I'll have the cheeseburger deluxe with an extra side of coleslaw," I tell her.

"I'll have the same but without the extra slaw," Christian states. The waitress leaves.

"So, a friend of mine, a girl from Boston, is coming to visit on Friday, and my mother wants you to meet her. But I want you to come over before that so that you can meet my family one-on-one. What night is good for you?"

"Slow down!" Christian excitedly responds. "First, who's this girl? Is she a girlfriend or an ex-girlfriend, hopefully?"

"Well, she thinks we're more than we are. Her family and mine have known each other for ages, and she thinks that we're destined to marry to preserve our family lines. I've never even kissed her except on the cheek. I think it would be very interesting if she met my b…" I stop short.

"Boyfriend? Is that what you were going to say?" Christian slyly inquires as he arches an eyebrow, a devilish look on his face.

"No, I—"

"It's okay dude, I'm not going to bolt. I feel like we're going in that direction too, but let's not get ahead of ourselves."

"You're right. I need to pump the brakes." I sigh, grabbing his hand harder.

"Now, about dinner with the parental units. I have exams this week through Thursday, so I have to study, including tonight, but I would like to come Thursday night, if that's good," Christian asks.

"Thursday it is, I'll tell Mary to slaughter the fatted calf."

"Mary? You call your parents by their first name?" Christian shoots me an inquisitive look.

"No, not to their face. Jack and I always talk about them in the familiar. Mom probably wouldn't care, but Dad's a professor, and he's used to being called 'Dr. Meade,' so I don't know how he would react," I explain.

"Your dad is a doctor? What's his specialty?"

"He has a Ph.D., not an M.D. His concentration is in anatomical sciences, and his research is in brain mapping. He teaches Gross Anatomy at the Medical School. Mom restores and preserves old houses. That's why we moved into Antioch; it's a project for her. What do your parents do in BB?" I question after delivering a rather boring diatribe.

"My parents own an accounting firm. They do the books for three quarters of the businesses in town. It's nothing I've ever wanted to pursue, but they have always given me the freedom to make my own choices. They're neutral about the band but are excited that I want to pursue pediatric medicine."

"Jesus, Dr. Meade is going to love you!"

We discuss our families, friends, and experiences for over an hour. After lunch, we walk together down Main Street toward the Jeep. I realize that our date is almost over. As we approach the car, I notice an alley between two buildings. Quickly seizing on the moment, I grab Christian by the shoulders, pull him into the alley, and seeing that no one was there, I kiss him full on the lips. Christian resists at first, probably from my abruptness, but then eases into the kiss and even gives me a little tongue before it is over.

"You're a bold one, Mr. Meade," he says, wiping my saliva from the corners of his smiling mouth.

Collecting ourselves, we walk toward the Jeep but then continue past it, stopping at the car parked in the next spot, a 1964 Mustang convertible. Christian pulls a key ring from the pocket of his khakis and inserts the key.

"No way! Is this yours?" I ask.

"Sort of...it's Dad's car, but I've been told it is

mine when I go to college."

"Christian has a muscle car! Jack Sr. is really going to love you!" I state as I feel the finish on the hood and the door. "Is it okay if I call you while you are studying or are you zee type that doesn't like deestractions?" I inquire in my exaggerated German accent.

Christian, laughing at my ridiculous accent, answers in between breaths, "No, I don't mind. You are not a deestraction!"

We both get into our convertibles. Looking over at him, I smile. He smiles back. Donning a pair of Wayfarers, he guns the engine. I slip on my Ray Ban Aviators and fire up the V6. It's official: we are the teenage protagonists in a John Hughes movie. The gay one.

As I drive up the driveway and into the garage, the bald eagle is still sitting in the same tree it was perched in this morning. Why was this bird taking residence at Antioch? What was it looking for? After purchasing new film while in the village, I hope to get a photograph of it.

****

I went to bed right after dinner. I'm almost in slumberland when the temperature drops significantly in the bedroom. Huddling under the covers, I prepare for what is about to come. Soon thereafter, the brilliant glow of Angelus is burning through my eyelids. Barely able to squint, his spirit descends onto the balcony and sails through the French doors like there wasn't anything there. Floating past the doors, he continues to sail right toward me. Lifting his ethereal right hand, it connects with my forehead. The familiar cold sensation speeds through my face and I'm unconscious. The second dream sequence begins like the first.

Chapter 13

Angelus and Lazarus
Portrait
June 14, 1919

I couldn't get Lazarus out of my mind. I wanted to spend more time with him, to see if he felt the same connection that I did that day. We obviously come from very different worlds. I had to think of a clever way to see him more, rather, than simply being part of the correspondence between our fathers.

The next day, I decided to ride out to the lighthouse to make a proposition. First, I made sure that I would look my most handsome. Applying a dab of Bryll cream to my comb, I slick my hair straight back to keep my long, blond hair in place behind my ears. My attire for this event includes a long sleeve, billowy white shirt, striped breeches, and leather lace shoes without socks.

It was a beautiful day. The sun shining brilliantly on my face and the wind at my back, the breeze pushes me along as I ride along the coastal road to the lighthouse and up the same rocky path to the cottage. I dismount, lean my bike against the wall of the cottage, and knock on the door. This time there is an answer. Lazarus appears at the door, handsome in his simple white shirt, trousers, and braces. His hair was dry now and combed away from his face to reveal the contours of its oval shape. He looks both pleasantly surprised to see me and perplexed as to why I'm there. This made me feel more confident in my mission.

After a few moments of no one talking, Lazarus finally speaks. "Angelus, why are you here?"

Gathering my composure, I nervously make my proposition. "I would like you to draw me. I liked the sketches I saw in your book. You have talent. I want to sit for you, as they say. I'll pay you."

Breathlessly, I finally stop talking. I said everything I wanted to say, but the smooth proposition I had envisioned in my head, it was not. Lazarus stares at me for what seems to be an eternity. His face is a mixture of confusion and concentration: eyebrows crossed and his sensuous mouth slightly pursed.

"You want to pay me to draw you?" he says with a tone that has more than a hint of disbelief.

"Ayuh, I would be your first commission. I think that's what they call it when someone pays an artist to do original…uh, art," I say ineffectively. His stilted response does not surprise me.

"I can't do that. I'm not that good. I draw for myself. I don't share."

Unable to contain myself, I blurt out, "Ayuh! You are! And you won't have to share it with anyone else because this is just for me!"

This revelation seemed to change his mind as the quizzical look on his face softens and he delivers his final answer, "When do you want to do this?"

"Today! It's bright and sunny, the kind of light I think that artists like…at least, that's what I have read," I awkwardly answer, hoping to convince him about my enterprise.

The expression on his face changes again. He's back to the same intense look of concentration. Turning away from me, leading with those broad shoulders, he walks a few steps, turns around again, and responds, "I've a few hours this morning before I've to meet my papa. Where did you want to pose?"

Pose? Is that what they call this? "Anywhere along the ocean. I was thinking that I could sit on a rock or something with the ocean behind me. It could be right here or on the grounds of Antioch...what do you think?"

He thought for a few seconds. "I think I know a place. It's about halfway between here and your house. Let me get my pencils and pad."

Lazarus placed his charcoal pencils and his sketchpad in a white cloth satchel with a long strap that he wore around his neck and across his chest. We ride out along the coastal road on our bicycles about a half mile from the lighthouse when Lazarus signals me to turn left, and we pedal through a meadow and down into a clearing that is surrounded by large boulders. Laying our bikes against a large boulder, we walk into the clearing. It was a perfect spot. A scenic rocky bluff with the lighthouse and the point in the distance on the north side, and in the southern exposure, the other side of the bay with the faint outline of the rooftops and steeples of the town. It was the kind of setting where a great work of art could be created.

Looking around for a place to sit, I find a group of rocks with large semi-flat surfaces. Making myself comfortable on a slab of granite, I watch Lazarus search for a place to sit as well. He settles unto a rock about five feet away that has a flat ledge, about the height of a standard straight-back chair. Pulling the cloth bag's handle from around his neck, he retrieves his sketchpad and charcoal pencils and lays them down on the ledge. He looks in my direction. I can see that he's studying the view in front of him. He walks over to me.

"How did you want to sit in this portrait? Do you want to look in my direction or would you rather look away, toward the water?"

"I really didn't think about it that much," I respond.

It was true. I had not thought that much about this, only that I wanted to get to know Lazarus better and thought this was a clever way to spend time with him. Lazarus raises his fist to the bottom of his chin; he's thinking.

He moves closer and points to the rock's flat surface, "Lie down on your side, your right side, and bend your knees with your legs folded next to each other."

I did as I was told. Lazarus then approaches and deliberately moves my legs slightly so they are supporting each other better. His strong hands felt good moving my legs.

"Now, I want you to put your right elbow and arm on this rock." He pointed to another large rock that was adjacent to the one I was sitting on.

Following his directions, I was now lying on my right side, putting the weight of my lower body against the boulder's flat surface and with my right arm resting on the other boulder. I was supporting the weight of my upper body. He then reaches toward my face and tilts my head so that I'm looking toward the sea, with the lighthouse and the point just out of my sight. It was a comfortable pose for now, but I knew that these hard surfaces were going to hurt eventually.

"You seem to know what you want. I mean, 'posing' me like this way."

"Have you ever heard of a statue called the *Dying Gaul*? It's a very old statue of a warrior who has been stabbed in his side and dying from his wound. He only has enough strength to keep his head and neck up by leaning on something with his arm. He's looking down at the ground as he waits to die. I saw it in an art book at The Metropolitan Museum of Art in New York." Lazarus has a look on his face that's as serious as the description of this statue.

"Do I look like I'm dying?" I joke.

He smiles slightly and shakes his head. "No, of course not. But you inspired me." Turning his head away from me toward the ocean, he says, "I think the statue is beautiful."

Taking that as a cue, I lean upward, uncross my legs to get my balance, unbutton my shirt and remove it. "Ayuh, don't let anyone tell you that Maine doesn't get hot in the summer. Besides, I'm sure the man in the statue was naked. All those statues from ancient times always seem to be of naked people."

I realize this would be the first time that Lazarus would see me partially naked, and I want to give him a proper show. Taking my shoes off, I lay them next to my shirt.

Pretending to warm my muscles because I would be sitting still for a long time, I stretch, flex, and rub my muscles accordingly. Raising my arms above my head to show off my hard-muscled arms and shoulders, I look down at the pale skin and light blond fur of my well-developed chest. Lowering my arms, I caress my chest muscles, lightly grazing my pinkish nipples. After I rub my chest muscles to warm them, I slide my hands down to my abdomen, and in a swirling motion, massage my abdomen, brushing the trail of light fur that begins at my belly button and disappears into my trousers. When I was done showing Lazarus what I had under my shirt, I assumed the earlier position for the drawing. I looked up fleetingly at Lazarus and thought that I had an admirer. I was surprised by what he said next.

"You're going to get sunburn your skin is so white."

Is that all he saw from my "show," my lily-white skin? "Probably, but you need a base before you get a tan, and the only way to do that is to burn first! But you wouldn't know that as you were born with golden brown skin." My impending burn gives me an idea.

Throughout the time I was being drawn, I could sense that Lazarus was not just seeing me from an artist's point of view, not just studying me as a subject but as an object. Occasionally, I would catch him staring at a part of my body like the toes of my feet or my nipples and not looking at my entire body. He would quickly dart his eyes to look at the crotch of my breeches, and then look up again. I sensed a mutual attraction.

After posing for about an hour, I start to feel hot. My arms and chest have become pinkish. I was sunburned across my entire body except where my breeches had covered me.

"I'm afraid that is all I will be able to stand today. I need to get something for my sunburn before it gets bad," I explain as I move from the boulders.

Slowly putting my arms through the sleeves of the shirt, I gingerly place the cloth against my sunburned shoulders and back. Leaning down, I retrieve my shoes and slowly slip them around the pinkish flesh of my toes. The burning sensation of the leather against my sensitive skin is intense. While I put my shoes on, I hatch the next step of my plan, "I have a salve at home that stops the burn, but I'm going to need some help putting it on, and the servants are out for the day."

"I need to get home. My papa is expecting me," Lazarus states as he closes his sketchpad, gathering his pencils into the cloth shoulder bag.

"I still have you for another hour and the house isn't that far. Come on! I can also give you a down payment," I say as I'm straddling my bicycle.

Lazarus reluctantly agrees and follows me back into the main road toward Antioch. Five minutes later, we're at the bottom of the long driveway of Antioch. Turning into the driveway, flanked by pillars of stone, Lazarus pauses slightly before he proceeds uphill toward my ancestral home. I knew he had seen it many times, as he had to ride by Antioch on his way to the lighthouse. I told him to park his bicycle in the garage so that it would not be in the way of my father's car if he should come back.

We enter through the front door of the house, and I immediately peel my shirt and breeches off as I make my way to the downstairs bathroom under the staircase, wrapping a towel around my waist. Spying on him from the bathroom door, I watch Lazarus as he walks hesitantly into the foyer slowly, turning in circles as he studies the immense room and the staircases that climb up to the attic and widow's walk. As he stood and stared in awe, I retrieve the small tub of cream for my sunburn from the medicine cabinet.

Motioning for him to follow me into the room to the left of the staircase, we make our way through the foyer, the library, and into the parlor. Walking to the bar cart, I pick up a decanter of whiskey and two glasses, pour each of us a shot of whiskey, and hand one of them to Lazarus. "This will help to take the sting away while I put the cream of my sunburn. Bottoms up!" I say as I down my shot.

I motion for Lazarus to drink his shot quickly. Following my lead, he quickly downs the caramel-colored liquid and makes the most terrible face, which causes me to laugh aloud and cough as the whiskey is still burning my throat. It was obvious Lazarus had never had hard liquor. I pour myself another shot, down it quickly and extend the bottle toward him to see if he'd also like another shot. He did not.

"I don't want to get any of the salve on the furniture in here. Let's go to my room where I won't have to worry about it," I say as I cross into the foyer.

He slowly follows me up the grand staircase to the second floor, down the hall and to the third room on the left, my bedroom. Sitting down on the chair next to my desk, I place the tub of cream on it. Scooping a generous portion onto my fingers, I massage it gently into my shoulders, wincing slightly. A few seconds later, Lazarus enters my bedroom with that same look of awe he had when he entered the foyer. I continue to apply the salve to my upper arms and work it down to my forearms, as he examines my possessions. He makes a beeline to the immense four-poster bed, feeling the curtains that hung from each corner.

Delicately spreading the salve across my sunburned chest, massaging my hard nipples discretely, I move my hand down to my belly and swirl the salve across my stomach. At this point, Lazarus is studying the woodwork of the headboard as he sits down quietly on the edge of the bed. I apply the cream to my face gingerly, especially my nose, as this has always been a problem area for sunburn and the eventual peeling afterward. I stand up, grab the salve, and walk toward the bed.

Sitting on the bed next to Lazarus with the tub of salve in hand, I hand it to him and complete the last step of my plan. "Hey, I need help with my back, I can't reach it. Could you please help me?"

Surprisingly, without hesitation, Lazarus agrees, and I turn my body so my back is now facing him. Dipping his hand into the small tub to get a generous portion of the salve, he places his fingers on the skin of my shoulders and begins to massage the cream into my burnt skin. His aggressive touch makes me wince at first.

"Ow, that's too hard. Gently."

"Sorry! Is this better?" he asks as he lightens his touch considerably.

"Ayuh, much better."

His large hands and long fingers lightly massaging my skin and muscles relax my shoulders into his hands. I purposefully moan quietly each time he touches my skin. Picking up on the cue, he begins to massage the cream with slightly more pressure across my shoulders, applying some of it to the back of my neck below my hairline. Moving his hands up and down along the spine of my neck, I bend my neck forward giving him more access. His hands massage the salve between the shoulder blades along my backbone and into the shoulder blades. I continue to moan quietly.

His powerful hands gradually descend into the lower back, causing me to arch my spine and bend at the waist. It feels so good to have hands touching the skin along my waistline, just above the towel. I straighten my spine as he moves his hands toward my mid-back, and then something unexpected happens.

Lazarus begins to massage the front of my shoulders across the collarbones, an area that I had no problem reaching myself. I feel my cock moving beneath my towel. Then his large hands descend to my chest, rubbing my muscular breast in a circular pattern. Opening my mouth to catch my breath, I let out a soft, low noise in the back of my throat as his fingers lightly swirl over my nipples. Hearing the moaning, he proceeds to take each nipple gently between his thumb and index finger of each hand and gently twist. I moan louder as he twists each nipple with more force.

Quickly, I turn myself so that I'm facing him. Slowly moving my face closer to Lazarus's face, I gently kiss his large perfect lips. A soft noise like a sigh emanates from this being as he lets me kiss him. His breathing is becoming more rapid as I sensuously move my lips over his. He moves closer to me. I can hear him breathing heavily through his nose. Opening my mouth slightly, my tongue lightly moves over his lips. Lazarus moans. He parts his lips; his tongue touches mine. We push our tongues against each other. We both moan loudly.

Moving my hands slowly along his chest, feeling

the large muscles beneath his shirt, I undo the buttons and pull his shirt down over his shoulders, touching Lazarus's chest as we continue to kiss. Massaging the hard muscles of his chest, I use my thumbs to feel the space between each muscle. Lazarus groans. Finding his nipples, I squeeze them gently between my thumbs and index fingers, which makes Lazarus groan even louder.

My hands travel to his belly, caressing the defined muscles I had seen when he was drying himself off in the outdoor shower. His mouth breaks from mine as his breathing quickens. I move my hands further down his belly until I touch his crotch. Lazarus lets out a low cry. Rubbing his wooden-like cock through his trousers, Lazarus lets out a low cry and starts to gasp for air.

Suddenly, Lazarus grabs my hands and pushes me away from him on the bed. "This is a sin; we will go to hell!"

With a determined look on my face, I move in again, grab the back of his head and forcefully kiss him with my tongue again. Moving my hands back down into his crotch, I undo the buttons on his trousers. Grabbing his freed cock between the fingers of my right hand, I slowly rub up and down the length of it. Lazarus's breathing becomes faster again.

I get an idea. Dipping my right hand into the tub of salve on the bed, I quickly move my hand up and down his cock, trying to do it the way I like it when I do it to myself. Lazarus is breathing even faster, whimpering and groaning. I could tell by his breathing and his sounds, that he was ready to spill his seed. Suddenly, Lazarus takes a deep breath and lets out a high-pitched cry, muffled by my mouth, as his seed spills over my hand.

Moving my face away from his lips, I watch the strange expression on his face as he yells, panting through his mouth. Pulling my towel off, I grab my hard cock, and using his seed and the salve, I move my hand up and down my cock. Pulling Lazarus toward me, I kiss him deeply on the mouth. Uncontrollably, I bite Lazarus's bottom lip as I spill my seed onto my stomach.

Screaming in pain, Lazarus breaks away from me. Licking his lips, tasting the blood spurting from his lower lip, Lazarus looks at me with confusion and anger. Slowly moving toward him, gasping for air, I kiss his lips gently. Lazarus is hesitant at first, but then allows me to continue. Swirling my tongue along Lazarus's lower lip, licking all the blood from his mouth I swallow it.

Moving my mouth to Lazarus's right ear, I purr, "So?"

****

I wake up, sweaty and out of breath. I have ejaculated in my basketball shorts again. Two wet dreams in two weeks, that has not happened since I was…13 years old? Slipping off my basketball shorts, I wipe the jism from my pelvic area, throw the shorts in the corner, and proceed to sleep commando. Rolling over on my stomach, I bend my right knee, rotating the hip on the same side so that my thigh is parallel with my torso, my usual sleeping pose. I can feel my slowly deflating erection against my pelvis. I'm asleep in seconds.

Chapter 14

Antioch
June 10, 1983

I woke up naked and with dried semen in my short hair. As I lay in bed, I wondered if this was going to be a nightly thing. Angelus would take me on a dream journey into one of his past sexual encounters, my body would experience everything he did, and I would end the dream with an orgasm. It was amazing, my own private gay porno a la the turn of the century. Like if you crossed an Oscar Wilde play like *The Importance of Being Ernest* and a Jeff Stryker porno. I was enjoying these romps through Angelus's sexual past, and the orgasms were incredible.

Then I contemplate what to wear to sleep at night if this does become a daily thing. Nothing? Then my spunk gets all over the sheets, and I wash my sheets every day. That wouldn't raise Mary's suspicions! Bathing trunks? Would the lining wash the ejaculate out more easily? Or continue to do what I'm doing now and keep a supply of basketball shorts ready? After settling on the latter, I shower, dress, and walk downstairs for breakfast. Mom is making eggs Benedict, a special treat on the weekend but never made on a Monday morning.

"So, what's the special occasion?" I inquire, pouring my coffee.

"No special occasion, I just want to show my family how much I love them. I know this move affected you most, making you leave before your senior year…I'm glad you're making new friends…and of course, that gruesome death last week, discovering…I'm going to stop. Enjoy your breakfast, Andy." She kisses me on the forehead.

Suddenly, I remember my conversation with Christian. "Oh, speaking of new friends, I invited Christian over for dinner Thursday night. He's finished with his exams on Thursday. Is that all right?"

"Thursday? Sure, I wasn't planning on anything elaborate. I've a phone meeting with my publisher, but it isn't urgent. I think I can rearrange some things so that I can make a nice dinner. I can't wait to meet this young man," Mom states, pouring the Hollandaise sauce over the poached eggs stacked on Canadian bacon and English muffins.

"I think you're going to like him. He's very artistic, musically, and otherwise. I know Dad will. He wants to go to medical school to be a pediatrician. Jack has already met him, and thought he was cool," I gushed.

"Well, I'm sure we'll be as smitten with him as you are. Tell him to come at six p.m. We'll start with some appetizers," she suggests.

I nod, and then I thought about the word "smitten." An interesting choice. Was Mary insinuating something or was she just being light in her speech…and dare I say it, gay?

I remember something else I want to tell her. "Oh, the Bart's Bay Players are doing *Blithe Spirit* this summer, and they perform at the Bartholomew Theater. They stop showing movies at night during tech week and for two weekends. I think I'm going to audition for Charles."

Mom responds and then begins an impromptu art history lecture. "That's great, honey! That theater is gorgeous; I had a tour of it last week. The Gilded Age finishes are intact for the most part, and I offered my consulting services for any restorations they want to pursue. I suggested a few they may want to consider. Old Vaudeville houses in that condition are hard to come by. Acoustically perfect and elaborate flourishes make the space exceptional."

Listening to her description of the theater, I realize it is my turn to wash the dishes. Dad and Jack are coming down later, so I must wait until they are finished. In the meantime, I walk out to my car to retrieve the flyer about the audition.

I notice that our fine feathered visitor is perched in the same tree as Sunday. Remembering that I had bought new Polaroid film in town yesterday, I run back into the house, grab the film and the Polaroid Instamatic off my dresser, load the film into the camera, and rush back downstairs to the driveway near the garage.

Aiming the camera at this creature, his eyes beaming directly at me through the viewfinder, I take the shot and wait for it to develop, shaking the Polaroid to activate the chemicals. The image of the eagle is blurry again! Branches and other flora that surround the eagle are perfectly clear, but the main subject is a black shapeless mass that looks like it is moving, vibrating. It wasn't moving, no fluttering of wings, however, when I snapped the picture. Curious. I conclude that this phenomenon has only one possible explanation: my camera must be broken.

"What do you want?" I ask the bald eagle, looking directly into its eyes.

The eagle turns its' head to the right, away from my gaze momentarily, but then it immediately turns its head back to look directly at me. Cocking its head forward, it stares at me with those predatory golden eyes; the effect is chilling. Raising its impressive wings and then ruffling its feathers, it makes a majestic squawking noise before it takes off, flying high into the summer sky.

I knew that it would be back. It has a mission at Antioch. It could be something as simple as scoping out prey for lunch, but I have a feeling that it's more than that. Everyone in the family has examined it while it's perched, but it only looks directly at me when I approach. I have never been a bird person, more of a cat or dog type of guy. However, this bald eagle is slowly changing my mind.

I showed everyone the three different photographs of the eagle this morning: explaining that each picture was taken during a different time at a different tree and that I changed the film before the last try. Everyone agrees the Polaroid camera is at fault. What else can it be? Dad volunteers to take it to a camera shop near his school, as he didn't think there was an official camera store in Bart's Bay. I acquiesce and give it to him.

****

After dinner, I phone Christian. "Hey! How are your exams going?"

"Good. My chemistry exam was a bitch, a ton of word problems, but I think I weathered it well. How are you?"

"Good. I tried to take a picture of that eagle I told

you about, with the new film I bought yesterday, and it still turned out blurry. Dad is taking it to a camera shop near his school…he didn't think there was a camera shop in BB," I explain.

"He's right, we have our share of 'fix-it guys,' but I don't know of any that specialize in camera repair. Hey, what time do you want me for dinner on Thursday if that is still good?" Christian asks.

"Mom said six p.m. She said we will start with some appetizers. 'Foncy.' You must be special," I brag, using an affected British accent.

I hear Christian laugh. "You're crazy!"

"She has been extra nice to me lately. I think she feels guilty about uprooting me from my old school and the…incident last week. She also used the word 'smitten' when describing how I felt about you. It was weird. She has never used that word before to describe my feelings toward anyone. Do you think she knows?"

"Did she say you're smitten with me?"

"Not exactly. She said that she thought the family would be as smitten with you as I was," I clarify.

"Oh, that's totally different. I wouldn't be too worried. Are you close to your mom…I mean, how do you think she will take it when you…come out?" Christian queries, his tone becoming more serious.

"I think she will be cool. I think my whole family will be. Jack already knows, remember."

"Then what are you waiting for?"

"I don't know…the right time. When I find that special dude…maybe soon," I confess, a smile breaking out across my face.

Silence. Five seconds later, I hear him respond quietly with a slight trepidation in his voice. "All right, lover boy, I need to get back to the books. I'll see you at six on Thursday."

"Ayaaah," I respond. I can hear Christian burst out laughing on the other end.

"I'm trying to learn your infernal dialect. Did it sound close?"

"No, but we can work on it Thursday. Later."

****

I was ready for bed, deciding on the b-ball shorts for my sleep attire. However, this time I have a box of Kleenex under the bed. Lying on my back, almost asleep, the familiar cold vapor rushes across my exposed chest, making my nipples uncomfortably erect again. I pull the top sheet over my chest. Angelus materializes, but this time he's floating next to me in bed. Lying on his left side, hovering above the sheets, he's facing me as though he's going to make love to me. I turn my body slightly to the right so that I can study this floating Adonis, staring at his stunning face and the hair that frames it. His hair is hanging evenly on both sides, defying gravity like the rest of him.

I stare into his mesmerizing, ethereal eyes. He stares back. Glancing downward at this naked statuesque, ethereal body, his long sculptural feet are pointed as if he were standing on tiptoe. His legs and thighs are folded together, and his well-endowed and anatomically perfect penis hangs naturally from his body, sprouting below a patch of downy short hairs. The hands are rotated so that the palms face outward. His flat muscular stomach transitions into a well-built chest, and because I'm so near to him, I can see that he has a light dusting of chest hair in between his pectoral muscles. The sinewy arms connect to broad shoulders, which blend effortlessly into his long, elegant neck. And of course, that magnificent face.

Looking at his body, I'm reminded of the "Anatomical Position," the universal position for studying anatomy that my dad referenced when I was learning the parts of my body. After I finish admiring his body, lifting my eyes to meet his stare, his ghostly head slowly moves toward me, as if he's going to kiss me. I close my eyes nervously to receive his kiss, not knowing what this is going to feel like. To my surprise, he places his lips not on my mouth but on my forehead. I feel the icy sensation spread across my face, from where his lips touched my forehead to the bottom of my chin, and then I begin tonight's dream.

Chapter 15

Angelus and Lazarus
Antioch Beach
June 16th, 1919

Two days after my first sexual encounter with Lazarus, I could not get him out of my mind. The feel of Lazarus's lips on my mouth, our tongues... Why had I never thought that a tongue could feel that good? How it felt to have my chest touched. He had the most wonderful hands. The excitement I felt when I touched his shoulders and chest and his submission to my touch. The feeling of being intimate with someone so handsome and giving them the ultimate pleasure.

My father asked me to meet him in the morning at his office to collect some documents that needed to be delivered to Erasmus Benedictine. Enthusiastically, I rode my bicycle into town, a little more than three miles from Antioch, as I would have another excuse to see Lazarus. My father's shipping company offices were in the 153 Fishing Industries building on Main Street, near Main Square, the municipal center of Bartholomew Bay. The local government buildings, including the town hall, were also located in this square.

With the papers in hand, I proceeded to get on my bicycle to make the journey to the Bartholomew Bay lighthouse when unexpectedly, a strong hand grasps my shoulder. It is Lazarus standing before me, smiling. It takes every bit of restraint I have not to grab him and kiss him full on the lips in front of the citizenry of Bart's Bay. Giving him the customary handshake, albeit it was much longer than I would shake any other man's hand, and with a big smile, I engage with him.

"What a nice surprise! What are you doing here?"

"I'm here to collect some papers from town hall for my papa."

"That's funny, my father has asked me to deliver these documents to your father," I state gleefully as I held the papers out to Lazarus. "I guess I won't need to make the trip out to the lighthouse…because here you are, and I can give them to you!" Instantly, I knew that I wanted to spend the day with him.

"Are you free today or at least this morning?"

"I'm free until this afternoon!" Lazarus responds with excitement.

"Great! I was thinking of going to the beach in town today, but there's a beach in front of Antioch. It's much more private than the town beach. We won't need our bathing trunks there. Does that sound good?" I slyly suggested.

Lazarus contemplates my proposal for a few moments, noticing he had mixed feelings about something, but then he agrees to the plan. "Yes, that would be nice. Are we going to walk? I came to town with my papa in the skiff and I don't have my bicycle."

I thought for a moment about how I could ride my bicycle and he could walk by my side, but then it came to me. "You can ride on the handlebars while I pedal!"

Lazarus is studying me and the bicycle, most likely figuring out if I'm large enough or have the strength to support him. Then he smiles and proceeds to put his papers in the knapsack that I had brought for Angus' documents. Hoisting myself over and then straddling the crossbar, I keep both feet on the ground to keep the bike steady. Lazarus then puts his right foot on the bolt that connects the center of the front wheel to the bar connected to the handlebars. Placing his hands behind his back on the handlebars, he pushes himself above the bars and sits on them evenly, holding on with his hands, and keeping his feet on the large bolts on either side of the front wheel.

Once he was settled, I put my right foot on the pedal, stood up and pushed off at the same time. It was wobbly at first and we had to shift our weight to keep the bicycle balanced, but we finally achieved our goal, and I was pedaling down Main Street with Lazarus on the handlebars. He's lighter than I thought he would be, and eventually, we start to gain speed. When we hit a bump or hole in the road, Lazarus leans back onto my chest and shoulders, an acceptable closeness between men due to the circumstances, which makes us laugh.

It's a beautiful day with the sun beaming down on our faces. Riding through the main square of town and onto the coastal road, we pass the row of identical one-story houses on the outskirts of town, waving occasionally to its residents when possible. Pedaling furiously to gain speed before we reach the big hill, I pedal up the steep summit with all the strength I have, our last obstacle before reaching the driveway to Antioch. Once we finally reach the summit, I relax my tired legs as we coast down the other side of the hill, gaining speed quickly.

As we near the bottom of the hill and Antioch,

seemingly out of nowhere, a baby lamb walks into the middle of the coastal road. Immediately, I apply the brakes and we skid sideways. Lazarus flies off from the handlebars and into the pasture to the left of the road. I go down with the bicycle in the middle of the road. Recovering quickly with a few cuts and bruises, I notice that Lazarus is not in sight. Panicking, I start to search in the pasture, shouting his name. I quickly spot him not far from the road, lying face up, and I run over to him. Kneeling next to him, Lazarus's eyes are open, but unresponsive to my voice.

Grabbing his hand, I try desperately to rouse Lazarus by talking to him and patting his hand. "Lazarus! Lazarus! Are you all right? Can you hear me?"

Tears well up. Brushing the hair away from his face, I kiss him gently on the lips. There is still no response. Crying and yelling his name hysterically, I pull him from the ground using his shoulders, and hug him. Tears tumble onto his neck and shoulder. Still holding him, I kiss his cheeks, his forehead and then...

I hear a giggle. Lazarus is smiling, directing his gaze into my eyes. He laughs louder. I release him from my grasp. I'm angry for a moment, realizing he has been conscious the entire time, but then I smile, ultimately relieved he was not hurt.

"Ayuh! You little shite! I hope you enjoyed scaring me like that!"

Still smiling and laughing, Lazarus responds, "Yes, I did actually. I wanted to see how much you liked me."

"I like you very much," I say, staring into his eyes.

Kissing his full, soft lips, and looking into those beautiful brown eyes, I embrace him again. Holding him close to me for what seems an eternity. Giggling and embracing each other, we lose our balance on the steep hillside and start to roll together down the hill. Feeling every rock and crevice on the pasture floor, we are heading toward the road.

At the edge of the pasture and the road, we unclasp ourselves and stop rolling, each of us landing on our back. Lying there, still laughing, and recovering from our roll down the hill, we hear the unmistakable bleat of a lamb, "Baaa baaa!" We both look up to see the baby lamb peering down at us. It looks directly at us, bleats again, and then runs off clumsily into the herd of sheep that have been grazing in the pasture.

Gathering our things, spread over the pasture, and the bicycle lying in the road, we decide to walk the remainder of the way to the beach. The bicycle seems to be working fine, but we are both a little shaken to attempt to ride someone on the handlebars again. The path to the beach is parallel to the property line of Antioch. The bay's shoreline is close, so it did not take us long to reach the sandy edge.

Once I spy the water of the bay, I initiate a race to see who can get to the water first. Running between boulders and over dunes, I start to remove my clothes as I get closer to the water's edge, starting with my shirt. As each piece of clothing came off, I let it drop wherever it landed on the beach.

Looking back, I notice that Lazarus is following my lead. By the time we reach the water, all we had on was our breeches. Quickly pulling them off as we dodge the waves, we toss them onto the beach. Neither one of us is wearing anything under the breeches. Running into the water completely naked, we both dive into the breaking waves to get used to the freezing water. Shrieking when we emerge out of the frosty ocean, we both made comments about how cold the water was, like "I think my cock and balls disappeared!"

We knew that the best way to keep from feeling cold was to keep active. Lazarus would spot a wave and, lying flat on his stomach while paddling his arms, he would catch the crest of a wave and ride its momentum toward the beach, sometimes riding it onto the shore. He seems to be an expert at riding waves like this; he never got close to the rocky part of the shoreline. He then shows me how to do it. I had some success, but mostly I'm being crushed by the waves because I'm under them rather than on top of them.

As the morning changes into afternoon, the tide changes and the bay's water becomes calmer, allowing us to swim parallel to the shore and play in the water. We take turns dunking each other under the water until we're exhausted.

Treading in shoulder-deep water, Lazarus attempts to float on his back, his arms spread out perpendicular to his body. Floating on the water, his lean, muscular body, and his outstretched arms remind me of the image of Jesus on the cross, only Lazarus does not have a cloth covering his midsection, he is completely naked. His cock, smaller than when I saw it for the first time in the outdoor shower, is lying against his abdomen and the sack of skin that held his balls was pulled closely to his body. My naked Jesus looks almost angelic, like an angel that has fallen from the sky and landed in the ocean.

Treading in the water next to him, I move closer to

Lazarus's stomach as he floats on the water. I stare at his cock; I have never seen one this close before. It looks like mine, but it is light brown, and it is thicker. The large knob at the end is a shade lighter than the rest. The water beads on it like it does on the skin of his stomach and chest, reflecting the sun light. Moving my head toward him, I quickly place my lips on his cock. I do not know why. Immediately, there is thrashing in the water as his hips buck and disappear under the water.

I hear him call out, "What!" Once he realized it was I, he exclaims, "God in Heaven, I thought a shark was eating my cock!"

I'm laughing uncontrollably. Seeing that he has recovered from his "attack," I swam over to him and kiss him on the mouth. I then suggest that we continue what I started on shore. He bashfully agrees and we swim back to the beach. Walking out of the water, we gather our clothing from the beach. I motion for him to walk toward a rocky area on the east side of the beach.

Unbeknownst to Lazarus, this group of boulders conceals a narrow strip of beach. Placing our clothing on the sand to form a bed of sorts, I drop to my knees and lay down with my back on top of the clothing. The shadow of my lover is coming toward this patch of beach hidden from the rest of the world. With the sun behind him, Lazarus looks like the handsome naked man that I had first seen outside that shower. Lazarus drops to his knees and lays down on top of me, meeting my mouth with his. As we kiss, moving our bodies against each other, our cocks hard as wood, rubbing against each other. The friction feels incredible.

"Before we go any further, we need to do this fast, before the tide comes in and we get caught between these rocks and drown," I state as we move toward more physical activity.

At once, Lazarus moves his head toward mine, and while looking at me in the eyes, his head slides down to my chest where he kisses and licks my chest. I moan. Moving from the rib cage to the belly, he kisses and licks the inside of my naval before his tongue traces the trail of hair from my naval to the patch of blond curly hair above my cock. His fingers are around my cock, and suddenly, I feel a wet enveloping sensation around it…my breathing gets more rapid. I'm going to spill my seed. I warn Lazarus and he moves his mouth away as I lose control and scream. Panting to catch my breath, pulling Lazarus toward me, I kiss his mouth deeply. I place my hand on his face and circle his lips with my fingers, "That was a surprise." I then continued what I had started in the water…we were able to finish before the tide came in.

Chapter 16

Antioch
June 11, 1983

When I woke up the next morning, I was exhausted. I thought to myself. Why? Then I saw the wads of balled-up tissue lying on the floor next to the trash can, my lame attempt at disposing of the evidence. Rolling over on my back, I then yawn. I wonder. How many sexual trysts with Lazarus is Angelus going to share? The dream journeys are hot, but they drain me of as much energy as if I had participated in the sexual act myself. I contemplate if I have the stamina to do this every night, and I am an eighteen-year-old dude!

I stop thinking, get out of bed, grab my towel hanging on the back of the door (another practice that I had employed to expedite the clean up after my nightly ritual) wrap it around my waist, and proceed to the bathroom for a quick shower. In the shower, I start to think about all the places Angelus has taken me while in my dreamscape: the rocky area near a meadow where Lazarus sketched Angelus, the lighthouse that Lazarus lived in, and now the beach in front of Antioch where they gave each other pleasure in the rocky intertidal zone. I've not seen these places. I decided then that today I would explore the grounds of Antioch and the bay shoreline to find these spaces that were sacred to them. I put on jean shorts, a grey t-shirt, a Navy-Blue Lacoste windbreaker and my LL Bean duck boots, something every Mainer has for wading through the intertidal zone and the snows of the long winter.

After fixing a quick breakfast of oatmeal with raisins and brown sugar, I fill a thermos full of coffee with cream and sugar and leave the house through the front door. The first stop: Antioch Beach. I knew that the cliffs behind Antioch were too steep to access the shoreline, so I would have to make my way down the long driveway to access the beach from the coastal road like Angelus and Lazarus did in last night's dream.

As I turn from the stone walkway to the driveway, I'm alerted by the high-pitched call from our friend perched in the tree next to the garage. I was so preoccupied with my mission, that I had forgotten that it might be there. Looking at it for an instant, I remembered that Dad has taken my camera to the repair shop.

"I will get you my pretty," I say to the beast, using my best Wicked Witch of the West voice, and continue down the driveway.

Looking over my shoulder about every 100 feet from the tree to see if it still looking at me as I progress down the driveway, I confirm it is. When I make it to the entrance of the driveway, flanked by the two stone gates, I make a sharp left turn and cross the grassy shoulder of the coastal to tall grasses and large boulders scattered about. The boulders become much larger and more numerous as I approach the shore. I can hear the waves crashing against the rocks.

Then I see the water of the bay lapping at the beach in between two groups of large boulders. Climbing through the narrow opening onto the beach, I see the entire arc of the bay's coastline from the beach in front of Antioch to the lighthouse on the left and the outline of the northernmost buildings from the town on the right.

Bending down, I pick up some of the sand. It is brown and coarse, typical of the New England coastline. This is the identical view of Antioch Beach that Angelus had shown me the night before. I wade out into the surf and the water is freezing, splashing against my legs. I had remembered that Christian told me that the only way you can enjoy the water in Bart's Bay, or in Maine in general, is to get numb first, as it never gets above the mid-50's Fahrenheit, even in the summer.

Envisioning how cold Angelus and Lazarus must have been when they were completely naked in this frigid water, it certainly would have woken them up, but I don't know how interested in sex I would have been! They were heartier back then, I thought.

I venture north along the beach into the rockier area to find their intertidal patch of sand. Carefully climbing the enormous boulders looking for the thin strip of beach sandwiched between rocky outcroppings that was in my dream, I cannot find it. I come up with two possibilities: it is still high tide and their patch of sand in the rocks is submerged or the coastline has changed in the last 64 years, and it doesn't exist anymore.

Climbing back down from the rocks onto the narrow shoreline, I look out toward the ocean beyond the bay. The water is so tranquil. Peaceful. Closing my eyes, I listen to the rolling waves as they hit the shore and splash against the rocks. Taking a deep breath through my nose, savoring the smell of the ocean air, I think to myself: this is a remarkable place.

My next stop would be the rocky bluff along the cliffs where Lazarus drew Angelus. After doubling back from the beach, traversing the driveway, and moving past the garage, I walk out toward the cliff in the backyard. Reaching the edge of the precipice, I peer down the steep slope of earth and rocks to view the beach I had just visited. The boulders look so small. I then turn around to look at Antioch. The afternoon sun is illuminating the contours of the mansion magnificently. The turrets frame the three stories of the great house majestically like a medieval castle, while the widow's walk towers over the entire edifice.

Walking north along the cliffside in search of the rocky bluff, I soon encounter the thick forest of evergreens next to the grassy backyard. I look for the entrance to a trail but cannot find remnants of any kind of path, deducing that either there was never a trail along the cliffs or that it's overgrown with vegetation. I decide to forge my own path through the presumably virgin territory walking along the exposed grassy areas of the cliffside and navigating the trees that grew into the cliffside by either climbing around tree trunks or using the branches as a ladder to get over the most difficult terrain.

After walking for about a half a mile, I finally reach a clearing, a meadow bordered by an outcropping of large boulders on the cliffside. Bartholomew Bay lighthouse and the point can be seen in the distance.

Walking through the meadow, the search for the configuration of rocks that I had seen in my dream was the mission. Approaching the lighthouse, a large group of rocks with flat surfaces emerges. Within this rocky promontory, I explore the boulders looking for the horizontally flat surface that Angelus laid across for his portrait. I discover a boulder that matches that description. The view of the bay and the lighthouse from this rock, the composition of the scenery, the lighthouse, the point and the bay were exactly as I had dreamt it.

Sitting down on the flat surface of the rock, I turn my body and lift my legs so that my feet are on the slightly sloped surface. I then lay across the flat surface of the rock on my right side in the same position Angelus held when he was immortalized. Noticing an adjacent rock that juts into this space that is as high as my elbow in this position, I remember that Angelus's right elbow rested along this shelf of rock in the portrait. Resting my right elbow on the rock and turning my head toward the sea, I imitate the pose in the portrait. I smile. This is the view I saw through Angelus's eyes in the first and third dreams. Turning my head forward to the other rocks, I discover the other flat rock where Lazarus sat as he sketched Angelus.

At that moment, I feel a sense of reassurance that my dreams are not a figment of imagination. I have never physically seen this place, yet I knew it was here. Everything I had experienced felt so real. Before, I thought could all of this have been part of an elaborate ongoing dream? The ghostly encounters before the visions, could they also have been part of the same dreams? Schizophrenia? A chill ran down my spine.

The next location to explore would be the grounds of the lighthouse. As I walk toward the meadow that borders the coastal road, suddenly, the light from the sky becomes dimmer and the wind picks up. There is a low rumble of thunder in the distance. It is one of Maine's infamous thunderstorms, storms that seem to come from nowhere and wreak havoc on the coastline. I knew what was coming next.

Deciding that the path along the coastline would be too treacherous to run along, and that running into a forest is not a good option, I run across the meadow toward the coastal road, and along the shoulder toward Antioch. The rain starts to pour. It's about a ½ mile to the entrance of Antioch by my calculations, enough time and distance to be easily hit by lightning.

As I run, I remember the story my grandmother had told me about how the Governor of Virginia's son was killed at the beach when lightning struck the zipper of his bathing suit. That was always adequate motivation for me to run as fast as I could during a lightning storm.

I finally reach the entrance to Antioch, run up the driveway, and cut across the front yard toward the front door. Running up the stairs to the front door, the first flash of lightning and the ominous sound of thunder two seconds later, the storm is close! I'm soaked to the core and dripping in the foyer. I call out to see if anyone is home. No one answers. Running up the grand staircase to the bathroom, I strip off my wet clothes along the way, as Angelus did on the day he was sunburned, turn on the shower, and stand under the hot water to get rid of the chill.

****

I went to bed later tonight than I had for the previous three days. Maybe it was the excitement of running through the thunderstorm that had boosted my epinephrine, the more scientific name for adrenaline (a result of living with a neuroscientist), and I was still on a natural high. It could have been my discovery of some of the locales of my dreams. My subconscious relieved that I wasn't imagining everything happening to me during my dreamscapes, and I felt at ease. On the other hand, had I simply had enough rest to repair the damage to my body, the damage from stress produced last Thursday? Regardless, I'm feeling better physically and mentally. Moreover, I'm going to see Christian in two days. Maybe the excitement of seeing him is keeping me awake.

As I prepare myself for tonight's journey, I think about Christian and what he means to me. Before I journey too deep into my analysis, a wave of frigid air envelops my chest, neck, and face. Angelus appears before me, floating above me as he had done before. As his face materializes above mine, I notice that he doesn't have the same contemplative expression he had before. This time he looks saddened. There are tears in his ethereal eyes. At least, they look like tears.

Can ghosts cry?

As I look into his eyes, a large tear forms in the corner of his right eye; but instead of it falling down his face, defying gravity as I expected, it leaves his eye and falls onto my forehead. I immediately fall asleep.

Chapter 17

Angelus and Lazarus
Secret
June 17th, 1919

Lazarus came to Antioch the next day after our tryst on the beach. He walked over to deliver some seafaring reports my father requested. I see him walk up the driveway and I hear him knock on the door. Our manservant, Edward, answers the door as was customary. I didn't want to see him. I listen to their conversation from the foyer, Lazarus talking to Edward about delivering the reports and then inquiring if I was home.

I really want to talk to him, to touch his face, to kiss those large soft lips, but I can't. Edward states that I'm not available. Lazarus asks if I'm all right, explaining that he had met me at the lighthouse earlier that week. I couldn't take it anymore; I needed to see him and to make him leave before I started to cry. I walk to the front door.

"Edward, it's all right. I'll talk to him," I say from behind the door. Edward leaves, slowly looking at me as I place my right hand on the door, keeping it only partially open.

"Angelus, I started to worry," he confesses as he peers through the crack in the door. Are you going to open the door?"

I open the door slightly so that he can see the left side of my face, the right side hidden by the door. He instinctively pushes on the other side of the door further and he catches a glimpse of my right eye.

"Your eye! What happened?" he asks with concern.

He sees the large cut across my eyebrow. So, I open the door to reveal my entire face. His beautiful face changes to an expression of horror when he sees mine.

"Angelus, what happened to your face?" He gasps. He's seeing all my wounds: the large gash across my right eyebrow, my blackened right eye, the bruises across my right cheek and the cut on the right side of my upper lip.

I lied. "I fell down the stairs this morning going to breakfast. My face hit the side of the banister. My back is sore from the fall, so I think I'm going to rest today. I'll come to the lighthouse in a few days when I'm feeling better."

Lazarus, with a look of concern on his face, pleads, "Are you sure I can't help you with anything? I don't have to be back home until this afternoon."

"No, I just want to go back to sleep."

Lazarus looks at me with those big, soulful eyes. I want to put my arms around him and hold him. I cannot do it.

"I have to go now. I'll see you at the lighthouse in a few days," I say as I attempt to close the door.

Then he grabs my left hand with both of his hands and looks at me for a moment, and then I pull both of my hands away. I continue to close the door as I look into his sad, handsome face.

He knew the truth.

Chapter 18

Antioch
June 12, 1983

As I wake from the dream, I feel an icy presence around my eyes and cheeks. Touching my face, I notice that the cold sensation is wet, realizing the droplets are tears, and they are streaming down my face. I had been through something very different tonight. Something more personal.

Most people would say that listening or reliving someone's sexual adventures would be the most intimate thing anyone could share. True, you reveal many of your vulnerabilities when you are seeking ultimate sexual satisfaction, and you need to be able to trust that your sexual partner will keep your sexual preferences confidential. However, revealing you're being abused by a parent must be the most difficult, the most intimate thing a person can face. Angelus had revealed this to me, and Lazarus knew that Angelus's father abused him.

Up to this point, I had thought of my nightly romps through Angelus's episodes of his sexual awakening to be physically, and mentally pleasurable, but this dream changed the game. I now saw the tragic figure developing before me, the young man who may have committed suicide to escape the hell he lived every day with Angus Bartholomew. To escape a society that would not accept he could romantically love another man. Alternatively, was he the young man who was murdered by his abuser? I wonder how long it will be before Angelus will tell me the truth. Flashbacks will lead me to his death.

****

I return to bed with trepidation, wondering if this was the end of the flashback dreams for the night. I had grown accustomed to the supernatural adventures that Angelus had taken me in the last few days because they had all been full of the sexual discovery and romantic love he had experienced in the past. Earlier tonight, a darker side of Angelus's past was revealed that I was not ready to confront. It was uncomfortable and personal. I knew more about who Angelus was and the sad circumstances that could explain why he died so young.

As I lie in bed, I start to contemplate the possibilities. What part of Angelus's past would he take me to tonight? Something pleasant? Something tragic? Assuming he was going to take me anywhere.

I had my answer soon. Sensing the familiar cold mist in the room, Angelus slowly materializes, but this time he is standing next to my dresser, and he's pointing to his portrait leaning on top of the dresser. His ghostly finger is pointing to something specific in the portrait. Squinting in the dark, leaning closer to the dresser, I can now see that it is the signature of L.B. in the lower right-hand corner of the drawing. As soon as I realize this, Angelus moves with lightning-fast speed from the portrait on the dresser to hovering next to me in bed. He then places his entire hand on my forehead, and I'm asleep again.

Chapter 19

Angelus and Lazarus
Lazarus's story
June 20, 1919

As I promised, I saw Lazarus at the lighthouse three days later. My face had healed except for the cut over my right eye. Because my ribs and back are not as sore, I can ride my bicycle. I make my way to the cottage and knock on the door, but the door opens before I finish knocking. There stands a handsome man with a smile on his face. A beautiful smile.

Once inside the door, Lazarus grabs me and hugs me fully against his body. He moves his head next to mine on my right shoulder. We stand there in this embrace for what seemed to be minutes but probably was more like seconds. Then he moves his face so I'm staring at those big, brown eyes. Lifting his left hand to my right cheek, he gently touches it, running his fingers softly along my cheek to the corner of my right eye and then down to the right side of my upper lip. Watching me to see if I have any pain. I do, but I have learned not to show it. Moving his hand to my chin while looking into my eyes, he moves toward me and gently kisses my broken lip with his soft mouth. He pulls back slowly and we both smile. Walking into the main room, I look around to see if anyone else is there.

I ask, "Is your papa or anyone else here?"

"No, he's in town. He will be there all morning."

Surveying the layout of the main room, I notice the door to the left of the kitchen, walk and point to it. Lazarus does not respond. I turn the knob and open the door slowly, revealing a room with a bed. The bed is on the right side of the room next to a window, and there is a fireplace in the left corner. A large wardrobe sits against the other side of the door with a small desk next to the wardrobe. The furniture is simple and sturdy like the furniture in the main room.

"Is this your bedroom?"

"No, this is my papa's bedroom. I slept in here with Mama and Papa when I was young until Mama died. I was nine," Lazarus explains. "Do you want to see where I sleep?"

I nod my head. Lazarus then opens a door to the right of the kitchen, which is the same one I had seen him go through when he went to change clothes the first day we met. Through the doorway, there's a large spiral stairwell made of white stone, with a black handrail spiraling next to the stairwell. Lazarus walks to the right of the stairwell toward a closed white curtain. He pulls back the curtain and walks inside the space. I follow him into the space, the wall inside is curved like the exterior of the lighthouse. There is a thin long bed with a woolen plaid blanket and a flat pillow. Next to the bed is a small wooden desk with artist's supplies and a candle.

"This is where I sleep when the weather is warmer. During the winter, it is too cold to sleep here. The heat from the fireplace cannot reach, even when the door is open. Those days, I sleep in front of the fireplace on the couch with my blanket and pillow. I'm responsible for keeping the fire going in the fireplaces in the main room and in Papa's bedroom, so there is always a lot of firewood piled up in both rooms. If they go out then we would freeze to death," Lazarus explains.

After Lazarus's explanation of his living quarters, I feel ashamed. I have so much, and he has so little. I will never complain about anything again. I sit on the bed and Lazarus does the same. Moving my left hand onto his right thigh, he grasps my hand with his right hand.

I ask him, "Tell me about your Mama."

Lazarus began his tale by telling me about his mother.

"Her name is Elizabeth, actually she was born Elizabeta, but she liked the name Elizabeth more. She was born in New York City, in a place called Greenwich Village, much bigger than Bartholomew Bay. She lived there with her brother and sister, my Aunt Helena, and Uncle Bacchus Santopietro. Santopietro was my Mama's Christian name.

"Papa met Mama in New York when he was in the Navy. He was visiting New York while he was on something called "shore leave." He met Mama in the summer of 1900. Papa found out that Mama was going to have a baby after he returned to sea. He married her two months later when he got back to New York. He told me he married her to keep her an honest woman. I still do not know what that means. After they were married, Papa had to go back to the Navy. Mama stayed in Greenwich Village with her sister and brother. I was born on April 17, 1901. Mama gave me the name Lazarus; it was her grandfather's name.

"My papa found out that I was born when he was at

sea. Papa told me that another seaman told him that a lighthouse keeper was looking for someone with experience in the Navy to learn how to become a lighthouse keeper and to take over the duties of the lighthouse in the next year. This seaman did not want to be a lighthouse keeper, so he asked my papa if he would be interested. The seaman told Papa it would be a good job for someone with a family.

"The lighthouse was in the town where this seaman was born and raised, a place called Bartholomew Bay, Maine. Papa met the lighthouse keeper, Jonas Brunt, while Papa was on shore leave again. He liked Papa and offered him the job. Papa quit the Navy when he got the job.

"He sailed on a boat owned by your father, Angus, from Bartholomew Bay to New York City to take us back here. This voyage was the first time that Papa saw his son. We all sailed back together to Bartholomew Bay in the summer of 1901. The trip was hard on Mama. I learned when I got older that she almost died when I was born. She was not well when we sailed from New York, and she had to take care of me while she was sick. She got better but she was never healthy.

"We lived in the lighthouse until I was eight years old. I remember how beautiful she was, but she could not do as much as Papa wanted her to because some days she was too weak to do the chores. I had to help Papa when she could not. She always had a cough, but it got worse. She died from something called respiratory failure in 1910, when I was nine years old.

"When she died, Papa and I sailed back to New York, and he left me with Aunt Helena and Uncle Bacchus in Greenwich Village. He told me he could not take care of me and keep the lighthouse at the same time, so he was leaving me with Mama's family. Papa never got married again. He seemed to like being alone. I cried when Papa left me in Greenwich Village. I lost both of my parents in the same month.

"I lived in Greenwich Village for the next eight years. Aunt Helena and Uncle Bacchus loved me very much and took good care of me the best that they could. They showed me more love than Papa ever did.

"Aunt Helena was a seamstress for a fashion house in the Fashion District of Manhattan, the island in New York City where Greenwich Village and many other neighborhoods were, where they make expensive clothing. She was beautiful and full of life; I heard another man say that she had a zest for life. We lived in a two-bedroom apartment in a building referred to as a 'brownstone,' on Christopher Street with Uncle Bacchus. Aunt Helena had many friends in our apartment, most of them men, and some I called uncles, although they were not related.

"Uncle Bacchus was an artist, but he did not make a lot of money from his art, so he worked as a bartender in a restaurant in Greenwich Village. He was very handsome and masculine, a word that I heard another man use to describe him. I slept in the same room with Bacchus, unless he had a friend stay the night, and then I had to sleep on the couch in the parlor.

"Like my Aunt Helena, he talked a lot about art and music. They would take me to the park and talk about the statues, about the artists and their history, and the history of some of the buildings. We also went to the amazing museums in New York City like the Metropolitan Museum of Art where I learned about and admired the great artistic works. My favorite area in the museum was the room with the statues of the Greeks and Romans. Bacchus told me that these statues were of 'real men,' and that we were the modern Italians, descendants of these strong men: the bold Roman nose and the powerful, strong bodies. It was these statues that made me want to be a better artist. Uncle Bacchus died of liver disease when I was sixteen years old. Aunt Helena died of tuberculosis one year after Bacchus. I had no other family in New York City, so I had to come back to Bartholomew Bay and work for my Papa."

Lazarus finishes his tale and looks at me with those sad eyes. I reach with my right hand to his face and brush the hair from his forehead so that it's perfectly in place with the rest of his dark brown hair. Rather than talk about the sadness that was in each of our lives, I wanted us to be happy.

"Show me the top of the lighthouse. I bet you can see Portland!"

With that suggestion, we get off the bed, and I follow Lazarus. Walking through the curtain of his nook, we start to climb the steep limestone stairs. Lazarus did not use the railing as he bound up the stairs, but I did because I was not used to the steepness of the stairwell.

We continue to climb the spiral stairs, but it gets harder to climb as the angle of the stairs increases. Finally, after what seems like 100 stairs, we reach the top. The opening to the stairwell has two iron bars on either side that Lazarus uses to hoist himself up into the watchtower.

Next to the bars is the large lamp that is used to illuminate the searchlight: six thick panels of glass arranged in a hexagonal pattern around a large black lantern-looking structure. Apparently, these glass panels rotate around when the lamp is lit and magnify the light. The interior of the watchtower is composed of glass panels, a door made of glass and wood, and the same white stone that the rest of the tower was made of.

Lazarus led me through the door and onto a narrow balcony that wraps around the top of the tower. The balcony has a circular railing that is as high as my waist. I hold onto the railing and use it to guide me around the top. The view is incredible. It's a clear day, not the typical Maine morning when the fog rolls in and can stay indefinitely.

Directly in front of us is the gradual slope of the point as it projects into the jetty, marking the northern border of Bartholomew Bay. Walking southward along the balcony, at about three o'clock from where we entered the balcony, the rooftops and the steeples of the two churches in town are visible. Bartholomew Bay is not a big town, but it looks even smaller from the top of the bay. Turning to five o'clock, the widow's walk, the turrets, and the peaked roof of Antioch nestled in the trees come into view. At six o'clock, the green meadow and the rocky bluff were where I posed for my portrait.

"Hey, there is our place!" I say as I point to the bluff, "You haven't finished my picture."

Lazarus is behind me looking at all the same sights I'm describing. When I show him the bluff, he reaches over and puts his hand on mine while it rests on the railing. He rests his chin on my shoulder.

"The light is good today. I can probably finish it if I have a couple of hours. Can you sit that long?" he asks while rubbing my hand.

Turning around, I smile at him, grab his other hand, and say, "Race you to the bottom!"

We walk along the path and onto the coastal road to the meadow. Running across the meadow, chasing each other, we challenge each other as to who could get to our special place first. Lazarus beats me. I didn't know he was that fast, and he was carrying his pencils and pad in his cloth bag. Truth be told, I'm not a good runner. After we settle ourselves into our respective places, I remove my shirt as I had before and pose in the same position, lying on the flat slab of a boulder and leaning with my right arm on a rock. We're there for about an hour when Lazarus looks up at me from his sketchpad.

"I think I'm finished."

I jump off the rock and sit next to him, nudging my body next to his with my head practically lying on his left shoulder as he holds the sketchpad. Looking at it, I could not believe the likeness I saw.

"That's me? I look like—"

"This is what you look like to me. You are perfect, like an angel," he interrupts me.

Staring at the portrait of myself, I remember something I wanted to say earlier. "Angus is going to be away tomorrow and isn't coming back until the next day, and Edward is traveling with him, so I have the house to myself tomorrow night. Would you, or can you, stay the night in Antioch with me?"

Looking at me, he smiles, and then kisses me lightly on the mouth. I have my answer.

Chapter 20

Antioch
June 13, 1983

Mom is making her famous Maryland-style crab cakes for dinner tonight. Her secret? She uses only backfin crabmeat, nothing from the claws or body, and Old Bay seasoning, a spicy paprika-laced seasoning that Maryland natives put on all their seafood. She's also making her homemade macaroni and cheese made with elbow pasta, milk and butter, and then topped with slices of Vermont cheddar. The meal is completed with steamed green beans and Caesar salad.

"Wow, Andy will have to invite friends over more often if we eat like this," Dad declares, kissing Mary on the cheek.

"Well, this is our first dinner party in the new house, and I thought it should be special," Mom explains.

I watch them talk about the details of the meal for a few more minutes when I hear a knock at the door. I race to the door to find Christian on our doorstep. He's dressed somewhere between his new wave/punk rocker attire and his "good boy" church-going togs: a purple polo-style shirt that is tight across his massive chest and biceps, a Navy cotton web belt, slightly faded jeans, and the brown docksiders with no socks he wore when I saw him after church. His strawberry blond faux hawk is tame, though it had some height; the bangs are swept across the right side and tucked behind his right ear. In a word, he looks "adorable." I step toward him as he stands on the doorstep closing the door behind me to leave just a crack.

Lifting both of my hands toward his face, I frame his strong jawline between my thumbs and fingers and kiss him hard on the mouth. Holding my mouth on his for a few seconds, he grabs my arms with both of his hands and squeezes. I break away from our kiss and look into his eyes.

"I'm so glad to see you. I missed you."

"I missed you too. It was hard to study and not think about you," he adds.

Cleaning off any saliva that may have collected on my mouth with the back of my hand, I motion Christian to do the same. I then re-open the door and usher us both into the foyer where we're surprised to see my father standing on the other side.

"Hi, I'm Jack Meade," he states, extending his hand toward Christian.

"Christian Gutmann, pleasure to meet you," he says, firmly gripping my father's hand.

I'm relieved to see that Christian gave him a good grip as Dad has stated in the past that he doesn't trust any man that gives a weak handshake.

"Gutmann, that's German for 'good man,' right?" Dad inquires.

"That's right. Some of my relatives have changed it to the English translation, but my papa says it reminds us of where we came from, our heritage," Christian proudly contributes.

Dad smiles and then extends a hand in the direction of the living room. "Come in. What can I get you to drink?"

"Uh, just a soda would be great," Christian answers.

"You sure you don't want something stronger? We have a well-stocked bar?" Dad suggests.

"Ayuh, rum and coke then."

"Roke and coke it is," Dad says as he prepares Christian's drink.

At this time, Mary walks into the living room and extends her hand. "Hi, Christian, I'm Mary Meade, I'm so happy to meet you, Andy has told me a lot about you."

"Nice to meet you, Griff...ah, Andy has told me a lot about you," Christian states, shaking Mom's hand.

Mary notices Christian's confusion over the name she calls me and clarifies her moniker as she puts her hands on my shoulders. "Andy is our nickname. My maiden name was Griffin...it's a long story." "Excuse me, I'll be right back," Mary states as she leaves the living room.

Jack Jr. enters the room, walks toward Christian, and extends his hand. "What's up, Christian?"

"Good on you, Jack," Christian responds, shaking Jack's hand and patting him on the shoulder.

"So, Andy tells me that you are interested in medicine," Dad inquires.

"Ayuh. Pediatrics. I'm interested in studying the prevention of natal transmission of viruses from mother to infant, especially deadly viruses like HIV," Christian explains.

"That's a fast-developing field. I'm sure that you

will have no problems finding a lab with funding for that kind of research," Dad contributes. "I have a few colleagues who have connections to the AIDS Research labs at the National Institutes of Health; I can give you their information and mention your name if you like."

"That would be great, thank you!"

Jack Jr. changes the subject. "Some of the guys on the football team saw your band last Friday, said it was wicked rad!"

"Thanks, it's fun. It's nice to exercise the other side of my brain," Christian comments. "Music is in my blood. Mama is a soloist at our church and Papa plays the piano in a jazz combo."

Mary returns to the living room with a tray. "We're starting tonight with an appetizer, scallops que sera: scallops, Gruyere cheese and dill on toasted sourdough bread rounds."

We attack the tray. Mary's a good cook, but her appetizers and hors d'oeuvres are legendary. Between four men, the tray of scallops que sera is history within minutes. We sit in the living room for a while longer, while dinner is cooking. Mary re-enters the living room.

"Jack, could you please set the table? Dinner will be ready in ten minutes," she announces.

Jack Jr. leaves the room. Dad then stands up and states that he's going see if Mary needs any help and walks in the direction of the kitchen. Christian and I are alone in the living room.

"Your parents are wicked nice," Christian exclaims.

"Yeah, they're all right," I say sarcastically.

With that, Christian, with an exaggerated slow-motion movement, lightly punches me in my arm. I grab his hand, pull him closer to me, and then after looking around quickly, gave him a quick peck on the lips.

"Dinner's ready, boys," Mary yells from the dining room.

We had a fantastic dinner. The food was delicious, and the conversation was stimulating. Dad and Christian talked a lot about the latest medical research and clinical applications in medicine. We all talked about the Reagan administration and "trickle-down economics." Christian specifically voiced his dissatisfaction that Ronald Reagan refuses to use the word AIDS, as it is ravaging communities that he doesn't feel are worthy of his notice. Christian, Jack, and I talk about modern music: comparing how the current independent music scene is reflecting the response to the conservative media and the treatment of the AIDS crisis devastating the art community the same way that most of the music of the late 60s and early 70s was used as a protest to the Vietnam War. By the end of dinner, we all have a good idea of where everyone stands on most of the topics of discussion, with only minor differences in thought and philosophy, particularly regarding the comparison of music from the 1980s and 1970s. Mom and Dad are not exactly hippies but were sympathetic to the cause.

Mom tops off the dinner with her signature dessert, dark chocolate souffle. She makes them individually in something she calls ramakins, small white ceramic bowls. They are delicious by themselves, but if you pour sweet cream on top of the souffle, it causes the chocolate interior to collapse, and the sweet cream mixes in with the melted dark chocolate. It is wicked delicious!

Dad told us that when we eat chocolate, it releases two neurotransmitters (chemicals that link your nerve cells with each other) in your brain called serotonin and dopamine which gives you a calming serene effect and a pleasurable effect, simultaneously. The same mood-altering substances that are released during sexual arousal. In other words, eating chocolate, especially dark chocolate, gives you the same feeling as falling in love, or at least being horny.

I wasn't sure if it was the chocolate souffle or the fact that Christian is getting along so well with my family, or that he's hot as hell, but I felt like what was developing between us was more than typical teenage infatuation. I haven't known him very long, but I really like this guy. Am I... falling in love?

It's getting late, and even though Christian has finished his exams, he still has school in the morning. "Thank you so much for inviting me. Dinner was amazing!"

Mom hugs him tightly as he was leaving. "It was our pleasure, and it was wonderful to finally meet you. I'm sure this won't be the last time."

Dad shakes his hand. "Christian, it was a pleasure. Good luck with your exams."

Jack puts his right arm around Christian's right shoulder, squeezes it, and turns to him. "Dude, I never knew you were so solid? We could use you on the front line...later." Then he let him go.

I look back at Jack and smile. "Cute," I say to Jack, escorting Christian to the door.

Closing the front door behind us, I walk Christian to his car. The moon is full like the night we kissed on the beach. I grab his hand at the end of the path. We're holding hands when I see his '64 convertible Mustang parked in the driveway next to my Jeep, and think, when am I going to get a ride in my boyfriend's muscle car?

Once we reach the car, Christian turns toward me. "I had—"

I stop him in mid-sentence, planting my mouth on his. It starts out as an innocent kiss but then evolves into something much deeper. The kind of kiss we shared on the beach. As we explore each other's mouths, I get excited. I can feel Christian's endowment coming to life as well. We are getting into heavier petting when I realize we cannot go any further.

"We better stop, or I won't be able to go in the front door," I say in between gasps for air.

"You're right. I don't have an extra pair of anything to change into." Christian pants as he adjusts himself.

"We need to make another date to go to the beach or my bedroom, or…the widow's walk, anywhere but here," I suggest, holding his broad shoulders in my hands, still breathing hard.

Christian opens the driver's door and rests his left forearm on the doorframe. "Ayuh, tomorrow is the last day of school. Can we get together this weekend? Oh, that friend of yours from Boston is coming."

Christian's simple, nonchalant stance next to the car is so innocent yet sexy. I can't resist. Placing my right elbow on the doorframe, next to his, I lean into Christian, kissing him lightly on the lips.

"Trista is very sociable. I'm sure she'll love to meet some of my new friends, especially someone like you…cute, strong, smart…I'll call you after we make plans."

Christian smiles at me with that mega-watt grin. Firing up his muscle car, the roar of the engine suits his personality: strong, fearless, and classically handsome. Putting his seat belt on, he leans his left arm against the open window frame.

"I will never forget you, Griffin Meade," he purrs.

I watch him as he backs out, making a 180-degree turn and heading down the long driveway of Antioch. Walking back to the house along the stone pathway, looking at the different shapes of the stones, thinking I'm the luckiest dude in the world when…my perfect world is rudely interrupted by the violent sound of metal crashing into a wall. Instinctively, I turn my head around toward the sound. I see smoke rising, reflected in the moonlight, from one of the large trees lining the driveway. Running closer to the smoke, I see the rear bumper of the Mustang. By this time, Mom and Dad have come out of the house to investigate.

"Call 911," I yell at them as I run down the driveway.

As I run toward the car, the eagle that has haunted Antioch suddenly appears out of one of the trees, screeching at me, its yellow eyes glowing in the moonlit night, staring at me…as if it's warning me not to go any further. I jump back momentarily from the screaming bird, but then I collect my wits; I cannot be stopped from running to see if Christian's still alive.

Tears stream down my face as I witness the destruction. The left side of the hood is crushed against one of the larger oak trees that border the driveway. Steam fills the air and water spurts against the oak and what remains of the left side of the hood. I look through the driver's side window. His torso is restrained by the seatbelt, his head resting on the steering wheel. There's blood coming out of his mouth, and he has a large gash across his forehead. He's conscious, moaning and crying, saying nothing.

"Christian, Christian, can you hear me!" I plead through my sobbing, the shock of seeing my boyfriend mangled in his car. "Hang on, an ambulance is coming!"

He turns his eyes toward me without moving his head, those sweet ice-blue eyes barely open, looking at me, pleading with me to tell me what happened. The blood slowly trickles around his eye socket and streaks down his sharp cheekbones. I want to clean the blood from his beautiful face, but I'm afraid to touch him, as he might have a broken neck. I remember that you never move anyone in an accident unless the person is in danger of drowning or burning or asphyxiating in a fire. He begins to close his eyes.

"Don't you close your eyes, Christian! Don't you close them! I can't lose you! I think I love you!" I shout to him, tears pouring down my face, running into my mouth, making me hoarse; I'm ugly crying.

He opens his eyes again. I swear this time his eyes look larger and more expressive. I imagine he's thinking the same thing: that he loves me also. The sound of a siren is heard, coming from the coastal road. Looking up, I see the red lights of the fire and rescue truck coming up the driveway.

"They're here, Christian, everything is going to be okay. They're going to take care of you, you're going to be all right!" I blurt out, snot running down my nose into my mouth.

The paramedics are behind me tapping me on the shoulder telling me that they would take good care of him. "What's his name?" one of the paramedics asks as he opens the door.

"Christian, his name is Christian."

"Christian, you're going to be all right. We're going to place something on your neck to keep it from moving in case you have a broken neck," one of the paramedics explains as he carefully places a backboard against the back of Christian's head and neck, wrapping the strap of the backboard around his forehead, as he lay across the steering wheel.

Simultaneously, the paramedics feel for his carotid pulse, check his pupils with a penlight, and place an oxygen mask on his face. One of the paramedics cuts the seat belt from around his waist and wraps another strap from the backboard across his chest. The paramedics continue to talk to Christian while they carefully move his torso.

"All right, Christian, we're going to keep your head and neck from moving as we lift you from the car, so please don't move."

The paramedics slowly move his head, neck, and upper body away from the steering wheel, his neck in alignment with the backboard. Sliding his upper body with the backboard onto a gurney, they gently pivot his lower torso and thighs. They lift his lower body from the seat and slide his legs and feet onto the gurney. The paramedics strap him into the gurney. Inserting scissors into the collar of Christian's polo shirt they cut through to his waist, pulling each half of the shirt away from his broad chest.

One of the paramedics uses a stethoscope to listen for heart and lung sounds. "Good breath sounds, heart rate is elevated, tachycardia."

The other paramedic has a blood pressure cuff around his left bicep, "B.P. is 150 over 100, and pulse is rapid."

As they load him into the ambulance, red lights swirling above it, the paramedic speaks to me. "We're taking him to Brunswick General. Are you his family?"

"No, he's a friend...he's my boyfriend. I'll tell his family. His name is Christian Gutmann, spelled G U T M A N N. I'm Griffin Meade."

"Okay, Griffin, he's in critical condition, but I think he's going to make it," one of the paramedics says as he places a hand on my shoulder. "We'll know more about his condition when the ER evaluates him."

The paramedics then jump into the back of the ambulance, and with the siren screaming into the night, the ambulance turns around and heads down the driveway. By this time, I notice that Mom, Dad, and Jack are behind me in the driveway. I walk toward them. Falling into Mom's chest, she hugs me hard against her. I start to sob again. I can feel Dad and Jack's strong arms surround me as my entire family embraces me. Walking back to the house to call his parents, I notice the bald eagle is still looking at me as I make my way to the house. Then it strikes me: did the eagle have something to do with Christian's accident?

Chapter 21

New Brunswick Hospital
Brunswick, Maine
June 14, 1983

Christian sustained a broken mandible (jaw), a concussion to the left frontal lobe of his brain, broken transverse processes at cervical vertebrae 6 and 7 on the right side, a subluxation (dislocation) of the left shoulder joint, and contusions to his abdomen and chest from the seat belt. This is what Dad was able to get from the attending ER physicians at New Brunswick Hospital. He went into surgery immediately to wire the left mandible together and to repair the broken vertebrae. The doctors were concerned about general anesthesia after sustaining a head wound, but he had internal bleeding in his facial area and that had to be stopped.

The surgery was successful. He's now resting in the Intensive Care Unit because of his concussion and trauma to his face and neck. He's still unconscious, but the doctors said his vitals are good and they believe that he would wake up eventually.

I'm not able to go into the ICU to see him, but his parents, Wolf and Sarah Gutmann, were and they told us how he looked. I had been able to contact them after the accident by calling Christian's home phone number several times. It was late, and they had gone to bed. We explained to the Gutmanns what had happened at Antioch, that he was being transported to New Brunswick Hospital, and that we would meet them there to answer any questions they had. They were incredibly cordial considering the circumstances, but of course, suspicious that Christian had run into a tree on our driveway on a clear moonlit night.

The police also had questions about the accident, inquiring whether he had been drinking, or acting erratically before he left our house. His parents told us that his blood alcohol level was tested, and it was below detectable levels that were considered to lead to impairment. I'm sure they wouldn't have revealed that to us if that wasn't the case. I concluded that Christian either had not drunk his entire rum and coke, or that he had a high tolerance. He had only the one drink. Dad had called his lawyer, and after the Gutmanns shared the blood alcohol test results, he said that we were in the clear legally.

Sheriff Roberts impounded the Mustang. They were going to run some tests on the car and take casts of the tire tracks to see if they could figure out what had happened. They had also taken loads of photographs at the scene to help them with their investigation.

When the Gutmanns came out of the ICU, they told us that Christian's jaw had been wired shut to promote the healing process. He's wearing a cervical collar around his neck to keep his neck straight after the vertebrae surgery, and he's wearing a sling around his shoulder to help with the shoulder dislocation.

It's early in the morning, and the Gutmanns look exhausted, so Dad and Mom ask them if they would like to get some breakfast in the hospital cafeteria and they obliged. We're all on the elevator when I notice that the sole ICU nurse on duty comes out of the ICU and is standing at the nurse's station. Christian is the only patient in ICU; New Brunswick is a small hospital. No one is attending the ICU. I quickly get off the elevator and tell everyone I must use the restroom and I'll be down in a minute.

The elevator doors close, and I walk over to the double doors of the ICU, gently pushing them open. I creep inside stealthily. It's practically empty except for one patient in the corner. Christian is propped up in bed. I move closer to his bedside.

He has a large bandage wrapped across his forehead and around his head, his strawberry-blond hair peeking out above the white gauze. He has black circles under both eyes and severe bruising on both cheeks and around his jaw, probably from the force they had to apply when wiring his jaw together. His lips are cracked. I can barely make out his facial features under the swelling, but I see enough of that handsome face to know it's Christian.

Seeing his naked chest for the first time, I notice large purple bruises across his chest and flat abdomen where the seat belt caused trauma. Intravenous tubes are attached with tape to his right forearm, near the bend in his elbow. The top sheet is covering his lower torso, just below a trail of curly blond hair under his navel. I can see the impression of his penis under the sheet, even soft, it is impressive. I had felt it against my thigh, but this was my first visual.

I move a chair near the bed closer and sit down. I look down at his right hand, motionless next to his thigh covered with the sheet. I hold his hand, and it is colder than I expected. Enclosing my fingers around his, squeezing tightly, tears well up in my eyes as I look at his broken body. I begin to cry.

I then find myself talking to an unconscious man in between sobs. "I don't know if you can hear me…I'm so sorry this happened to you…you have to wake up Christian…I think…I think I love you…we're…we're just getting started."

Breaking down completely, I'm unable to talk anymore. Suddenly, I feel a twinge in my hand; Christian's fingers squeezing mine. I put my other hand over his and cup it. His hand responds to mine by straightening his fingers, feeling his fingertips on the palm of my hand. Looking at his face, there's a small flutter in his eyelids. As they lift slowly, I can see a sliver of his ice-blue eyes. Lifting his lids further, I can see that the whites of his eyes are severely bloodshot from his trauma. I smile at him through my tear-stained face. He's looking back at me; his expression reflects his pain and bewilderment.

He tries to speak. "Hmm," but then his face contorts into more pain.

"Shh, you can't talk. Your jaw has been wired shut…you broke your jaw. I'm so happy that you woke up…"

I start to cry again, but this time they are tears of relief. I then hear the nurse talking to someone outside the door. Quickly I rise from the chair and place it back into its original place. "I have to go. I'm not supposed to be in here, you know, not your family…not yet," I say as I smile and laugh quietly. "I will be back soon."

Picking up his hand, I kiss the back of it, curling

his fingers together, and lay his hand down next to his thigh. He looks at me as I leave, his ice-blue eyes slowly following me as I walk toward the door. Looking back at him for a few seconds, I see my boyfriend… a beautiful man. Peering through the plate glass window of the ICU doors to see if the hall is clear of the nurse, I walk through the door.

Chapter 22

Antioch
June 14, 1983

Leaving the hospital, we soon realize that no one
has called Trista about what happened the night before,
and that this, obviously, is not the best time for a visit.
Her plane is due to land at 9:30 a.m. in Portland and it
is 9:00 a.m. Luckily, Portland is only about a half an
hour drive from Brunswick, so we drive the Volvo
station wagon directly to the airport.

Trista Morten is an ex-girlfriend of mine (more on
her part) from Boston. Her family and my mother's
family have been close for generations, with various
Mortens marrying Griffins, so our bloodlines are woven
together like a big spider web, but we're always sure
not to marry someone that is any closer than a second
cousin. We're upper crust New Englanders, part of the
New England aristocracy and/or American Royalty.
When we intermarry, we do it correctly, not like the
gentry, say in the Ozarks?

Trista has been pursuing me since we were
children, playing husband and wife/mother and father,
when she forced me to play "house" or "mansion" or
whatever you want to call it, stating that we shall be the
next Griffin-Morten marriage. She also has a wicked
sense of humor and talks like a sailor when she has too

much to drink, which I have witnessed at many social events, especially at school. She attends a preparatory school for girls outside of Boston that is a feeder school to the Ivys.

Trista is a very pretty, petite brunette. Her hair is shoulder length and always pulled back with a purple velvet headband. She has skin that is creamy white with a rosy hue; a "peaches and cream" complexion. She has deep green eyes that are surrounded by the longest eyelashes. Her nose is thin and sloped, that slightly hangs over her plump upper lip. Her upper lip is doubly curved, referred to as a "Cupid's bow. High cheekbones and a slight cleft in her chin, a Morten trait, accentuate a triangular shaped face. Her long slender neck, thin body and small breasts remind me of the body of a ballerina: graceful and fluid.

We meet Trista in the baggage claim at the Portland airport. She's wearing a variation of her usual Preppy uniform: purple headband, a plaid skirt cut just above the knee, this one green and purple, a white blouse with a green ribbon tied around the collar that matched her skirt, a purple cardigan with a crest of some sort over the breast pocket, her requisite string of pearls, white knee socks, and purple Sperry sneakers.

"Griffin, dahling," she purrs into my ear in her hilariously affected accent, embracing me.

"Hi, Trista," I respond somewhat curtly. "How was your flight?" A customary question that I really didn't care about the answer.

"First class, of course, the flight people were lovely," she comments as she identifies her rather large suitcase on the luggage conveyor belt, not typical for a weekend in Maine.

Dad and Mom each take a turn hugging Trista. Dad picks up her suitcase from the baggage carousel and we head toward the car. There's an unusual silence in the car as we drive back home.

Trista stares at us, puzzled. "You all seem troubled. What's happened?"

We explained what happened to Christian and that we had been up all night at the hospital trying to do what we could. Understanding our predicament, she apologizes for the inconvenience of her visit at such a terrible time. Trista has her faults, but she has always been a sympathetic person.

Mom responds for all of us. "You have nothing to apologize for, Trista. We're happy to see you and have you at Antioch this weekend. We'll have a lovely weekend. How's your mother?"

"Cynthia is...well, Cynthia," she drolly responds.

Mom laughs. As cryptic as Trista's answer is, she totally understands what Trista is trying to say. A moment of levity is welcome this morning. When we finally arrive at the driveway of Antioch, Trista reacts to seeing the mansion.

"Well, look at this...absolutely palatial. I'm expecting Miss Havisham to walk into the garden any minute."

As we pass through the pillars of the driveway entrance, I train my gaze on the left window in the backseat, preparing myself to see the tree that Christian crashed into. There it is, still brandishing the scars of missing bark and gouged wood. In the daylight, the tire tracks imprinted on the grass and earth are visible.

Then I remember the eagle. I examine every tree along the driveway to see if the eagle is present, perching on a branch, staring at us as we come closer to the house. It is not. Jack sees us coming up the driveway and meets us at the garage. Trista bounds out of the car and wraps her arms around Jack.

"Oh my God, Jack Meade, you're all grown up and gorgeous," she says with a high-pitched shrill in her voice.

I pick up Trista's suitcase from the trunk and carry it into the house. Mom and Jack give Trista the downstairs tour as I bring her suitcase to the guest room on the second floor, the first room on the right, across from the bathroom we would share for the weekend.

I drop her suitcase on the bed, and as I turn to leave, I stop and sit down on the bed. I need to collect myself. It's the first time I've been alone since the accident last night. I feel like I want to cry, but I don't. I'm drained of tears sitting in the silence. Then I hear Trista and Jack's voices as they ascend the staircase. I get up and walk to the door of the guest room to meet them in the doorway.

"I put your suitcase on the bed, the bathroom is across the hall, and my room is next to the bathroom," I explain.

"Jack, can Griff and I have a moment?" Trista says as she slowly closes the guest bedroom door. Grabbing my hand, Trista pulls me to the bed and forces me to sit down. "So, tell me about this Christian," she inquires while sitting beside me.

She's staring at me waiting for an answer. I stare at her for a moment and then answer, "He's a new friend, my only friend here so far...we met at orientation, he's in a new wave band, he's a cool dude...and he hit a tree last night leaving after dinner."

"I'm so sorry, Griff. You said that you were at the hospital, was he hurt badly?" she asks with genuine sorrow in her voice.

"He's pretty messed up. Broke his jaw, got a concussion, dislocated his shoulder, bruises all over…but he's conscious, I think. I snuck in the ICU, talked to him, and he opened his eyes," I say, choking back the tears I didn't think I had a minute ago.

"That must have been hard. But he's lucky to have a friend like you," she says as she cups my face in her hand.

She then kisses me softly on the lips. I let her and then pull away slowly, so as not to offend her, and stand. Opening the door, I gesture toward the hallway.

"Let me show you the rest of the house," I say as I sigh in the hallway out of her sight.

****

The rest of the day includes tours of the house, grounds, and a walk on the beach. Mary made lobster rolls for lunch to provide Trista with an authentic regional dish of Maine, unlike most inadequate copies in Boston. She loved them so much that she ate two. For dinner, we have a selection of local fish: poached salmon, grilled swordfish, and tuna steak.

There's a lot of conversation, mostly about college. Trista volunteers that she's going to pursue a double major in Theater and English, and she's applying to Wellesley, (surprise surprise!), Trinity College, a few Ivys and two "cute" schools in Virginia, Sweet Briar and Hollins, where she could board her mare Parksley. She learns that I'm still intending to pursue a Theater degree, but that I hadn't decided if I was going to return to Boston or go beyond Massachusetts, say the left coast?

We talked, drank, and ate until the wee hours of the night. It was good, if not for one reason: it kept my mind off Christian, lying in that hospital bed, alone, and in pain. Exhausted and slightly tipsy, I go to bed early. Wondering if I'm going to be visited by Angelus, I wonder what effect alcohol will have on my dreamscape.

I was passed out when Angelus and his cold aura entered my room. For some reason, I must be awake for him to enter my thoughts, so he had to wrestle me out of my stupor. I'm not sure what he did, but I'm awake, and his face is in front of mine. He has the same serious expression on his face but there's something in his eyes that is different. Bending his head toward me, he touches his ethereal forehead to mine and an icy sensation spreads across my forehead. I'm asleep again.

Chapter 23

Angelus and Lazarus
Summer Solstice
June 21, 1919

The next morning, I woke to see an image of myself that was not a mirror. Lazarus had finished my drawing and I had placed it standing up on the dresser next to my bed. We had agreed the day before to meet in the meadow next to "our place," the rocky bluff and the patch of grass where Lazarus had immortalized me. It was to be late in the afternoon, as Lazarus had to complete his chores at the lighthouse earlier to have the rest of the day and night with me.

It was going to be another beautiful day. I could see the sun and white puffy clouds through the windows of the French doors to the balcony. I decide to walk along the rocky coastline from Antioch to the bluff after lunch, much earlier than we had agreed to meet.

I saw Angus before he left for his overnight trip to receive any instructions he had to give. He did not have many, except that I was to stay out of his good liquor, and there were to be no parties with the townsfolk. He asked me what I was going to do for meals, as Edward would not be there to prepare anything. I told him I would eat whatever I could find or maybe go into town

to get a lobster roll. He did not seem to care where or what I would eat, which was normal. Then he did something different. He walked over to me, grabbed me by the collar of my shirt, and moved his face closer to mine.

"Do not embarrass me, do not disgrace our name, or you will regret it," he warned rather sternly.

Calling Edward to bring down his bags, he went out the front door. Angus had talked to me like that before, but usually after he had been drinking. He was completely sober. There was something different about the way he talked to me. It was as if he was daring me to do something, which would warrant punishment.

Trying to make myself forget the expression on Angus's face and his warning, I left the house.

Wearing a white, loose-fitting collared shirt with the sleeves rolled up to my elbows, brown breeches, and brown leather shoes without socks, I walk through the backyard and into the small forest of trees on the north side of the property. I'm also carrying a surprise for Lazarus. As I clear the small forest going northeast, the coastline that borders our property appears, and I walk along the natural trail of the cliff.

I come to the meadow Lazarus and I had run through the day before. Walking over to the rocky bluff, I find the boulder I had posed upon and lean Lazarus's surprise against another rock. I lay down on the flat slab. The sun feels warm on my face but the breeze from the ocean keeps me from getting hot. Falling asleep as I wait for Lazarus, I have an interesting dream while sleeping peacefully in the mid-afternoon sun.

While sleeping on the flat stone slab, the screech of

a large and powerful bird awakens me. Its enormous wings cast a shadow over me as it hovers above. The sun is so large and bright behind this bird that I must shield my eyes from the sun's rays, even in the shadow of the large bird. The bird then hovers closer, its talons moving closer to my face. All I can see are the bird's large sharp talons and its powerful feathered body coming closer and closer...and then I feel something touching my face. I scream, "NO!"

I awake to see Lazarus's face over mine. His expression is one of concern. His hands are on my shoulders. "Angelus, it's all right, it's all right," he says with a comforting voice.

Quickly raising myself off the boulder slab, I sit on the edge of the rock, sweating and breathing rapidly. Sitting next to me, Lazarus places his left arm around my back. Gently pulling me closer so that my head is buried in his chest. My rapid breathing calms down. He continues to stroke my head.

"Shh, it's all right now. I'm here."

I'm breathing normally now. His firm muscled chest, soft cotton shirt, and his fingers stroking my head feel good. It is also a warm day and I need to cool off or become overheated. I raise my head from his chest.

"I had the strangest dream that a large bird, I think it was an eagle, was trying to grab me and take me... into the sun, it was so big, I have never seen the sun that big... and just as it was about to get me, I felt something touch my face..." I profess.

"I put my hand on your face to wake you up. You were screaming and moving your head back and forth. Sweat was all over your face. I got scared. Your face is so red," he explains, as he places his hand on my shoulder. "I think you might have been in the sun too long and got too hot and that is why you had that dream. When I get a fever, I dream about terrible things."

This was a side I had not seen in Lazarus. The comforter. A gentle man. This was new for me. I laid my head on his shoulder, overcome with emotion but feeling better about my dream. Looking at him, I remember my surprise. "I almost forgot. I brought a surprise for you, for us."

With that announcement, I reach over the boulder and produce a bright red kite. It's made of pine wood strips and dyed butcher-block paper with a tail made from white cloth. The ocean breeze blows the tail into Lazarus' face as I hold it: a good omen.

"I have had this since Christmas and have been waiting for the perfect day to fly it, and when I looked at the sky today, I knew this was the day. Have you ever flown a kite before?"

"No, but I used to watch other boys fly them in Central Park. That is a big park in New York City."

"It's not hard, but you have to coordinate two things: the amount of string and wind. There is a lot of string on a spool like this, so when your kite starts to fly you can let it go a long way into the sky, letting the string unravel as the spool spins. The wind, which we have plenty of today, will determine how much string is used," I explain as I show him the spool with the string. "Let's do this in the meadow; we'll have more room to run."

We walk up the bank of the bluff into the meadow. I held the kite and Lazarus held the spool of string. Immediately, a swift wind gusts across the meadow, rattling the paper kite. It does not take a lot of running to get the kite to lift into the air. Quickly, the red kite ascends high into the sky. I tell Lazarus to watch the slack of the string, or he will have to run to get it to tighten and lift the kite further. Luckily, there's enough wind today to keep the right amount of tension on the string. It's an amazing sight. The bold red color of the kite reflecting the sunlight, it looks as if it were on fire!

Then out of nowhere, we hear a rumbling in the distance. Turning to look for the sound, we can see the dark clouds gathering in the northeast toward the lighthouse and the point of the bay. It's not uncommon for these thunderstorms to appear suddenly off the coast of Maine, even on the most beautiful of days, and they're usually loud, electrical, and dangerous. Lightning from one of these types of storms struck and killed my father's brother, Angelus Bartholomew II, for whom I'm named, so I'm aware of the danger that they can cause.

I tell Lazarus to start cranking the reel of the spool to coil the line around the spool, but the wind is so strong, it's making it difficult to do so. Taking over the task, I crank the spool, but the kite only comes in about halfway when the string breaks and the kite goes flying southward toward Antioch.

The dark storm clouds move in fast, so the whole meadow is cast in shadow. I knew we had to get out of the open field, and the lighthouse is the shortest distance for shelter. Then I remember that we have Antioch to ourselves, and I change my mind.

"Let's run to Antioch. We need to run toward the woods along the path on the cliffside, to run as fast as we can because lightning can hit tall trees until we get to the backyard. There you'll see the door to the back porch of the house. Follow me," I shout to Lazarus as the wind whistles loudly.

Feeling the first raindrops, I knew we had to go right away. Then the rain starts to pour down on us. It's a hard rain, and within seconds, we're soaking wet. We were close to the small forest near Antioch, when I hear the unmistakable call of a bird of prey.

A large bird is flying toward us. I stop running. Standing in my muddy tracks, I quietly look up at the sky as the rain stings my body. I cannot believe what I'm seeing. It's the bird in my dream! I cannot move, mesmerized by the sight. Lazarus has stopped running; he's also looking up at the massive bird in the threatening sky. My eyes fixate on the bird's flight. The lightning flashes reveal that it's a bald eagle, a big one, and it is caught in the winds of the storm. It calls out again, but it does not come any further toward us on the cliffside, staying high above the trees.

Lazarus grabs my shoulder, startling me from my gaze, and yells, rain dripping into his mouth. "We need to keep going: it's not going to bother us!"

At that time, a jagged bolt of light lights up the sky, illuminating everything around us like a full moon shining down on the forest. Two seconds later, a loud crackling boom echoes over the sea. The storm is moving closer. Looking at Lazarus, I signal to him to run toward the woods where the eagle is circling. We make it into the thick small forest.

As lightning crackles in the sky, and thunderclap follows, we carefully watch to see if any trees have been struck down in our direction. We can still hear the call of the eagle as we get closer to Antioch. Finally, we make it to the edge of the woods. Stopping shortly to catch our breath and gather strength, we determine the back porch is about 100 feet from where we stood. I give the signal and we make a mad dash through the backyard, as lightning lights up the open sky and thunder crackles above us. We leap onto the back porch.

I open the back door on the porch and we walk slowly into the mudroom. We stand in the middle of the room trying to catch our breath, leaning on the walls to help steady us as our chests heave, gasping for air through our mouths. We look at each other as our breathing rate slows. We're soaking wet, our clothes are drenched, hanging uncomfortably off our bodies. Lazarus's wet shirt is plastered to his chest. I can see the impression of his well-developed chest and his brownish nipples poking through the sheer white fabric. It's also uncomfortably cold in the mudroom.

The wet clothing next to my skin is giving me the chills, so I begin to undress. Unbuttoning my shirt, I remove it and drop it on the floor. I then unlace my shoes and kick them over into the corner. Unbuttoning the fly of the breeches, I peel them from my wet thighs and toss them onto the floor as well. Standing in wet white boxer shorts, I pull them from around my waist and toss them onto the pile of clothes. I'm completely naked. My cock looks smaller than usual, as it is always colder in the mudroom than the rest of the house.

Lazarus follows my actions except he folds his clothes as he removes them, placing them on a bench. Standing naked in the mudroom as well, he looks like a Greek statue without a fig leaf, a statue that has fallen off its pedestal. His cock looks bigger than mine. I had never noticed that before. As I open the door to the kitchen and motion to Lazarus, he grabs his folded wet clothes and shoes and follows me.

Walking completely naked through our kitchen and dining room, leaving wet footprints on the kitchen tile and oriental rugs, we pad into the grand foyer, dripping water unto the tile floor as we approach and climb the grand staircase to the second floor. We walk down the hallway into my bathroom where I pull four large, thick white towels from the shelf inside the closet, giving two of them to Lazarus when he returns from putting his clothes in my bedroom. Wrapping one of the towels around my waist, I place the other one over my head; Lazarus does the same. I turn the knob for the hot water and scalding water pours into the tub, instantly producing steam. With the towel hanging over my head, I kneel next to the tub.

"Come over here and place your face into the steam with the towel over your head like this. It's the quickest way to get warm. I don't want you to get sick."

Lazarus does as I instruct. He's kneeling next to me with the towel over his head. We both inhale the hot steam, letting it warm the cold skin of our faces and necks.

"Do you feel warmer?" I ask as he continues to kneel next to the tub.

"Yes," he states, his voice muffled by the thirsty cotton towel.

After steaming for a few minutes, I lean over the rim of the tub, turn the knob for the cold water, until the temperature of the water coming from the large silver faucet is comfortably hot, not scalding, and then flip the drain closed. With the hot water filling the tub, the steam in the bathroom is thick. I pull out a fresh bar of soap from the medicine cabinet, hidden behind the fogged mirror, and place it next to the tub.

I remove the towels from my waist and around my head/neck and step into the tub when the water reaches the halfway mark. Submerging my body all the way under the hot water, I instantly feel warmer. Lifting my head and shoulders out of the water, I look over at Lazarus looking at me.

"Come on in, there's plenty room for the both of us."

Standing up, Lazarus removes his towels and carefully places his left leg into the water, anchoring his left foot onto the bathtub floor. Because he's shorter, he must sit on the edge of the bathtub to get both of his feet completely onto the floor of the tub. I sit up and bend my legs to give him room on the floor as Lazarus slowly lowers his body into the water.

"This is the biggest bathtub I've ever seen," Lazarus states as he soaks in the tub up to his chest, his legs bent, and knees above the water.

"Ayuh, this was the bathroom that my father had when he was my age. When his father died, and he inherited some money, he had the old bathtub replaced with this one. Came from Boston. It is called a ball and claw tub, and it is made of iron and porcelain. If you think this is big, wait to you see the bathtub in Angus's bathroom. Long, hot baths in big bathtubs are about the only thing that I've in common with Angus."

Realizing that I was bragging and remembering that Lazarus had to take baths from water boiled from the fireplace in the lighthouse cottage, I stop talking. I move closer so that my feet are on either side of his bottom. I rest my legs against the outer edge of his thighs and his feet rest under my legs and bottom.

I'm now able to move my face closer to his. I give him a light kiss on his right cheek. It felt warm. Then I kiss his left cheek. It also felt warm. Kissing his full lips gently at first, I tenderly grab his fuller lower lip with my teeth. I pull away slowly and smile.

I make a bowl shape with both of my hands, fill it with bath water and pour it over Lazarus's chest and shoulders. Taking the soap, I place it on his chest and rub it in a circular pattern. He closes his eyes letting out a big sigh. I move the soap in a bigger circle until it is touching his right nipple. He moans louder. Touching the sensitive knob of flesh lightly with my thumb, Lazarus starts to breathe faster. Soaping and touching the left nipple with my other hand at the same time as I touch the right nipple, Lazarus is breathing loudly through his nose.

I look down in between his thighs to see if his cock is getting bigger. I see the tip of it is poking above the water. I move my hand beneath the water and wrap my fingers around it. He stops breathing loudly for a moment.

I place the soap on the edge of the tub. I grab both sides of the tub and hoist myself out until I'm towering above Lazarus. Walking backwards one step along the bathtub floor, I kneel into the tub, inside of Lazarus's knees as he's now stretching his legs along the bathtub floor. I move my arms into the spaces between his arms and his chest, placing my palms flat against the tub floor, lowering myself so that my thighs are on the inside of his thighs, my wood-like cock rubbing against his as my chest rests on his chest.

Lazarus wraps his arms around my back, holding me closer, my face hovering above his. I kiss him on his large soft lips, my tongue opening his mouth, our tongues dance with each other. Lazarus's hardness, rubbing against mine, feels amazing as we move our bodies against each other.

Then a thought came into my head. In one of my father's books, the ones he hid under his bed, I had seen a drawing of a naked man and a naked woman on top of each other in this same position. The caption under the drawing said, "missionary position." I was younger then and I did not know what that meant, but I knew that it had something to do with what had to happen to have a baby. "Sexual intercourse" was the title of the chapter. In the picture, the man's cock was inside of the woman, an opening large enough to fit the man's cock. I learned later in the book that this is the same opening where babies are born.

I stop kissing Lazarus and move my hands so that they are under his thighs. Cupping them, lifting and separating his thighs and legs out of the water. He places each of his feet onto opposite sides of the rim of the bathtub. Lazarus is in the same position as the woman was in the missionary position. I move in closer to his body and begin to kiss him again. His hard cock is pressing against my belly and my stiff cock starts to rub in the space between the two halves of his bottom. The sensation feels good. Lazarus starts to moan louder as I rub faster in the tight space. He seems to like this feeling. The friction from the water makes the rubbing down there more difficult as we continue, so I stop.

"Let's get in my bed," I whisper into his right ear.

I get to my knees and then carefully stand up in the

tub. I hold out my hand to Lazarus and help him to stand in the tub. Stepping out of the tub, we dry ourselves off. We walk holding hands into my bedroom and over to my four-poster bed. I place Lazarus's folded wet clothes on the floor next to the bed and pull the bedspread back.

Lying down on my back, I motion Lazarus to lie on top of me. We begin to kiss deeply as we did in the bathtub. Then Lazarus places the palms of his hands on the bed, lifting himself from me so that he's looking into my eyes. Moving his head down my body, he kisses and licks my neck, chest, nipples, belly, pelvis and on the flesh in between my legs. It all feels amazing, but I cannot get that image of the missionary position out of my head.

I sit up, grasp him around the waist with both hands and quickly roll Lazarus over so that I'm on top of him. His thighs and legs are fully apart with his feet around my back as his legs squeeze. Supporting his lower back with my arms and lifting his hips off the bed, I rub my hard cock in his bottom like I did in the bathtub. Rubbing my cock on this soft, smooth skin feels good. Lazarus starts moaning again. Then, for a second, the end of my cock moves into a smooth hole and Lazarus yells. It feels amazing but I pull it out. He's looking at me with a strange look on his face, confused about what I just did. Suddenly, I remember something I had heard from boys talking in the village, something called "buggery," when a man sticks his cock into the arsehole of another …was this buggery what we were about to do?

I then remember something else that the boys said about buggery, "Be careful of men that spit on their cocks, they'll get behind you and stick it in your arse."

I spit into my hand. Lazarus is looking at me and wondering what I'm doing. I then rub the spit on the end of my cock. I spit again onto my fingers and rub it around his arsehole. Leaning down, I whisper into Lazarus's right ear.

"Ready?"

Kissing him deeply, I push my wet cock into his arsehole once more, and Lazarus yells again, but it is not as loud. My mouth is over his, muffling any sounds he makes. Then my cock moves further, and it is completely inside his body. Lazarus has a pained expression, but he is also moaning.

The warmth of his body and the tightness around my cock feels so good. I then begin to move my cock in and out. This feels even better. Lazarus seems to like it more and has stopped looking like it hurt, moaning louder. My breathing increased, moving faster in and out of Lazarus. I feel like I'm going to spill my seed.

Suddenly, the door in my bedroom slams against the wall. The next thing I hear is Angus's angry voice as a pair of large rough hands grab me around the throat and pull me from the bed and onto the floor. I try to shield my face as I feel bony muscular fists punching my neck and head as he's screaming.

"Perversion! How dare you bring this filth into my house?"

With his hand, he pulls my hand away from protecting the right side of my face and batters it with his fist: hitting my cheek, my nose and crushing my lips against my teeth.

"You will never be a Bartholomew from this day forward! I will disown you for disgracing this family!"

Blood trickles down my face, into my mouth. I try to stand up but immediately fall to my knees, dizzy. Angus continues to beat on my back and yell at me, but I cannot tell what he's saying now. The horrible words he has said to me are pounding in my head along with the throbbing pain of the wounds he has inflicted there.

He leaves the room screaming, and I can hear him stomping down the hall. Suddenly, remembering Lazarus, I look up to the bed, but he's not there. Abruptly, a blast of cold air hits my back as I'm wondering where he went. Turning my body to search, I see that one of the doors to my balcony is open. I examine the floor next to the bed. Lazarus's neatly folded clothes are not there. He got away! It was all I could think. I did not hear Angus call his name, so I prayed that he was not recognized in my bedroom or caught climbing down from the balcony.

Slowly standing, I use the bed and stumble into the hallway, naked, and bloodied. I can hear Angus cursing downstairs and glass smashing. He's drinking, and it would only be a matter of time before I would become the target of his rage again. Leaning my broken body against the wall outside of the bathroom, *No more. I will not let him beat me one more time and then throw me out of his house and his family. I will not give him the satisfaction.*

Staggering down the second-floor hallway, slowly using the wall to guide me toward the second-floor stairwell, I use the banister to pull myself up the stairs, step by step, until I finally reach the third-floor landing. Supporting my weight against the banister on the third floor, I grip the handrail and struggle to inch myself forward toward the wall of the short hallway. I lean against the wall and stumble to the end of the hallway to the narrow stairwell of the widow's walk. I pull myself up the stairs by using the railing to the widow's walk door. I push it open and fall through to the balcony, almost losing consciousness.

Crawling, feeling the rain pelt my naked skin, I reach out into the darkness to find the iron guardrail that surrounds the walk. Finally, my hand collides with one of the sharp points of the guardrail. I grasp the spike by the cylindrical base. Then with all the strength I have left, I manage to stand up next to the guardrail. The raindrops, propelled by the fierce wind, hit my skin like bullets, producing unbelievable pain as each drop bounces off my wounds. Standing there, naked, bloodied, bruised, and in pain, I summon the courage to make my last stand.

Leaning over the guardrail, I tumble over it and my left leg catches the spikes on top, tearing at my leg furiously. I fall three stories to the stone pavement below. As I fall, I feel weightless, floating, relieved of any pain for a few seconds as the rain and wind envelop my body. Then I feel the crushing jolt of the impact of the hard, unyielding stone against my head and neck. Darkness.

My head split open when I hit the ground. So severe was the damage to my head that the other wounds that Angus had made were impossible to detect. My naked, broken body lie in a pool of blood next to the back porch, the porch I had run to escaping the storm only hours ago.

Angus would discover my body hours later after he sobered up. He had come home that night because the business deal he traveled for had failed. He was drunk before he got home. The county coroner ruled my death a suicide. No one questioned the cause of death, and no one ever spoke of it again until after Angus's death 20 years later.

I'm condemned to this house and the grounds for eternity for committing the mortal sin of taking my own life. Antioch is my Hell.

I feel like this is the end of the dream, when suddenly, I'm transported back to my bedroom. I'm not awake, still in my dream state but not in one of Angelus's flashback episodes. I'm standing, wearing the same basketball shorts I went to bed in. Angelus is standing in front of me, naked as he always appears, a serious look on his face.

"Griffin, I have kept you from waking up because this is the only way that I can talk to you."

It takes me a minute to realize the importance of this moment, as this is the first time that Angelus is directly communicating with me, not through dreams, not through imagery, but having a one-on-one dialogue in my head.

"Now you know my life's story. I had to show you everything, no matter how painful it was to me, so that you would understand what it is that I'm asking you to do. Because I took my own life, a mortal sin against God, my spirit can never leave this house or the barrier that surrounds this house. I cannot ascend to heaven to be with my Lord. My spirit must dwell on this earthly plain for eternity. This is my purgatory…my Hell.

I have been banished to this place, but I do not want to be here alone anymore. My Lazarus is still alive, but he's old and sick and is near death. I need you to bring him to Antioch. He must commit the mortal sin of taking his own life before he dies so that he cannot ascend to heaven and be with me, forever."

I cannot believe what Angelus is asking me to do. To be an accessory to a suicide! I struggle to find the words to answer his macabre request.

"Angelus, I know that you love Lazarus. It may be the most beautiful love story I have ever witnessed, and I know you're alone...but what you're asking me to do...I can't be part of someone's suicide...how could I convince someone I don't know to end his life?" I plead.

"Griffin, I knew from the moment you entered Antioch that we were kindred spirits, that you knew the love between men, and that you would understand what it is not to have that love. You are my only hope."

"Angelus, please, I cannot do this."

The expression on Angelus's beautiful face changes. His eyebrows knit together in a menacing shape. His eyes glaze over, serious and determined. His once beautiful mouth morphs into a cruel form. He then threatens me. "I want Lazarus to be with me forever! I will not be denied this any longer. I will not let ANYONE keep us apart any longer! You have witnessed what I can do. I took the life of that miscreant for his blasphemous speak, for offending my name. I can do it again!"

My worst fears were realized at that moment. Angelus had murdered Anvil Millstone. Then I thought about Christian.

"Did you hurt Christian? Did you hurt the one I love?

****

A flash of light and I'm awake. Sweat pours down

my face, and my hair is wet with perspiration. My chest heaves heavily, beads of water collect in the valley between the pectoral muscles and across the abdomen as it flexes up and down. I'm slightly dizzy, disoriented, and chills run through my body, as if I had a raging fever that just broke. Abruptly, a bright beam of light shines on my face and burns my eyes. Shielding them with my hand, I can barely recognize the sun's rays penetrating the bedroom, peeking through the sheer curtains of the French doors. It's morning. My journey with Angelus lasted the entire night.

I turn over in bed to escape the sun's beaming light, grab the pillow, and stack it under my face. I lie there thinking of all that had happened to me last night. I remember everything. What Angelus had revealed about his death. Why he was haunting Antioch. What he asked me to do with Lazarus Benedictinc. The truth about Anvil Millstone's death. That he did not answer my question about Christian's accident.

"How can my life ever be normal after what I know?"

Chapter 24

Antioch
June 15, 1983

I stayed in bed until noon. No one came to my bedroom to wake me up or check on me. We'd been at the New Brunswick Hospital until the early morning hours on Friday dealing with Christian's car accident and his trauma, so it was understandable that I might need a few more hours of sleep. However, I wasn't asleep. I was lying in bed still contemplating what Angelus had shown me and asked me to do. I hear a gentle knock on the door.

I groggily answer, "Come in."

The door opens and it is Mom. "Honey, good news. Mrs. Gutmann called and told us that Christian is conscious and out of the ICU and has been moved to a regular room. He's responding well to treatment. She said that Christian indicated that he was anxious to see you. I have the room number and the phone number when you are ready."

"Thanks, Mom, I'll be down in a minute."

"Honey, I know this has been a rough couple of weeks. If there's anything you need, please ask."

I shake my head, trying to hold back the tears. One escapes and runs down my cheek, which I quickly wipe off with the heel of my hand. Mom slowly closes the door, watching me through the narrow opening.

I have a short cry and then gather myself. So many emotions. The most important thing is that Christian's recovering from his accident. Being the son of a neuroscientist, I know there are so many things that can go wrong after traumatic brain injury. I decide to go downstairs and make a phone call to the hospital.

As I'm pulling the covers off, Trista comes bounding into my room and jumps on the bed. She's wearing her signature purple headband, purple cardigan with a white t-shirt underneath and pink Capri pants. She's barefoot, revealing a pedicure of bright purple nail polish. Lying on her belly, her knees are bent, and feet are bouncing back and forth against the bed.

"Griffy, do get out of bed, the day awaits!" she teases me as she pulls the covers toward her. "Oh, can I get a look at little Griffy?"

I pull them back even though I'm not naked. She doesn't need to know that. "Trista, will you control your hormones for one minute!"

"Only if you get out of bed. Oh, I heard the good news about your boyfriend!"

"What? What the hell are you talking about?"

"Ooooh, me thinks he doth protest too much. It's so obvious that Christian's more than a friend to you. The way you talk about him, really touching…Relax, Griffin. I have known for a long time, and I don't care, sweetie," Trista confesses. She continues with her diatribe. "How did I know? Well, remember that time at Bootsie Anderson's pool party, and I dragged you into the cabana? You were the first boy that I gave access to my 'pussoir,' and you looked at it like it was an alien. That is not the normal reaction of a straight, horny, teenage boy."

I looked at her dumbfounded.

"But…you have always said that we were destined to be married, to unite our families…"

"Oh, I think we should still get married. Let me explain. I've no delusions about what marriage and love are. Cynthia has been married three times, supposedly for love, and she's still miserable. Oh, I want to be in love… but it doesn't last, and it certainly isn't the sole reason you should get married. No, marriage is more about logistics…family lines, wealth, property…you know the way it has been for thousands of years. Moreover, to satisfy ourselves, we can have as many lovers as we want. You can have your boy or boys, and I can have mine…I have a penchant for Latin muscle hunks, construction workers…you know the type. The only thing I ask, dahling, is that we have a munchkin or two to carry on our bloodline."

I could not believe what I was hearing. "But…how if I'm—"

"Oh, Griff sweetie, all I ask is that you let me climb on top of you when I'm ovulating…I'll do all the work and you can think of Emilio Estevez or whoever…we'll have the most divine children. Our looks, brains, and money, they would be unstoppable!"

I can't respond.

"So, now that you have your Christian, why don't the three of us plan on going to schools that are near each other so that we can keep up the illusion that you and I are hot and heavy while you two really are hot and heavy! Do you think Christian would go for that?" she asks, batting those crazy long eyelashes.

"I'm not sure where Christian wants to go to

school. I know he wants to be pre-Med…he's smart, takes all AP courses. I know he mentioned schools in Boston, and I like E's theater program, but he may want to stay local or go to a small liberal arts school in a small town." Then I realize the absurdity of what I'm saying, "Wait, this is crazy to be talking like this, we just started dating!"

"Griffin, dahling, think about it. Do you want to stay in this dreary old house with a magnificent view of the sea in this adorable, but boring little village, with your beau for the rest of your life, or do you want to live in an amazing city like Boston where the gay community thrives? Don't you miss all the fabulous parties, the theater, art, society?"

She makes a convincing argument. Trista's attention focuses on something on the dresser. Realizing she has spied the portrait of Angelus leaning on the top of the dresser, she rolls over to the edge of the bed, stands, and retrieves the framed picture. Sitting down on the bed again, she crosses her legs and scrutinizes the drawing.

"Well, who do we have here? You are a handsome devil. Do we have a Romeo? Or is it Iago."

I cannot tell if she's being rhetorical or if she's asking me. I think for a moment if I should answer her. She has been so honest with me so I decide to divulge some history.

"He was the grandson of the man who built this house. He committed suicide when he was eighteen years old by jumping off the widow's walk."

"Why? He was so gorgeous. How could anyone that beautiful be that selfish, depriving the world of his magnificence? On second thought, I think he was more of an Iago, something in the eyes," she pontificates.

"All right, this has been…stimulating and revelatory, but I need to call the hospital and check about visiting hours," I say as I roll out of bed.

Standing, I lift the framed picture from her hands and settle it back on the dresser, realizing that I'm wearing only my basketball shorts, which do not do a great job concealing my semi-wood. Why was I excited? The talk about having sex with Christian?

Trista is ogling me now. "Oh my, little Griffin isn't so little after all. That will be fun someday."

"Out!" I demand. "I'll see you downstairs. Maybe we can have lunch in town, after I take a shower."

I slip off my b-ball shorts, put on a pair of boxers, a pair of jeans, a t-shirt and then trot downstairs into the kitchen and ask Mom for the hospital phone number and room number. I pick up the rotary phone in the living room, dial the number, and get the directory.

An operator eventually responds. "New Brunswick Hospital, how can I direct your call?"

"Hello, I would like you to connect me to room 209, but can you tell me the visiting hours first?" I inquire.

"Eight a.m. to eight p.m. for family, ten a.m. to six p.m. for general population," the operator informs.

"Thank you. Could you connect me to room 209 now?"

The phone rings once and then I hear an older female voice. "Hello?"

"Hello, Mrs. Gutmann, this is Griffin Meade. I was told Christian wanted to see me, and I was wondering when it would be a good time to visit."

"Hello, Griffin. Christian is not able to speak, but

he's able to communicate through writing. He has requested to see you as soon as possible. He's very insistent, and I'm afraid that the stress is going to make him weaker. Could you come today or tomorrow?" she desperately pleads with me.

"I can come today, in about two hours."

"Good, I'll expect you around three. I'll tell Christian."

"Great, I'll see you soon."

I'm about to hang up when, unexpectedly, I hear something loudly thumping down the grand staircase, something heavy rolling and banging against the wall and the stairs as it falls toward the bottom. Then a singular harsh thud when the object finally lands on the foyer floor.

I turn my head toward the foyer to see what the object is that has landed at the end of the staircase. I see a small river of blood spreading out across the tiles of the foyer floor. I drop the phone. Slowly walking toward the source of the river, I fall to my knees when I see the sleeve of a purple cardigan shrouding an arm. I yell in horror at the top of my lungs at the discovery. Trista's body is grotesquely contorted, the right side of her face flat on the floor, eyes still open. The base of her neck is at a ninety-degree angle with her head, pieces of vertebrae protruding from the skin of her neck, blood streaming across the floor. Her torso remains on the first four stairs.

The room starts to sway. Feeling dizzy and nauseous, I double over and vomit on the foyer floor. Abruptly, the room gets darker, and then it is black.

****

I see Mom's face; she's placing something warm,

soft, and moist on my head: a compress. I'm looking at the ceiling, and something is holding my head elevated. My head hurts and looking into the light makes it worse. I reach my hand toward the source of pain in my forehead, and I feel something soft and textured—a gauze pad.

I hear voices coming from behind me and the sound of a camera clicking rapidly. I attempt to sit up when Mom gently pushes my shoulder down to stop me.

"Andy, sweetie, lie down. You have a nasty cut on your head. You got it when you collapsed. The paramedic said you are going to be fine, but he wants us to monitor you for the next twenty-four hours," she quietly explains.

"Mom, what's happening behind me?"

"The coroner is examining Trista's body, and the police are taking pictures," she answers quietly, a tear forming in her eye.

I then hear the squeaking of wheels on the tile floor and a metallic rattle. "What is that sound?"

More tears form in her eyes. "They just wheeled in a gurney to take Trista's body to New Brunswick Hospital. I called Trista's mother and she's on her way to identify the body. They require a relative for an official identification, apparently."

Tears stream down my face, each sob, the action pulling on my bandaged forehead, wrinkling, and irritating the skin of my wound. This elicits pain from beneath the gauze pad. Then Sheriff Roberts appears.

"Hello, Griffin, are you feeling any better? Well, enough to answer a few questions?"

Quickly wiping away tears, I nod subtly. I answer a

series of routine questions about our relationship and the last time I saw her alive. He asked me what I had heard or seen when I discovered the body, which wasn't much. He asked me what Trista might have been doing on the second floor when everyone else was on the first floor. I told him that I was calling the hospital to find out when I could visit Christian Gutmann when I heard something falling down the stairs.

"Yes…there has been a lot of…unfortunate events around here lately. How is Mr. Gutmann doing?" Sheriff Roberts inquires.

Realizing this was the only good news of the day, I respond, "He's out of the ICU, and recovering well, it seems. I was going to visit him this afternoon…Wait, Mom, did you call Mrs. Gutmann and tell her—"

"Yes, I did," Mom says.

"Well, that is it for now. If you remember anything else, please call. We'll know more after the autopsy tomorrow. Take care of yourself, Griffin," Sheriff Roberts says in a comforting tone.

I can feel his large hand gently rubbing my left shoulder, and then the sound of his shoes tapping the tile floor walking away. The coroner and the rest of the police leave soon after that. By this time, Dad and Jack have entered the living room.

"Dad, can you help me up to my room? I want to lay down in my room."

"Sure, sport. Jack, help me with your brother." He kneels next to me on the couch.

Sitting up slowly, Dad and Jack lift me from the couch. Crossing the foyer to the staircase, I realize there is no sign of Trista's blood. The coroner or someone had thoroughly cleaned the floor.

Jack and Dad then help me up the stairs, one step at a time until we're on the second floor. We head down the hallway, passing the guest room, bathroom, and enter my room. After they helped me to the bed, I climb under the covers with my clothes on. Dad leans down and kisses me on the forehead, resting his mouth for over a moment.

"You rest, sport. You have been through enough for a lifetime." Dad stayed in my room and watched me the rest of the day.

****

I wake up in darkness, with no idea what time it is. As far as I was concerned, it could be p.m. or a.m. The cold mist filters into my bedroom. I don't want to see or talk to Angelus, but too weak to move. I think about screaming, but I would have to explain why I'm yelling in the middle of the night. I'm sure that whatever reason I came up with, no one would blame me due to what I had been through in the last three days. But it is too late, Angelus's face appears before me as I lie on my back, his entire ethereal face approaching and entering mine. I'm unconscious instantly.

****

I open my eyes and we're both standing on the balcony. Angelus is nude, as usual. It is nighttime, brightly lit by the moonlight of a full moon. There's no sense of cold, as it is not real. Am I dreaming, or is this a supernatural state of consciousness? We are both silent for a while.

"What happened today, Angelus?"

Angelus turns and looks directly into my eyes. A wave of energy brushes against my face, penetrating my head. Angelus gives me my answer.

I can see Trista walking down the hallway toward the staircase. As she steps onto the first step, I see his ghostly arm reaching out to her, touching her shoulder. As she turns her head toward the arm, there's a look of sheer horror on her face. She opens her mouth to scream, but nothing is coming out. Instead, there is the appearance that she's choking, gasping for air, clasping her hands over her left breast, desperately grabbing at her clothes. Then her eyes roll back into her head, and she collapses onto the stairs. She tumbles, limbs flailing in every direction as she somersaults down the entire staircase. The motion is accompanied by the sickening sounds of her body thumping against the steps, banister, and wall. Bones crack as her head and body smash into an unnatural position.

Abruptly, the scene changes and I'm watching myself and Trista talking in my bedroom. The perspective is from above, however, as if I'm floating above the conversation. Trista is talking while holding the framed portrait of Angelus.

"Well, who do we have here? You are a handsome devil. Do we have a Romeo, or is it Iago?…How could anyone that beautiful be that selfish, depriving the world of his magnificence? On second thought, I think he is more of an Iago, something in the eyes."

I try to interrupt the flashback from the previous afternoon, yelling at Angelus. "You killed her because she criticized you!" The vision continues without interruption. I'm now hearing her comments about our conversation regarding marriage.

It was obvious now. Angelus perceived her as a threat, a serious diversion to his plans. That is why he killed her. Angered, I confront Angelus about Christian.

"Did you try to kill Christian because you thought he was a threat too!"

I'm now floating above Christian's Mustang as he makes a three-point turn in the driveway. Then I follow his car as it drives down the driveway. Suddenly, I'm swooping down toward the car, moving in front and rushing toward the windshield to see Christian's face change to shock, his arms crossing over his face as the car veers off to the right. I hear the car crashing into a tree, I can see Christian's face bouncing off the steering wheel.

"Stop!" I yell. The film in my head ceases to exist, and I'm shaking, trying to gain my composure, "All right, I understand. I will help you. I will bring Lazarus to Antioch…to convince him to take his life…but you must promise not to hurt anyone else, especially those that I love."

****

Quickly, I'm in my bedroom, lying in my bed, no longer in Angelus's dreamland. The cold is gone and so is Angelus. Turning over on my right side to shield myself from looking at the French doors and balcony, I cry aloud. I want it all to go away.

Chapter 25

New Brunswick Hospital
June 16, 1983

The New Brunswick Hospital is a hotbed of activity for the Meade household. I'm here to see Christian now that he was moved to a regular room. There's another event taking place here in which our family is involved: Trista Morten's autopsy is being conducted in the basement of the hospital, the county morgue, this morning.

Trista's mother, Cynthia Morten van Rhys Dalton, flew into Portland last night. She has the heartbreaking job of identifying Trista's body and hearing the results of the autopsy. She brought a prominent doctor from Boston General, Dr. Milton Beckett, a family friend, to assist the Cumberland County coroner.

Mom and Dad are also here for the second time in three days. They will meet with Trista's mother after she identifies the body. Mary Griffin Meade would probably be the only person in the world who could calm her and explain to her what transpired.

All involved are anxious to learn the results of Trista's autopsy. Of course, I knew what was responsible for her death. Angelus's spirit confronted her at the top of the stairs, which either caused her to faint or have a heart attack, which led her to fall and tumble down the immense staircase. I have desperately tried to get that image of Trista's broken body lying at the foot of the stairs out of my mind, but it haunts me. I feel responsible. If I had agreed to Angelus's plan for Lazarus the night before she was murdered, perhaps Angelus would have spared her life. Perhaps not.

I've been standing outside Christian's hospital room for at least a minute, aching to see him, but I'm also afraid. Why does he want to see me, unsure if I'm ready for any more shocks to my system.

I finally open the door, giving me a view of the beds situated on the left wall; Christian is lying in the bed closest to the door. He's alone, awake, and looking at me as I enter the room. He still has the bandage across his head, the black eyes, the cervical collar, and his left arm is still in a sling. His right arm extends toward me, beckoning me to come closer.

I smile faintly, knowing that he can't smile back. Tears well up in my eyes as I slowly inch toward the bed. I lean down and wrap my arm around his back, his uninjured arm wrapping around my back. I drop my head delicately onto his right shoulder and start to cry. Circling his right hand over my back, occasionally lifting his hand to cup the back of my neck, he slides his hand down between my shoulder blades to circle more.

Through my tears, runny nose, and shallow gasps of air, I mumble into his shoulder, "I am so sorry, Christian."

A muffled high-pitched sound comes from the back of his throat as his chest convulses slightly, crying also. Lifting my head, seeing the tears streaming down his face, I gently wipe them away from his cheek, and then very carefully place a light kiss on his tear-stained cheek, the only part of his face that does not appear to have a bruise.

Even with all this trauma to his face, he's still a handsome man. He lifts his free hand to my face and returns the caress to my cheek. Our eyes are locked on each other, communicating the only way we can. Understanding how important we are to each other.

"How are you feeling?" I finally ask.

He shrugs his shoulders a little and slightly tilts his head because movement is hindered by the cervical collar. I take this as a sign that he's not in much pain. He then moves his hand from my face and making it into the shape that it would be to hold a pencil, he scribbles the imaginary pencil into the air.

"Oh, you want to write something?"

He slowly shakes his head affirmatively. I look around the room; there's a tablet of paper and a black marker on the tray next to the bed. I place the marker in his hand and lay the tablet on his lap that is covered with a sheet. His expression becomes more serious and determined as he begins to write. He then lifts the pad so that I can read it: YOU NEED TO LEAVE ANTIOCH!

My eyes must have appeared inquisitive because he places the pad down on his lap and starts to draw something. A face, but not a human face. It is long and thin, huge eyes, and the mouth contorted. The hair is long and thin, surrounding the ghastly-looking visage. I instantly recognize it. It is Angelus. Christian points his finger at the face repeatedly.

I play along. "What are you trying to tell me, Christian?"

He then lays the tablet down and writes something above the drawing of the face: THIS IS WHAT I SAW WHEN I CRASHED!

"This is the face of someone you saw on the driveway that caused you to crash?"

Christian, trying to rotate his head back and forth to say no, writes another word below the face: GHOST!

"You saw a ghost?"

He nods slightly. Then he writes something else: HAVE YOU SEEN IT?

"No," I lie.

His face looks relieved and crestfallen at the same time. Thinking about the vision and the intention of Angelus, I make a decision. Grasping Christian's right hand and enclosing both of mine around his, I look into his eyes, and warn him.

"I do not want you to ever come to Antioch again. It is not safe for you there!" He looks at me incredulously. "I am safe, but you aren't! I can't explain why I know this, but if you trust me…if you love me…you will stay away. I won't be there much longer," I calmly explain.

I realize I said the "L" word. He realizes it too. Tears filling those ice blue eyes, he slightly nods his head once in the affirmative. His tears form rivulets coursing around his prominent cheekbones. He looks scared. I'm scared, too. I stand up and cradle Christian's head next to my chest, being careful not to put any pressure on his bandage.

"I'll be all right; you just concentrate on getting better. I need you…I love you."

Christian melts into my chest, wrapping his unbroken arm around me.

Chapter 26

Antioch
June 16, 1983

The autopsy results reveal Trista suffered from a prolapsed mitral valve that had never presented any symptoms, and therefore, had never been diagnosed. It was surmised that she had a heart attack and then fell down the stairs. Mom remembered that Trista's father died young from a heart condition. Perhaps it was the same condition Trista had died from and may have inherited. Her body was to be flown to Boston later in the day once the coroner officially released it and signed the death certificate. Her funeral is Tuesday, June 18, in Boston. We will go as a family.

****

As we return home, I notice the eagle is back perching in his favorite tree. Knowing that it had nothing to do with Christian's accident, I have become intrigued as to why it was present at Christian's accident. The sound and vibrations of a car hitting a tree would cause such a disturbance in the environment that it would drive all animals away, except maybe carrion like turkey vultures or buzzards. However, the eagle was there, defiant, observing the scene, calling at me as I approached the accident. In retrospect, it seemed to be warning me about what I was going to see.

Was the eagle here to protect us or harm us?

Chapter 27

Antioch
June 17, 1983

Angelus did not visit me last night. Curious. Not an intervention to see if I had started my research into finding Lazarus Benedictine, whom he says is alive but did not know where he is in the world. Is Lazarus Benedictine still living in Bart's Bay? Maine? America?

After the shocking confession to two murders and revealing his deadly plan for Lazarus, I had a few unanswered questions for Angelus. Horrifying as they were, I understood his angry and selfish motivation behind killing Anvil Millstone and Trista Morten: one was for revenge and the other was to demonstrate his power. What I could not understand is why he attacked Christian.

It was no surprise for me to learn that Angelus could read my thoughts, as he had used my thoughts to manipulate me to become more sympathetic to the events of his life, his cause, and now to do his bidding. It was clear that he didn't have any remorse about what he did to Trista, as he used her death as both a warning of what he can do and what he would do if I didn't agree to find and bring Lazarus to Antioch. He had not revealed why he caused Christian to crash.

This question has haunted me since I learned that he was responsible for frightening Christian to the point that he drove his car into a tree to avoid seeing Angelus's ghastly face. I have been racking my brain to try to understand this cruel, demented act that could have killed Christian as well.

Did he intend to kill Christian that night or did he just want to hurt him?

I was rationalizing Angelus's actions as if he were a human, but he's not a human anymore; he's a disembodied spirit with a lot of pent-up rage over how he was cheated out of a normal, human life. The tragic circumstances of his life, in many ways, determined his afterlife.

Jealousy: Perhaps, he was jealous of the relationship that Christian and I were developing. On the night when Christian came to Antioch for dinner, he could sense that two men in this house were falling in love and that may have reminded him of the relationship he and Lazarus had, but was tragically cut short. Did Angelus covet me and not want to share me in the romantic sense with anyone else? That could also explain what happened to Trista. He heard her talk about her marriage plans for us. Although he knew I was not interested in the type of arrangement she described, he may have thought that she could wield power over me due to her money and social position. Angelus was also part of the wealthy aristocracy when he was alive. He was painfully aware of how the perception game was played.

Impediment: Maybe Angelus thought Christian would be too much of a distraction to me, that his needs would interfere with my task of finding Lazarus.

Angelus knew how exciting romantic love could be, especially the energy it required when it was between two men, and simply would not abide to the threat it could impose on his endgame.

Whatever his reason or reasons for causing Christian's crash, I was determined to confront Angelus regardless of the consequences. Therefore, the task at hand, find Lazarus Benedictine. Although Angelus had presented his plan for Lazarus on Friday night, the night after Christian's car crash, I had not had any time to start looking for Lazarus.

Killing Trista strengthened his hand toward my cooperation with his scheme to be re-united with his first love, but it also created a gruesomely chaotic situation in our house on Saturday that overlapped into Sunday when we had to deal with Trista's autopsy and family. I would also not be able to focus on Angelus's plot tomorrow, Tuesday, because we had to go to Trista's funeral in Boston.

When I thought of how I would go about finding Lazarus, what immediately came to my mind was the most basic and accessible tool for finding people: the phone book. After I showered and dressed, I made my way downstairs to search for our phone books. They're in a drawer of the table in the living room on which the rotary phone sits. There is a phone book for Bart's Bay, Freeport, and Brunswick, which is rather thin, that includes the yellow pages for all the businesses in Bart's Bay and neighboring towns.

There's another thicker phone book covering all of Cumberland County, including Portland, the largest city in Maine. I open the Cumberland County book and look under the residential listings for last names beginning with the letter "B." Soon I'm on the page that begins with "BE," scanning for the next letter and then the entire last name. Happily, there are only two listings with the name "Benedictine," and one of them had the letter "L" behind it. When I look at the abbreviated address next to it, I'm pleasantly surprised to see: "97 RT 1 Bart Bay." Could this be the end of my search?

I immediately write the address and phone number on a piece of paper. The other listing had the letter "S" after "Benedictine," and it is a Portland address. I write that address down and phone number as well in case the first listing turns out to be a false lead.

Looking at the maps included in the phone book, I recognize that RT 1 is also known as the Coastal Highway, the road that passes by Antioch and the main road to Bartholomew Bay. RT 1 becomes Main Street in town and then continues as the road to Portland. As I was planning to visit Christian at the hospital today, I'm also anxious to start my search so I can have time to drive to Brunswick.

Grabbing the paper with the address and phone number and my car keys, I jump into my Jeep and drive down the driveway to the intersection with RT 1. Antioch's address is 107 RT 1 and the first address on the way to downtown is the farm across the street, 106 RT 1. 97 RT 1 is close. Driving slowly into town, I watch for the numbers on the mailboxes, posts of porches, and above doorways along RT 1. Address numbers decrease as I get closer to town.

Approaching the row of similarly built one-story bay front houses on the left side of the highway made of weathered wood with simple porches and adjacent gravel driveways, I spy a house in the middle of the row with peeling blue paint and the number "97" on a post on the porch. Slowing down to get a better look, I drive a few blocks toward town and park.

The house with the peeling blue paint is like the other houses in the row that are perched upon a rocky cliff above the beach of Bart's Bay. The small front yard is decorated with various artistically crafted sculptures made from driftwood, sea glass, and other objects found on the beach. The porch is saturated with mobiles of sea glass and objects found from the beach and chimes made from metal tubes hanging from the eaves. I remember admiring the artwork at this residence while traveling back and forth to town thinking it was a cute bungalow.

As I survey the yard, I notice an old blue pickup in the driveway with rough spots and with three lines of words crudely stenciled on the outside of the driver's door. Stealthily moving closer to the truck, I notice that it is an old Ford, probably from the late 1950s. The lettering on the door reads, "Fix-it and Repairs— Lazarus Benedictine—207…"

I cannot believe my eyes. There's his name, as plain as day. Lazarus Benedictine exists, and he only lives a few miles from Antioch! It can't be this easy. Then another thought crosses my mind. It's now obvious to me that Angelus' power extends only to the grounds surrounding Antioch, at least only to the end of the driveway. Maybe Angelus knows Lazarus is still alive because he lives so close to Antioch, his center of power.

Being on this man's driveway, I realize I'm technically trespassing. I walk away from the truck down the short driveway and stand outside the house, admiring the artwork. As I return to my car, I keep repeating, "Lazarus repairs things." I'm sure that Mary needs help with simple repairs at Antioch, especially since she lost Anvil, so this could be my way of getting into Lazarus's house. The earlier thought I had keeps repeating in my mind. Can it be this easy?

I rush back to Antioch to pick up Jack, who is going with me to see Christian. As I drive up the driveway, the eagle is in his favorite tree. I now feel differently toward it after learning that Angelus caused Christian's crash.

Before Jack and I leave for the hospital, I look for Mary. She's in her makeshift office in the living room, going over the latest specs for the renovation of the library.

I approach her desk. "Mom, do you still need a handyman to do some repair work other than the restoration work?"

"There's some plumbing work in your bathroom and some minor electrical work on the third floor and the widow's walk, the work that Mr. Millstone was working on when...Why do you ask, do you know someone?"

"Yeah, I saw this old pickup truck in town with 'Fix-it and Repairs' on the side of the door and had a conversation with this nice old man...his name is, ready for this, Lazarus Benedictine, you know like raised from the dead Lazarus. But he was cool, and he's been a repairman for ages. Real salt-of-the earth kind of dude."

"Well, does he have any references or a resume?" she inquires.

"A resume, Mom? This guy is old school. I bet if

you ask anyone in town, they have probably had him fix something."

"All right, have him come Wednesday morning. There won't be any time tomorrow, as we're driving to Boston for Trista's wake and memorial service after my lunch meeting with Mayor Jenkins regarding my building permit," she explains.

"Great. I'll swing by his house tomorrow morning to let him know."

"Doesn't he have a phone?"

"Yeah, I think so, but I dig his house, it's full of all of his artwork," elaborating on my previous fabricated tale.

****

My visit with Christian is lighter than the previous visit when Christian warned me to leave Antioch. For one thing, his appearance is different. The bandage that had been wrapped around his head has been removed and replaced with a simple plaster that covers his stitches. Without the head bandage, Christian's fantastic strawberry blond faux hawk is free to fall around his handsome face. Because his cervical collar and neck surgery prevents Christian from turning his head, he's not able to comb his hair properly.

After Jack leaves the room to give us some time alone, I use the opportunity to comb through his hair to remove the tangles that have accumulated since the night of the accident. To avoid pulling his head, I hold his hair in my hand and gently pull the comb through the tangles. Christian appreciates the weird gesture. Jack notices the difference immediately when he walks back into the room.

We visit with Christian for another hour, but I

sense that he's tired, even though he states he's not, and we say our goodbyes. Leaning down, hugging him, I run my hand through his hair as I embrace him, careful not to put pressure on his neck or his head in its post-concussive state. I then kiss him lightly on the lips in front of Jack. To Jack's credit, he did not turn away; rather, he wells up, wiping the tears from his face before he hugs Christian as well.

****

I wonder if Angelus will make an appearance tonight as I drift off to sleep. He does not. He visits me in the middle of the night.

After he awakens me using the cold trick, I see him standing above me. After he lays his spirit hand on my forehead to open a lane of communication on the dream highway, I tell him of my discovery that Lazarus lives in Bartholomew Bay, only a few miles from Antioch. I inform him I plan to meet Lazarus in the morning and offer him employment at Antioch, doing minor repairs for my mother. Angelus seems pleased at the prospect that Lazarus will be returning to Antioch, the first step in his plot to re-unite with Lazarus for eternity.

I also communicate that I must attend Trista's funeral tomorrow, and that event will prevent Lazarus from coming as early as Wednesday, if he accepts the job. This perturbs Angelus, but I insist we must attend Trista's funeral. Angelus severs the connection, and I'm alone in my bedroom. I realize I forgot to ask him why he'd frightened Christian into crashing his car, but decide to leave it for another time.

I turn over and go back to sleep.

Chapter 28

Bartholomew Bay
97 RT 1
June 18, 1983

Instead of driving the few miles it takes to get to Lazarus's house, I ride my bike instead. I figure a job offer in Antioch, presented by a young man on a bicycle, might stir nostalgic memories of his and Angelus's bike rides, making him more likely to accept. It was a long shot. This was the only plan I had to convince him to come back to Antioch where he was the last person to see Angelus alive before he leapt from the widow's walk. Not exactly happy memories.

Approaching his house, I slow down to admire the unique artwork that separates his home from the other similar houses in the row of bungalows on that rocky cliff. Opening the wooden gate of the natural split rail wooden fence that surrounds the yard, I stop to appreciate each piece.

There is a birdbath to the right that is fashioned from pieces of commercial metal collected from the sea. The writing on the sides of the cans and signs are faded from years of floating in the sea or weathered from the surf on the beach. I can barely make out the name "Budweiser" on one of the flattened cans that made part of the bowl of the birdbath. The faded sculpture is a beautifully recycled use of man-made materials that will never break down and continue to pollute our seas. I remember a stand at an environmental fair in Boston that had similar artwork.

To the left of the gate is a very large weathervane, made from newer metal and pieces of faded discarded metal, but it also incorporates driftwood and other elements from the sea. I thought it would take an enormous house for it to be attached, as it is at least 4 feet tall. Like Antioch.

The main figure of the weathervane is a nautical mythological figure about 30 inches tall. As I can make out, it is half-human and half-fish. I move closer to inspect it. To my great surprise, I realize that it is a merman and not a mermaid. The figure is made from copper as the bluish-green patina is evident on the edges. The verdigris contributes to the nautical theme. The merman's features are both pressed into the metal and built with other layers of copper.

His face reminds me of Greco-Roman sculptures: a youth, as he has no beard, a facial feature that was attributed to a married man in Greek society, with a sharp pointed nose, high cheekbones, and thin lips. His shoulder length hair is made of layers of copper soldered together to give the three-dimensional illusion that it is flowing in front of and behind his shoulders.

His torso is made from a solid piece of copper that is engraved with tremendous detail to produce his muscular chest and abdomen. There are small-layered pieces of copper that produce each areola and nipple. The arms are made from separate pieces of copper in which the round deltoids overlap the torso piece, producing another three-dimensional illusion at the shoulder. Its biceps are generous and taper into more delicate forearms and hands, more feminine than the rest of the sculpture.

The fishtail is made from copper where the patina lent its greatest effect. Layers of scales soldered on top of each other, different layers of verdigris make the texture of a fishtail more authentic. The tail ends in four fins, two on each side, that are made of copper like the rest of the tail but also of the most beautiful blue and green sea glass, expertly cut into thin wavy sections. The transparent nature of the glass, when illuminated by sunlight, produces an underwater effect, as if the fins are floating in the water.

The box-like base of the weathervane is made from pieces of driftwood that surround radiating tubes of metal that meet in the middle, welded to a thick rusted iron ring that provides the support for the metal pole in which the sculpture is mounted. The arrows pointing in the four directions of the wind are also made of copper, with each of the letters designating north, south, east, and west being cut from recycled metal. The arrow pieces are soldered to an iron ring that surrounds the pole that allows it to spin with the wind current. Stepping back to get the whole effect of the sculpture, it is a work of art that could easily have been displayed in a museum of modern art. As I continue to admire the craftsmanship, the face of the merman kept reminding me of someone. As I study it more closely, it suddenly dawns on me: it is Angelus's face.

Other pieces in the yard are also noteworthy. There is another fountain next to the house, in which water spits into a basin from the mouth of a white plaster sculpture of a human face attached to a large plaster cornice. Most likely, this decorative motif crowned a large building or was cast to look like it fell from a building. I recognize it as a "Green Man" sculpture, a human like face surrounded by vegetation; in this case, there are large leaves and vines that surround the visage. The rectangular basin is made from driftwood on the outside, and a large oblong porcelain sink on the inside with fleur-de-lis accents around the lip, probably recycled from an old house, maybe the same one that the Green Man came from.

The last unique construction in the yard is a sculpture that has no alternative purpose, not a weathervane or fountain, but a freestanding piece of art. It is an abstract creation made entirely from large branches of trees, weathered driftwood in appearance. The intersecting branches are placed in such a way that they form a cone, wide at the bottom and narrower at the top. They are bound to each other by wheat colored twine that can only be seen from the interior of the cone. The soft gray color and the smooth surface of the branches give the appearance that the entire sculpture is made from weathered antlers. Antlers from dozens of male white-tailed deer, four, six, or eight-point bucks. It has an almost pagan appearance, an altar made for a god/goddess of the forest, where the sacrificial animal is placed at the top and then the entire altar is burned to please the god/goddess for a good harvest or appease the god/goddess so that it wouldn't do harm.

I climb the two short wooden steps to the porch to admire the various mobiles and wind chimes that hang from the rafters. The sounds from the chimes collectively range from the deep base of a cowbell to delicate, high-pitched tinkling from sea glass. When the breeze came through the porch, the cacophony that was expected did not come, rather, it was a soothing slur of metallic and crystalline sounds.

I walk over to the front door and give it a couple of swift knocks. No answer. I give it a couple more. Then I hear a voice behind the door coming closer. The door opens and there stands a man I recognize, the other man with whom I had become familiar during my dream adventures into Angelus's past: Lazarus Benedictine.

For a man who was over 80-years-old, he is remarkably handsome. A full head of gray hair that is cut short on the sides but longer on top, much like the style I remembered from my dreams. Skin that is darkly tan, and full of lines, nicely weathered like leather, but not overly wrinkled, that makes his face masculine and interesting. Gray eyebrows arch over deep brown bedroom eyes; eyebrow hairs that are a little too long, curling into his forehead. Long, lustrous eyelashes that match the new mature shade of hair surrounding his eyes. He has a bulbous nose that has been exposed to the elements for decades and become swollen and cauliflower-like, but not disfiguring. His lips are thinner and not as rosy, but an upper lip that still has the full shape of the handsome Italian in my dreams. His strong jawline is accentuated even more by the thinner skin covering his defined cheekbones. Wire-rimmed spectacles hang off his nose, giving him an old-world look.

He wears the same style of clothing that I remembered from my dreams, the same uniform he has worn since he was a youth. A simple blue long sleeved button-down shirt with the sleeves rolled up to his elbows, a white V-neck t-shirt, tan flat front cotton pants, and a thick black leather belt that matches his scuffed black leather lace up shoes.

He greets me at the door. "Can I help you?"

His voice is craggy but not unpleasant. A smoker's voice. A gravelly intonation that is common in people of his generation that were not aware of the dangers that the addictive habit posed.

"Hello, my name is Griffin Meade. I was driving by and saw all the amazing artwork in your yard, and I stopped to meet the artist—"

"They are not for sale," he says in a serious tone.

"As I said, I stopped to meet the artist, but then I saw the stenciling on your truck, and we need a handyman for some repairs. We are new in town, and I thought...if this man can create these amazing mechanical works of art, then he can fix anything."

"Ayuh, well that's different. Come on in," he says, gesturing for me to enter. "What kind of work are you talking about? I can fix anything except I don't know nothin' about computers."

I ease his mind. "No, it has nothing to do with computers. My mother is restoring our house, and she needs some repairs that are not part of the restoration. Some of the bathrooms need some plumbing, and the basement needs minor electrical work. She also said something about carpentry that is more foundational and not decorative."

"Well, that sounds like something I can handle," he says with a more pleasant tone. Suddenly, I hear the distinct whistle from a teapot coming from a room in the back. "Excuse me. I need to get that." He turns toward the sound. Turning back around to me, he asks, "Would you care for some tea?"

"That would be awesome."

Smiling at my response, he instructs me, "Please, sit down and make yourself comfortable."

"Thank you." I watch him walk with a slight limp to what must be his kitchen. I take this opportunity to survey the room.

I surmise that we're in the most formal room in the house as the furniture is of two main types. "Mission Style" also referred to as "Arts and Crafts," simple, timeless, well-designed, high quality furniture made from natural strong hardwoods and assembled using techniques perfected in the golden age of American furniture making. "Primitive," similar in theory to Mission, but even more plain and simple, and tending to be larger in stature. I'm sure that some of it had to be Stickley, the most famous brand of the Arts and Crafts type. These styles of furniture are masculine, practical, sturdy, and well made. There are also lamps and light fixtures that fit the style of the period.

My eye absorbs the layout of the room. There's a large stone fireplace on the right facing wall that is made from fieldstone and indigenous rocks, like those seen on the rocky shoreline of Maine. The fireplace has a mantel that is made from one large piece of dark, rough-hewn wood that could have been mistaken for a railroad tie. There are five wooden frames of differing shades of color containing black and white photographs on the mantel. In a word, this room is very L.L. Bean, a store in nearby Freeport, and a Mecca for Preps. I walk over to the fireplace to be nosy and get a better look at the people in the photographs. They are all vintage pictures from an earlier time. I move from left to right along the mantel.

The first photograph is a picture of a striking, ruggedly handsome man in a Navy uniform posed on the deck of a ship. I soon realize that it is Lazarus as a young man. In the corner, there is an inscription of June 1920. I remember from history class that this was the last year-end of World War I.

The second photograph is of a group of virile young men with their arms around each other's shoulders. They are shirtless and wearing white Navy issue trousers, the type with a flap over the crotch that buttons along three sides, posing on a beach in a tropical location. I recognize Lazarus as being one of the young men in the middle of the group.

The third photograph is a close-up of Lazarus with his arm around the shoulder of another strikingly handsome man. They are both shirtless, as in the previous photo, only the top of the trousers can be seen. The other man has dark hair, a square jaw, and matinee idol-like looks. He reminds me of a young Rock Hudson. The style of photography is reminiscent of the movie stills of old Hollywood.

The fourth photograph is a facial profile of the other man with dark hair and brooding good looks. It reminds me of the Hurrell style of photography made popular by movie stars in the 1930s. This personable type of photograph is not the type of picture that a man would have of another man at that time.

The fifth photograph is of Lazarus and the handsome man with dark hair, both smiling, leaning on the railing of the porch of this house in Bartholomew Bay. They are both wearing one-piece swimsuits with a tank top attached. In the corner of the photograph, the date July 1935 was inscribed. There are no other photographs in the room.

I hear Lazarus shuffling down the hallway, and so I move from the fireplace, sitting down in one of the Mission-style rockers. Lazarus walks into the room carrying a tray with a teapot, mugs, a selection of tea bags in a box, a bowl of sugar, a small pitcher of milk, two teaspoons and a dish with an assortment of cookies and sets it down on the coffee table in front of the rockers and loveseat.

"Ayuh, I have green, chamomile and Earl Grey, help yourself," he instructs as he settles into the loveseat.

Selecting Earl Grey, I place the tea bag in one of the mugs, pour the scalding water from the teapot into the mug and let it steep.

"Earl Grey, good choice. Notice that I serve the water in the pot so that it will be scalding. I was once told very curtly by an Englishman that tea is always served with piping hot water in a pot and never served as a tea bag in a cup with water already poured into the cup." Lazarus copies my actions.

"Now, tell me more about this job."

"My mother has made a career out of renovating old buildings, especially residential structures. The process is photographed and organized into nice coffee table books. In addition to the restoration of the architectural and decorative features, there's also a need for work on the foundational or the 'bones of the house,' including plumbing, structural carpentry, and electrical work. This is what she desperately needs as she has had some difficulty finding experienced people. You definitely fit that description."

"Your mother sounds like quite an accomplished

woman. I think I would be interested at looking at these jobs. Work has been scarce lately. Where is your house?"

This was the question that I was most nervous to answer this morning. While straining my tea bag in the mug with the teaspoon, I contemplate what I'm going to say. I decide to be upfront with him. As I pour milk into the mug until the color changes, I respond, "We live in the mansion at the top of the hill, Antioch."

"Antioch!" he states, with a surprised tone in his voice. "I'm sorry, I'm not interested in anything associated with that house."

"Can I ask why?" I query convincingly, even though I knew the answer.

"That house has caused a lot of people in this town a lot of pain, I don't want anything to do with having more people in that place," he states with a measured delivery that masks his obvious anger well.

"Mr. Benedictine, I know the history of our house is tragic, but we really need help, and I think you need a job."

I try a different tactic. "Let me ask you, when I came to the door and mentioned how much I admired your artwork, you assumed I was here to try to buy it, and you told me it was not for sale. Have other people tried to buy your work?" He was silent. "Why would people think that they could buy your art if you have made it clear, like you did to me, that it is not for sale?"

While preparing his tea, he responds with a humble tone, "I have had some financial problems lately, jobs are not as plentiful for an old man, imagine that," he declares with a demeaning chuckle.

"Mr. Benedictine, I don't want you to be forced to

sell your artwork. Please let us help you so that you won't have to. Come to Antioch tomorrow morning. We will pay you for your time, even if you decide not to do any job."

He puts his tea down and stares at the mug. At least he's thinking about it. After a long deliberation, he looks me directly in the eyes.

"What time?" he asks.

"How about nine a.m.? That gives you all day to work...if you take the jobs."

Shaking his head subtly in the affirmative, he takes a sip of his tea. I take a sip of my tea. We talk about a few other subjects in the news, how they relate to his history, and then finish our tea. I thoroughly enjoyed talking to Lazarus Benedictine, one of the most prominent players in my visions, and I understood what Angelus saw in him.

As I left his home, I thanked him for the tea and the conversation, giving him a firm, but not too firm, handshake. I mount my bike where I left it, leaning on the gate. Thoughtfully stepping down the stairs on the porch, Lazarus walks closer to me. He comments on the fact that I rode my bike, saying that was his only form of transportation as a boy. I smile at the reference and wave as I pedal away.

As I pedal down Rt. 1, I felt guilty. I'm bringing the proverbial lamb to the slaughter. Lazarus could refuse to follow Angelus's plot anytime, and because I'm not participating in this deed, I have nothing to feel guilty for. However, I know the truth.

While I was preparing to ride up the large hill before Antioch, I think about the range of Angelus's power. Stopping my bike, I stand next to the road to contemplate the situation. Angelus has demonstrated to me that he can read my mind anytime of the day when I'm on the grounds of Antioch, so being off the property is the safest time to contemplate his abilities. This is what I knew:

—Angelus has the power to enter my mind to reveal events from his past, but only during the night for some reason. I knew this because the last full dreamscape stopped when light from the sunrise came through the French doors in the bedroom.

—Angelus can read the mind of anyone that enters the grounds of Antioch, day or night.

—Angelus can manipulate things physically anytime of the day, as is evidenced by the murders of Trista and Anvil during the day and the decrease in temperature he causes when he appears at night.

—Angelus's power is limited to the grounds of Antioch, as he did not know where Lazarus lived; only that he knew he was still alive.

Before I mount my bike again, I try to block all of this out of my mind for fear that Angelus would know that I'm thinking about the limits of his power when I'm on the Antioch soil. I do the best I can. Climbing the hill using the strength in my legs and thighs, not thinking about Angelus as I struggle up the steep hill, I coast down toward Antioch, pedaling through the entrance gates and up the driveway. The eagle is not there. I stop thinking about Lazarus and Angelus. Mission accomplished. I need to get ready for another life-altering event: Trista's funeral.

Chapter 29

Boston
Trista's Funeral
June 18, 1983

The car ride to Boston was long and arduous. Travelling by car is especially difficult this time of year when Maine's tourist season is at its busiest. The various two-lane roads and bridges that are normally easy to cross are snarled with vacationers from all over the country which can back up traffic for miles through small coastal towns like Bart's Bay.

Trista's family was not particularly religious, so there was no church or synagogue involved in the wake or memorial service. The funeral home in downtown Boston is enormous with a seating capacity for hundreds which was what is needed as Trista's entire prep school class is present in addition to prominent members of Boston's social scene.

As I stated before, I don't drop names, but there were plenty of local politicians, industrialists, and celebrities who Cynthia Morten van Rhys Dalton had encountered in her rise through the social ranks. After three wealthy husbands, each wealthier than the last, many of these folks were indebted to her for her donations to campaigns, her entrepreneurial investments, and her ability to spot and sponsor rising talent.

Trista Morten's funeral would no doubt be covered in the *Boston Globe* tomorrow. The New England glitterati came dressed to impress. I'm especially impressed that most of the girls from her prep school attend at such short notice. She was very well liked, but that still normally wouldn't be enough reason to jet back to Boston from vacation locations all over the world like Majorca, Bordeaux or Positano.

It's interesting to see these girls wearing all black, as I have only seen most of them donning their preppy colors of emerald-green, pinks, purples, navy blue and burgundy. Although some of them did accent their hair with ribbons and barrettes in the subtler shades of the preppy color palette. Their hair and makeup are perfect. No doubt, they made time to see their stylists, after all, Trista would have expected no less for the social event of the season.

Cynthia looks stunning in her made to fit designer black strapless dress with matching cape and pillbox hat. Her hair is tastefully pinned into a chignon, and her makeup is nighttime casual. The Meade family wore black or dark suits, including Mary, in her jacket with wide lapels, black camisole, cigarette style pants, and low heel stilettos. Mom was raised in this world and still knew how to dress for an occasion. Make a statement but be subtle. You never know whom you might see, your publisher, an editor…

It is an open casket service. The coffin is made of a dark wood, probably walnut, in a classic style with gold handles, and the lining is a luxurious cream-colored silk. The coffin is drenched in a sea of flowers. Two large standing sprays of Trista's favorite flowers, blue hydrangeas and white roses, flank either side of the coffin. Surrounding these sprays are bouquets, vases, and baskets of the most beautiful arrangements that money can buy in Boston or flown in from New York.

Trista looks very cute, like she is on her way to go shopping at Jordan Marsh. She's a vision in purples and emerald green. Wearing her requisite purple headband, emerald green sweater, crisp white shirt, a deep purple ribbon bolo tie around the collar, purple and green plaid skirt, white knee socks, and purple suede slip-ons with gold embroidered crests. The funeral home did an amazing job with re-aligning her neck and vertebral column; there are no signs of trauma. The make-up covering any post-mortem bruising to her face, gives her the fresh "peaches and cream" complexion we all knew.

The service consisted of classical musical selections sung by a well-known soprano and eulogies from Cynthia, the family matriarch Rose Morten, and Trista's best friend, Bootsie Anderson. Each was heartfelt and authentic (authentic as this crowd can be) stimulating the appropriate responses of tears and verbal outbursts. Cynthia's remarkable waterproof makeup made it through an avalanche of tears; she was not going to be caught with raccoon eyes on page six. Then the floor opened for anyone who wanted to pay his or her respects. I wasn't planning to say something, but when the moment was presented, I feel like I have to represent our family.

Standing at the podium next to her coffin, I take a moment and look down at the lectern. I do not know what I'm going to say. I begin the slow thoughtful delivery of my impromptu speech.

"I have known Trista since we were put in the same playpen together. I cannot remember a time in my life when she was not an influence in what I did, not always in the same direction that she tried to guide me, but she was always there. She was the person you invited to a party if you wanted it to be fun. Her smiling face could light up a room and her deadly smart wit could shut it down at the same time. Trista was also a sympathetic, empathetic person who deeply cared about her family and friends. She would do anything she could to help them, making sacrifices that no one expected. She was an important member of our family. I will miss hearing 'Griffin, dahling'…her signature greeting for me. I will miss her. I loved her. We loved her."

I stop speaking as tears well up in my eyes. I don't want to cry. I have cried enough lately to last a lifetime.

Chapter 30

Antioch
Lazarus Benedictine Returns
June 19, 1983

We didn't get back to the house from Boston until late last night. Normally, we would have stayed in Boston with relatives but Mary had an important meeting in the morning with the local archivist in Bart's Bay. The archivist was going on vacation for three weeks, and if Mary postponed her meeting that would have backed up her schedule for a month for locating her source material for her book.

After the funeral and reception, we were physically and emotionally drained, so we all say good night to each other when we walk in the door. Angelus didn't visit me last night. Even though I had met with Lazarus, and he agreed to come to Antioch today, Angelus didn't interrupt my sleep to talk through a mind meld about what I had discussed with Lazarus.

I supposed he read my mind while I was sleeping to learn what he wanted, or not. I wondered if his absence had anything to do with the arduous journey we took to pay our respects to someone he responsible for killing. Angelus didn't appear to have remorse for any of his actions, but that didn't mean he wasn't clever enough to know when he was pushing the limits that could result in a less than effective outcome, namely, this tête-à-tête with Lazarus today. I didn't know how he was going to pursue that goal or how I would factor into the equation. Was I going to be a mere spectator or an active participant?

Mom's anxious to meet this handyman I recommended so highly. What she didn't know is that I had not actually talked to him at all about working at Antioch at that time when I mentioned his name. I was very lucky to have been able to find an angle to get him to come to Antioch: he needed money, and he didn't want to sell his artwork to pay his bills. Lazarus is expected at 9:00 a.m., and Mary's meeting with the archivist is at 10:00 a.m., so she made a breakfast spread. She does this for all the people she hires during her restoration projects, wanting them to feel welcome, and that will in turn, result in good work. Slightly manipulative, but she's a good businessperson.

While we're in the living room waiting, I hear a loud engine coming up the driveway. Looking out the window to investigate the cacophony, I spy the old Ford truck putting its way along the driveway toward the garage. Listening for the truck to cut off its engine, I approach the front door and wait for Lazarus to knock. After waiting an appropriate amount of time for an older man such as Lazarus to be able to walk from the garage to the front door, I went out to investigate.

I walk along the stone walkway to the driveway and garage. He's nowhere to be seen. Perplexed, I look around, and glimpse the figure of an older gentleman further down the driveway, closer to the entrance. He's looking up into the branches of a tree. I recognize the tree immediately. There it is, the bald eagle staring down at him, moving his head toward me when I get closer. Lazarus is studying the bird as I had done on occasion.

"Ayuh, that's quite a rarity, having a bald eagle perched in a tree branch that close to the ground. They prefer taller heights as it allows them to scout for food much easier like most birds of prey," Lazarus comments in his distinctively craggy voice.

"It's been in that tree and others like it since we moved in. I don't know why it's decided this is its home or its hunting grounds, but it is unflappable and has continued to stay," I say.

"I have seen an eagle like this before on these very grounds, when I was a young man. It was further down the cliff side toward the lighthouse, and it flew at us when we were running toward this house during a violent storm. It was very aggressive, swooping down on us, as if it was trying to keep us from going any further, but then it disappeared when we... well, that was a long time ago," he interrupts himself. "Let's see what needs to be done," he proclaims, walking toward the house.

Climbing up the stairs to the front door, he stops shortly before reaching the doorknob. I walk in front of him, open the door, and gesture for him to enter. He hesitates for at least 20 seconds before taking a deep breath and moving over the threshold. Looking up into the immense foyer, he focuses on the top of the grand staircase as if he's expecting someone to appear. When he realizes he's staring, he looks down and walks further into the foyer. I close the door and quickly walk in front of him.

"Mom is in the kitchen. She made breakfast for all

of us, her normal routine when meeting new people who will be working with her. Follow me."

Lazarus follows me to the kitchen, walking slowly but methodically, where Mary is waiting for us.

"Hello, Mr. Benedictine, I'm Mary Meade. Won't you sit down? I have made some breakfast for us before we get started. Coffee?"

"Thank you, but I already ate, so just coffee please," he responds. I wonder if he's anxious about being in Antioch and has a nervous stomach.

"Very well," she says as she pours him a cup of coffee. "Milk and sugar?"

"Ayuh, thank you." His hand shakes as he lifts the cup. "I have to tell you something, Mrs. Meade, before I get started. I'm nervous about being in this house. I was here many times as a young man. My father was the lighthouse keeper, and he did a lot of business with Angus Bartholomew. I knew Angelus Bartholomew, Angus's son...well. There was a lot of unhappiness here. Angus was abusive toward Angelus. I saw the bruises and cuts. After Angelus...died, no one could come into Antioch unless they were Angus's servants, so this house gained a reputation, and not a good one. When Angus died, no one in town wanted to come here, and no one wanted to buy the house, because Angus had made everyone afraid of it and him. So, you'll have to forgive my nervousness."

Then Lazarus reaches into his pocket and produces a bottle of pills. Shaking a couple of them into his hand, he pitches them into his mouth and swallows with a gulp of his coffee. He looks at the two of us with an earnest expression.

"I have a heart condition; I was told to take them

regularly and when I'm feeling anxious."

Of course, I knew more than Lazarus was letting on regarding his relationship with Angelus, but he did an effective job laying the groundwork if he decided not to take the job.

"I understand," Mom says. "I have heard the stories, and I'm learning the history of this house and the people of Bartholomew Bay. If I can do anything to make it easier for you while you're here, please let me know."

Lazarus nodded once and then looked at his coffee.

"The initial jobs are in the bathrooms on the second floor. Some of the plumbing needs to be replaced as the pipes are rusted and could break any minute," she states.

"Fine, let's see what we got," Lazarus says as he finishes his coffee, placing the mug on the table and heading toward the foyer.

Mary and I follow behind him to the foyer. He looks up at the staircase again. She walks in front of Lazarus and ascends the staircase. Once on the second floor, she walks down the expansive hallway to the bathroom next to my balcony room and we follow like well-trained puppy dogs. Mary explains what the bathroom needs by pointing to the various fixtures and pipes that need to be replaced. Lazarus apparently knew what she was talking about by his affirmative nodding and his questioning.

I lost interest so I retreat to my bedroom. Then I hear Mom leave the bathroom, the distinctive sound of her heels clicking on the wooden floor, walking down the stairs. Only one set of footsteps. I walk back into the bathroom to check on Lazarus. He's taking measurements with a tape measure.

"So, I see that you decided to take the job," I comment.

"It'll be a bit of a challenge, as the fixtures are vintage and will be hard to replace. I'm going to try to get originals, but we might have to be fine with reproductions," he states.

I nod. Lazarus is in front of the ball and claw tub. He pulls the shower curtain back slowly. I knew what was going through his head. This was where he and Angelus had shared a bath after the thunderstorm that led to the final consummation of their relationship. Through Angelus's eyes, I had seen the seduction of Lazarus: the exploration of his magnificent body and the pleasure that it brought him, the ecstatic facial expressions and sounds in the bathtub that must be resonating in his brain at this moment.

Turning away to hide my growing erection, I'm looking at the reflection of the back of Lazarus's head in the mirror above the sink. He's still looking into the bathtub. Then his head disappears. I readjust my view to see where he disappeared. He's kneeling next to the tub, presumably to take measurements or inspect something.

As I stare into the mirror, a fog begins to develop on the edges. Abruptly, the temperature drops in the bathroom, and I can see my breath. In the mirror, something else is developing in the reflection. It is Angelus's form materializing and floating above Lazarus. He's looking down at him. His hand is about to touch Lazarus's shoulder when I rush over to the tub. It is too late; however, Angelus makes contact, and Lazarus reflexively turns around to see what touched him on the shoulder. I'm standing there next to him.

"What is it, Mr. Meade?" he inquires.

"I was wondering if I could get you a drink. I'm going to get one downstairs," I say, thinking quickly.

"Ayuh, I'll be done with these measurements, and then I'm going to do some preliminary work on the drywall."

Leaving the bathroom, I walk down the hallway and see Angelus staring at me. He then quickly floats past me and into my bedroom. I follow. He's visibly angry by the expression on his face. I close the door once I'm inside my room.

"Angelus, I know you're angry, but I think contacting Lazarus this quickly is too soon. I was going to talk about your presence later when he feels more comfortable with his memories in this house. He already told us about some of his bad memories of this house, those involving your death, so he must trust us. It's just a matter of time," I plead.

Angelus then disappears with the same angry expression on his face. The portrait on the dresser falls over. Was that explanation good enough? I know that he can hurt me physically if he desires, but he does not. I'm sure I would learn more tonight. Angelus did not appear for the rest of the day.

I come back to the bathroom with two glasses of iced tea. The bathroom wall next to the porcelain toilet has a long, thin rectangular hole, in which pipes can be seen leading to the reservoir of the toilet. There are a few other holes in the wall where pipes can be seen.

"I brought you some iced tea. So, does it look like you can do what Mom needs?" I say, making small talk as I hand him a glass. Taking a sip from his glass, he nods his head. I sense an opportunity.

"I've been reading some of the Bartholomew family history, mostly Mom's research for her book about Antioch, and there was a question about how the young man Angelus died. The official record says he committed suicide, but others, including my friend Christian, think that his father pushed him from the widow's walk. Do you have an opinion?" I question Lazarus.

He looks at me, thinking for a while about his response. "Ayuh, I think he killed himself."

"Can I ask why?"

"His father was a coward. He beat Angelus severely, but he didn't have the guts to kill him. He wouldn't have anyone to torture if he killed Angelus," Lazarus responds with a dark tone in his voice.

"It sounds like you knew them well."

His tone changes, becoming curt with me. "Why are you asking me all these questions about the past? Have you ever heard the expression 'Let sleeping dogs lie'?"

"Well, since we have lived in this house, I have heard and seen some pretty strange things," I divulge. Lazarus's facial expression immediately changes to one of interest and fear at the same time.

"Have you seen ghosts, Griffin?"

"Yes, I believe I have. One. You're the first person that I have told," I confess, which was true.

"Was it the spirit of Angelus Bartholomew?" he says with a pained face staring directly into mine.

"Yes, I think it was him. It looked like a young man, and he was also...naked," I cleverly reveal.

Lazarus looks like he has seen a ghost himself at

that very minute. "The ghost was naked?" he repeats. "Did he say anything to you?"

"No." I didn't want to reveal anymore, I just wanted Lazarus to think that Antioch was haunted.

Standing there in silence, Lazarus finally speaks. "I have to find the supplies for this bathroom. Excuse me."

Lazarus leaves the bathroom and Antioch. The seeds have been planted, I thought, for future conversations. I hope.

****

After Lazarus's departure, I went to visit Christian at the hospital. As I got closer to his room, I can hear music coming through a crack in the doorway: the distinctive sounds of an acoustic guitar, a keyboard, a tambourine, and a drum. To my surprise, his band mates are also visiting this evening. Christian and his friends are playing their instruments quietly and dancing to unplugged versions of some of their covers. Christian still cannot speak but he's communicating with members of his band through their other language: music.

I join in the merriment, dancing around the room and with Christian, holding his hand as I twirl him like some demented version of square dancing. I have not seen him this happy in a long time. There's the faintest of smiles on his bruised and strained face. The band stays about 20 minutes longer singing and dancing. As his bandmates leave, they give him hugs and wish him a speedy recovery, stating they need him to get better so they can rehearse. He is visibly tired from all the activity, lying down in his bed as soon as they leave.

Sitting on the edge of the bed next to him, it never

crosses my mind that his band would have to cancel shows while Christian was healing. All I had thought about was that school was over, and he didn't have to make up any work. I had completely forgotten about The Wilde Boys. It was good to see him happy.

Tonight I didn't write anything in his notebook about Antioch, or ghosts, or his accident. We had a 'normal' conversation via writing that two people in love would have. How much we missed each other. What our plans will be for the summer. What classes we should take together in the fall. I really love him. I just want us to have a chance at a normal relationship when all of this is over.

The nurse peeping through the door states that we have five more minutes until visiting hours are over. Looking at him as he lies on his hospital bed, I think to myself how lucky I am. Standing up, holding his right hand in mine, I move our clasped hands to my heart and then up to my mouth, kissing the back of his hand. We both have tears in our eyes. Leaning down, I kiss him lightly on his bruised lips and whisper, "I would do anything for you."

****

I came home late from the hospital. Knowing there would be an unpleasant encounter with Angelus tonight, and since I was in such a great mood after seeing Christian, I made a detour into town, parking the Jeep and walking out to the municipal beach. It's a luminescent night, a fingernail moon so bright that it almost outshines the brilliance of thousands of stars in the Milky Way. Lying down on the beach, I stare at the stars. I think about taking a walk along the shoreline, but then I remember this crazy, true story of a couple that were taking a moonlight walk, somewhere on the west coast, when a freak tsunami-like wave came ashore, crashed into the man, and swept him out to sea. They found his body the next day.

I have always been overly cautious, never tempting fate when there is a distinct possibility of being harmed or killed, like skydiving. Nevertheless, here I am, in a situation that is potentially dangerous to me and my family, one I can't escape. A vengeful entity that has killed and hurt the ones I love.

Why didn't I tell my family what was happening when I had the chance on the way to Boston, when we were a safe distance from Antioch? Would they have believed me? More likely, they would have thought I was cracking up. The trauma after witnessing the violent deaths of two people and the car accident that almost killed my boyfriend. Was it too late to escape the inevitable?

I shudder to think what Angelus is capable of if his plan does not work. I try to wipe all of this from my mind and focus on the stars. A new thought crosses my mind.

If there is a heaven, is it above us somewhere in the vaulted sky? Angelus calls his entrapment in Antioch, his version of Hell or Purgatory. I would agree, but it's not the traditional Hell of fire and brimstone that most Christians are raised to believe. For Angelus, his Hell is a lonely place where he can observe earthly pleasures but cannot enjoy them. No wonder he's so desperate to find a companion to live with him in his realm. I do have sympathy for him. He had a terrible tragic existence and did not deserve what happened to him. He is due some happiness, but at what cost to others?

I pull into the garage of Antioch. As I walk across the stone path to the house, the eagle screeches at me. Turning toward the call, I see that the eagle is perched in the tree closest to the house, near the balcony of my room. This is the closest it has been to the house since its residence at Antioch. I stare at it for a minute. Its gaze is locked on me as well.

"What do you want?" I say aloud. As if responding to my question, the eagle stretches it wings out and snaps them back into place as it continues to stare at me. I don't know why, but I have a distinct feeling that it is going to play some part in this supernatural drama.

I slip into the house quietly. Mary had eased the curfew rules sensing I had been through a lot in the last couple of weeks, but I still didn't want to wake anybody. It is colder inside the house than outside. I instantly remember an acquaintance stating that is a good sign during the summer that the house is well insulated.

Creeping up the grand staircase, softly walking toward my bedroom, I see Angelus floating just above the floor. A translucent being that has the appearance of a nude youth, as if a statue made of smoke-filled glass has breached the natural boundary. He has been waiting for me to come home. I walk by him, open the door, and shut it. He moves through the closed door. Even though it's cold in the room because of his presence, I strip and jump into bed under the covers naked. Approaching me, touching my forehead with his ethereal hand, he communicates two messages to me:

Never interfere with his actions.

Lazarus must take his own life in two days, on Friday by midnight.

When he sees my perplexed facial expression, he discontinues the connection.

Chapter 31

Antioch
June 20, 1983

I awoke this morning with many thoughts racing through my head. The abrupt disconnection with Angelus last night made one thing very clear: I was neither to question any part of his plan for Lazarus, nor interfere with any of his actions toward the completion of that plan. Lazarus was to take his own life tomorrow. Friday. But why did it have to be tomorrow? Was it the date itself, June 21? Why was that date familiar to me?

I got out of bed, showering quickly as I knew that Lazarus was going to work on the bathroom this morning, toweled myself off, pulled on a pair of b-ball shorts and a t-shirt and headed downstairs for breakfast. Mary is in the kitchen reading the *Boston Globe* when I walk in.

"Is there anything about Trista's service or her obituary?"

"Yes, here is her obituary. There's a nice description of her memorial service as well," Mom says, giving me a section of the newspaper.

Mary had folded the paper to the page with Trista's obituary. There's a nice photograph of her, taken by a professional photographer, no doubt. It's not her school picture, as there is no uniform or school insignia. She's wearing almost exactly what she had been dressed in during her memorial service. Hands are folded in her lap. She would have approved. The write-up is a combination of her history/lineage, accomplishments, and details about the memorial service and the cemetery where she's buried. It also includes that the service was for family only and listed the charitable organizations people could donate to in her name. There are plenty of famous names and places dropped in the article.

"I agree, it's a nice memorial. She would have approved."

Dad and Jack walk in together from the porch after they had gone into town for breakfast, just the two of them, and had bought the *Globe*. It's summer and after commencement, the official end of the academic year at the university, so tenured faculty like my dad can make their own schedules when classes aren't in session. A nice perk that allows us to take vacations in the summer any time.

"Hey, where did you get a *Globe* out here?" I ask Jack.

"Hank's Café."

"I'm beginning to think that Hank's is sort of the nerve center for Bart's Bay," Dad comments.

"I don't disagree," I state. Remembering that I wanted to investigate why the date of June 21 was so familiar to me, I query Mom. "Hey, Mom, can I get a look at that history of the Bartholomew family again?"

"Sure, honey. It's in the blue folder on my desk. Why are you asking?"

"There's something about the date of June 21, tomorrow, that sounds familiar to me, and I think it had something to do with Antioch or the Bartholomew family," I reply.

"Oh, I think I know the answer. That's the date that Angelus Bartholomew committed suicide. I made note of it while I was compiling the history because that date is coming up soon," she explains.

There it is. The reason why Angelus wants Lazarus to kill himself tomorrow. It's the anniversary of his death. He and Lazarus will presumably be re-united on the day that Angelus died, on the day that he was condemned to Antioch for eternity. Now, so would Lazarus.

There's a knock on the front door, startling me from my daze. It must be Lazarus. He said he would return in the morning with his supplies around 9:00 a.m.

"Good morning Lazarus," I say, opening the door for him to enter.

"Good morning, Mr. Meade."

"Mr. Meade is my dad. You call me Griff," I state, correcting him. "Here comes the real Mr. Meade."

On cue, Dad appears and shakes his hand. "Good morning, Mr. Benedictine. I'm Jack Meade. I'm sorry I wasn't here to meet you yesterday."

"Please. call me Lazarus."

Jack Jr. then walks into the foyer, and he and Lazarus repeat the customary gestures. Sashaying into the foyer, Mom greets Lazarus with a cup of coffee in one hand and a sweet roll in the other. Grasping the breakfast treat, Lazarus strolls through the foyer into the kitchen with a satchel around his neck, presumably containing the supplies, and his toolbox. While drinking his coffee, he has a conversation with Mom about the copper pipes he's using and that he has a strong lead for the vintage fixtures in Portland.

Seeming to be much more relaxed today, Lazarus discusses the weather and other benign topics of conversation. He's getting along well with everyone. Realizing that the *Boston Globe* is on the table open to Trista's obituary, I quickly hide the newspaper so no one mentions Trista's death. We didn't need to be talking about death when it was so close to Angelus's death anniversary.

Taking his medication as he did yesterday, Lazarus repeats his regimen to Dad and Jack about his heart condition without the anxiety he experienced when he told us the story about Antioch earlier. After exchanging pleasantries, Lazarus excuses himself, stating he's glad to have met Dad and Jack, but it's time to work.

I follow him upstairs, carrying his toolbox and the supplies as he mounts the staircase. Declaring that he's appreciative of my help, he also states he could have done it on his own if he had to. I think to myself, thank God for these old salt-of-the earth types. After reaching the top of the stairs, we walk down the hallway to the bathroom. No sign of Angelus so far. I escort him into the bathroom when he makes a request.

"Mr....ah, Griffin, I think I might need some help with removing some of these pipes if you're able."

"Of course, my day is free, whatever you need," I answer enthusiastically, as this would give me the opportunity to talk about the next topic of persuasion.

Turning off the local water supply to the bathroom, Lazarus begins to dissect the copper piping that he's replacing. As I assist with the removal, holding a monkey wrench on some part of the pipe, I begin my next interrogation. I make sure the bathroom door is closed.

"Lazarus, I noticed the black and white pictures on your mantel, especially the photographs of the military. Did you join the Navy or the Coast Guard, I couldn't tell?" I inquire.

"Navy, I joined at the end of World War I when I was eighteen-years-old, so I was lucky I didn't have to go into battle."

"It looked like you had a close group of friends."

"Ayuh, even if we didn't see any fighting, the way the military works, you have to put your life in your fellow seaman's hands, and that's what brings us closer," he eloquently answers.

"Did you stay in touch with any of them after you left the Navy?"

He's silent for a minute while he continues to work, giving the illusion that he's concentrating on the job, but then he answers my question. "I did, one."

I dig deeper. "Is it the man…the picture of the man by himself, the portrait, the handsome man with dark hair?"

Again, a period of silence. I observe Lazarus' face. He's struggling to decide about telling me something. Then Lazarus begins to tell me about this man.

"His name was Zachariah Kingston…Zack, and he came to visit me in Bartholomew Bay…and decided to settle here."

"I liked the picture of you and Zack in bathing suits. It looked like you were good friends." Then I made the first leap, "Were you more than friends?"

He quickly turns his head in my direction and looks at me with astonishment. I can't retreat now. It's time to come out to Lazarus.

Reassuring him, I stumble my words, "It's okay….I like men…I have a special friend that's a man…I have a boyfriend; you're only the second person I have told. It feels good to tell someone."

Tears form in his eyes, and he wipes them away subtly with his sleeve. He goes back to work but then stops. Turning toward me, he faintly smiles and begins to tell me more of their story.

"He was in my crew, and we started out as friends, like the rest of the guys. Zack was from the south, Richmond, Virginia, the capitol. He had this accent where he used the word 'y'all' a combination of 'you and all' that we constantly made fun. I wound up using it sometimes—it is convenient. Imagine my 'Ayuh' and his 'y'all' being said in the same sentence." He chuckles. I laugh with him.

"I thought he was handsome. He thought the same of me. We soon realized that we wanted to be alone with each other more than with any of the other guys. To get to know each other better. We talked about our hometowns, about our families. We had a lot in common. We both lost our mothers when we were young and were raised by insensitive fathers that didn't want us…We talked about our favorite foods, about how I liked lobster rolls and how much he liked something called sausage gravy, which was a lot like S.O.S, 'Shit on a Shingle,' aka cream chipped beef on toast. S.O.S. is disgusting, so I could not imagine that something similar with sausage would be better. But it was! He made it for me when we came back to the states, many times.

"Ayuh, so one day our crew was assigned to

exercises at sea, but there had to be two of us to remain at the base to man the radio and other duties. It was seaman apprentice Kingston and me. One night after dinner, we started taking shots from a bottle of whiskey I had purchased from the commissary. We got drunk. Zack started to feel light-headed and so he got into the shower to make himself feel better, with his clothes on. I followed him to the showers to make sure he was all right, and when I saw that he had his clothes on, I started to laugh. He asked me to help him take his shirt and pants off, so he could cool off. I helped him get his shirt off but when I started to help him with his pants, unbuttoning the top buttons, he grabbed my hands, and moved them across his. He grabbed my face in his hands…he had large hands, and kissed me hard on the mouth. That was the beginning.

"When we finished our tour of service, we traveled all over the world together…sleeping in the same bed. We made plans to come back here, and we lived together in our house until Zack died from lung cancer when he was seventy-five-years-old. He smoked…like everybody did back then. But we had a good fifty-two years together."

I looked admiringly at Lazarus. "Did anybody know that you were a couple?"

"We lived openly from the day we came back to Bartholomew Bay. I would not accept anything less. I was not going to live in secret. I had already done that once. Folks around here tend to let people live their own lives. I think that's why Zack came here. We couldn't have lived as openly in his hometown in the South," Lazarus explains passionately.

"So, people accepted you as a couple?"

"I had enough business to keep food on our table. Zack worked for 153 Fishing Industries, Angus Bartholomew's outfit, for fifty years. We attended church together. I was the 'unofficial handyman' for the Bartholomew Bay Church of Christ. We taught Sunday School and cooked for the picnics. Zack had a beautiful baritone voice and sang in the church choir; not me, I'm tone deaf. I created my art, often donating pieces for auctions for local charities. We were in every manner, members of this community," he said with a defiant tone in his voice.

"You are role models. Not just for men like me but for everyone."

Correcting me, he adds, "We never wanted that. We just wanted to live our lives freely, like our Constitution guarantees. I'm glad that things are changing and getting better for your generation. But please remember that many didn't have the freedoms that you enjoy."

I stood there in silence in awe of this man. I almost forgot my mission. I soon recover and backtrack to something that Lazarus said and made the second leap.

"You mentioned that you had loved someone in secret one time before…was that with Angelus Bartholomew?" Lazarus looks at me incredulously, but it's evident by his facial expression that it's true.

"How…did you know? What did I say?"

"It was how you talked about Angelus yesterday when you shared with us about why you were nervous. I caught it because I'm more sensitive to how men talk about other men. I'm sure Mom didn't. I heard that Angelus was caught in bed with another man on the night he died…were you that man?" I ask, already knowing the answer.

Again, he looks at me as to how I would have known something about him that was so personal. The burden he must have had keeping this secret for 64 years was immeasurable. He sits down on the toilet seat, looking pale, about to faint. I wonder if it's his heart. I run to Mom and Dad's bathroom and get him a glass of water. Pulling out the bottle of pills from his pocket, I put two in his mouth as I had seen him do before and gave him the glass of water. He gulps down the water and starts to look better, the color returning to his cheeks. A few minutes later, he began to speak with some difficulty.

"Zack Kingston was the love of my life, but Angelus Bartholomew was my first love. I've never told another soul what happened the night Angelus died, not even Zack. I was there that night…Angus knew that his son was in bed with another man, but Angelus fended him off by taking the blows from his father so that he could not see me…I escaped, naked, through the French doors to the balcony and then jumped to the porch roof and then down to the stone patio. I ran all the way home to the lighthouse during a violent storm. I feared for my life.

"I didn't know what had happened until the next day when my papa told me that Angelus had jumped from the widow's walk. I didn't believe it, that Angelus killed himself. He loved me too much to do that. I wanted to tell other people in town, but Angus forbid anyone in Bartholomew Bay to discuss it…everyone was to accept that Angelus killed himself. Knowing that suicide is a mortal sin in Christianity, and that his son would never go to heaven. He was so powerful that people were afraid to say anything else. Until Angus died in 1939, the story was the same. It's only recently that I've accepted that Angelus could have killed himself to escape the cruelty of his father. That was more powerful than our love."

Lazarus, overcome with emotion, starts to weep. Kneeling before him, I place my arms around his back, embracing him, as Lazarus puts his head on my shoulder and cries. I pat his back as a parent would when comforting a child.

There it is, the confession Lazarus has been waiting to tell for 64 years. Catharsis, I believe that is the term, for what Lazarus Benedictine is experiencing. A cleansing of his soul. Lazarus cries for a while but eventually stops. Wiping the tears from his eyes, he goes to the bathroom in my parent's room to wash his face and remove any signs that he had been upsct.

We finish the plumbing in the bathroom, turn the water back on, and then Lazarus goes home. No one else is home during his ordeal, so he slips out of Antioch without anyone knowing what he endured today. I offer to drive him home, putting my bike in the back of the truck so that I can pedal home. He accepts my offer. He is 82 years old and has been through something traumatic that day. Reliving a sad chapter in his life, of a first love that was over as soon as it started.

I helped him walk into his house and then into bed so that he can rest. The style of the bedroom furniture matches the living room. I make him some Earl Grey tea and he takes a few sips before he gradually falls asleep. Then for some reason I feel compelled to kiss him on the forehead before I leave the bedroom. Guilt? Compassion? Pride? I want to make sure he's all right, so I wait in the living room for a while, looking at the pictures of Zack and company, exploring the other rooms in the house.

Thirty minutes later, I go into the bedroom and check on him. It was then that I notice a different picture of Zack and him on the Mission style dresser. It was taken when both were considerably older. Lazarus looked like an aged version of the sailor in the other photos, but Zack didn't look healthy. He was far from the stunning young man with the dark hair and the old Hollywood look. I guessed that the picture was probably taken during his battle with lung cancer. Lazarus was sleeping soundly by now, so I made my way out.

I rode my bike straight home; it took about ten minutes to get there. Riding my bike into the garage, I notice that the eagle is not perched in the tree near the balcony anymore. I run upstairs to shower and dress to see Christian. As I climb out of the shower tub, wiping down the mirror to see myself, I realize I made an extraordinary human connection today. I start to think more deeply but then notice the time and dash into my room to change. If I hurry, I can see Christian the last 30 minutes of visiting hours.

****

I make it to the hospital in record time. Timing on the two-lane windy coastal roads between Bart's Bay and Brunswick depends entirely on the drivers. If you have drivers that drive at the speed limit or over then you can get to your destination quickly. But if you get the resident(s) who regard the speed limit as exactly that, then those drivers tend to not only not go the speed limit but 5-10 miles below the speed limit. Your patience will be tested, as these roads, for the most part, are not passable because of the blind curves. Regardless, I made it in time for the last 40 minutes of visiting hours.

Christian is reading a medical book and slurping his dinner through a straw, when I enter his room. This time there is no band, family, or friends. Just us. He makes room for me on the edge of the bed. Sitting down, I lean over and give him a light kiss. He pulls me closer, and our kiss becomes more forceful and longer, our lips moving instead of just barely touching. After 30 seconds or more, we break apart.

"Well, I would say someone's feeling much better."

The corners of Christian's mouth curl as much as they could into a smile. Picking up his tablet, he writes a word, and then shows it to me: "HORNY!"

I start to laugh. "I can imagine, being cooped up here all day, looking at those sexy nurses, and all that time on your hands too…"

He puts his hand on my mouth to stop me from talking anymore. I extend my tongue and move it in circles on his hand. Instinctively, he pulls back, making a disgust filled face with what facial muscles would cooperate. He then picks up his tablet and begins to write something furiously; he shows me two sentences: "Discharge Saturday if examination goes well tomorrow!"

"That's awesome." I hug him gently, always careful of his neck brace.

He picks up his cup and sucks on the straw.

"How long will it be before you can eat solid food?"

He writes on his tablet for me to see: "Depends on examination can't wait bite into cheeseburger!"

I didn't want to keep doing this, me asking a question, and he, in turn, writing the answer on the tablet. Contemplating what conversation is relevant that will be mostly one-sided to avoid the back and forth. Then I decide to share the news about Lazarus.

"So, we have this new handyman who's doing some work for Mom and his name is Lazarus…"

Suddenly, Christian grabs my hand and writes down "Benedictine?" on his tablet.

"You know him?"

Christian nods his head in the affirmative, and then he writes: "Zack Kingston members of our church."

I had forgotten that Christian's family belonged to the Bartholomew Bay Church of Christ. The very church that the Bartholomew family had established and maintained through a trust fund. I excitedly tell Christian everything I knew about Lazarus and Zack.

"Lazarus told me about how he and Zack lived here as a couple, openly and how much the church and community accepted them. It was amazing to hear their story. They were together for fifty-two years! Living most of their life in Bart's Bay! You were lucky to have an example like them growing up. Did they make it easier for you to accept who you were?"

Christian answers using his tablet. "Yes, they were close to my grandfather…worked at 153…came to Thanksgiving and Xmas dinners…I was eleven when Zack died…cried for days."

I then ask Christian, "Lazarus said that Zack had a beautiful voice and sang in the choir. Did he help you with your music?"

Christian, nodding affirmatively, writes two words on his tablet: Inspired me.

We continued to talk about Lazarus and Zack for the next 20 minutes. I would bring up something from their past and Christian would comment on the tablet when he had new information to contribute. I kept thinking how unique and special this was; we were both excited to be discussing the lives of people who were not us. Role models for us. Maybe a blueprint for our life together.

Visiting hours are almost over. It's hard to leave Christian at the hospital every night, but I felt much sadder tonight for some reason. I knew he would be home soon and that I could hang with him the rest of the summer. Building our relationship. Coming out as a couple, like Lazarus and Zack. The world is full of possibilities for us. My first love. I started to tear up thinking about it. Christian notices and embraces me. Burying my head into his shoulder, I leave it there for what seems like a lifetime. We had been through so much already. *There isn't anything in this world that we can't fight together.*

I raise my head and kiss him on the lips, tears streaming down my face. "I don't know when I became such a pussy."

Christian laughs, his body shaking up and down, and then I laugh. I walk to the door and look at him. I think to myself. Here is my life.

****

I go to sleep early tonight. I'm exhausted. All the activities of the day had taken a toll on me. *Angelus could read my mind if he needed to know anything that wasn't discussed in the bathroom.*

However, Angelus had other ideas. Sometime in the night, I feel the familiar cold trick, and when I awake he's standing above me. Touching his ethereal hand to my forehead, we're back in dreamland. I look at him and telepathically ask him what he needs from me that he couldn't read from my mind. Looking at me seriously, he communicates that there's something he needs to reveal that's important, the reason why Lazarus has to take his life tomorrow.

"June 21 is the longest day of the year, the Summer Solstice. When I killed myself on this day sixty-four years ago, the longest day of that year, I think that is the reason why I was condemned to this place when my soul left my body. I learned the significance of this day to ancient civilizations after my death. This is the reason that Lazarus must die tomorrow. You must keep him on the grounds of Antioch until the sun sets tomorrow night."

I telepathically ask him, "What if he doesn't do it…there is always next year…" I was awake. I got the message. Failure is not acceptable. Angelus would not wait another day longer.

Chapter 32

Antioch
Summer Solstice/Litha
June 21, 1983

I awoke this morning conflicted. After what Angelus revealed to me about today's date and the ramifications that it carried, I was more confused than ever. Until last night, based on Angelus's condemnation to this house, I assumed that any person who killed themselves in this house would have their soul connected to Antioch and the grounds forever. I didn't know that it had to be on the longest day of the year. Why that made a difference was beyond my comprehension, but so much about the last few weeks has been beyond my comprehension.

Ghosts!

Ghosts that can read minds!

Ghosts that can plot their future!

Ghosts that can physically harm and kill!

Ghosts that can enter your mind and communicate!

Ghosts that can enter your mind and reveal events from their human past!

Angelus mentioned that ancient civilizations revered this day. I looked it up in my encyclopedia. It stated that this day was celebrated as a day of great fertility and creativity.

Perhaps, the creation that these ancient people referred to is the creation of a new kind of being, a spiritual being that can live forever. The longest day meant that the sun had the most influence on the earth on this day during the yearly cycle, and the duration of the sun's energy was at its most potent. Potent enough to bend natural laws, and capture souls that leave the body at death?

Does this happen everywhere in the world? Is it in specific locations on the earth? I remember what this dude at my former school who was into astrology and "New Age" stuff had told me about certain areas on the earth where the earth's energy is palpable, he called them "meridians," like the vortexes of energy that people swear to in Sedona, Arizona. Is Antioch built on one of these meridians? If so, then maybe the energy of this location coupled with the energy exerted by the sun on the longest day has an influence on our souls.

Some theologians have postulated that our souls are energy. Unethical experiments took place in the early part of the 20th century to determine if souls had mass. They weighed people at the exact time of death to see if they weighed less than before they died. The majority weighed around 21 grams less than they did before they died. They deduced that the energy that left the body at death, or the soul, weighed 21 grams. New Agers call the energy that radiates through our bodies "auras," energy fields with specific wavelengths that in turn, correlate to specific colors.

I felt different this morning, but I don't think it had anything to do with the sun. Today, a man that I have grown fond of is going to be confronted by the spirit of his dead lover and asked to kill himself so that his soul can be imprisoned in a house with that spirit.

Lazarus confessed his love for Angelus and his torment over not knowing if Angelus was murdered or committed suicide. These questions will be resolved today. As Lazarus told it, he ran from Angus Bartholomew, a man who had brutally abused his son for years, would most likely have inflicted violence on him as well if he had been caught. If Lazarus had been caught in the bedroom, the outcome of the evening would have been changed forever.

Several scenarios become possible. Lazarus could have been severely beaten or killed by Angus Bartholomew as he defended himself and Angelus. They could have beaten Angus as they defended themselves, severely injuring or killing Angus. The possibilities must have haunted Lazarus for decades after he learned Angelus died that night from a fall from the widow's walk, the only action that was never in question.

When Angelus appears to Lazarus today, undoubtedly, the main question Lazarus will want answered: Did Angelus take his own life or did his father take it from him? When Lazarus learns that Angelus killed himself, how will he react? When he learns Angelus struggled to walk to the third floor to leap from the widow's walk after he had been severely beaten and disowned by his father. That this same father had threatened to make sure none of his dreams for his life would ever come true. Will Lazarus's compassion for Angelus and his choice to end his life influence the man to do the same? Or will Lazarus be angry with Angelus for making the choice to end his life?

I started to think about Lazarus's life after Angelus and how that might influence his decision. Lazarus and Zack had a wonderful life together for over 50 years, living openly as a gay couple in a small town. They were members of a community that not only accepted them but also welcomed them to be part of it. A community that embraced what they could offer. A community that didn't shield their children from seeing a loving, romantic relationship between two men. A life that anybody, straight or gay, would desire. If Lazarus does believe in a heaven, would he take his own life, to commit the mortal sin of suicide to prevent his ascension into heaven, to be with Angelus in Antioch at the risk of not being re-united with Zack?

This question made me think of my own feelings toward Christian. If I had the same choice Lazarus will face today, would I do it if it meant uniting with Christian's spirit forever? Of course, there are many more variables in Lazarus and Angelus's story than in our burgeoning relationship. Still, the love I feel for Christian is strong, and at this time in my young life, I can't imagine not having him in it.

Lazarus's health is another factor. It's obvious that his heart condition is serious and something that will only get worse as he ages. Is he ready to be released from that pain? If he's given the opportunity to be released from a body that is old and worn, to be born into an existence where his corporeal self is of no consequence, will he take it?

Is this ethereal existence guaranteed? Just because Angelus's spirit was linked to Antioch for eternity when he ended his life, does it mean that this will happen again? Angelus is re-creating the elements that were in place when his soul was trapped in Antioch. The longest day of the year and the significance of that energy. The release of the soul or spirit from the body on that day. The mode of release. However, if Lazarus takes his own life on the longest day of the year in this location, does that guarantee he will be an entity that dwells in Antioch for eternity? Does that mean he'll be able to interact with Angelus if he's condemned to Antioch's grounds?

Why does Lazarus have to take his own life after sunset, as Angelus directed, if the energy from the sun is waning on the longest day? Does any of this have anything to do with the sun's duration on summer solstice, or is it the opposite? The days will now become shorter after tomorrow, signaling that the nights will now become longer until the winter solstice? Maybe that's where the energy is for this transformation, as the night has always been associated with the spiritual world in almost every culture. Perhaps, the celebration of the nighttime becoming longer is the same energy that trapped Angelus's soul when he died.

Besides the metaphysical, how am I going to keep Lazarus at Antioch until sunset, which will be around 9:00 p.m.? I can ask Mary if we can invite him for dinner, which I'm sure she would be inclined to do, as the Meade family has become fond of Lazarus as well, but will that keep Lazarus here until 9:00 p.m.? Lazarus also must agree to come, which I think he will. I'm sure it has not been easy after losing Zack to live alone for the first time in 52 years. He would probably welcome a home cooked meal with a kind, intelligent, open-minded family.

Today, Lazarus will literally face the most important question of his life. Tonight, I'll have completed the task Angelus planned for me in his grand scheme to be re-united with Lazarus. He has forced me to be part of this for fear of the people I love. He has killed my closest friend and wounded my first love. He's capable of much destruction. But it will all be over tonight…one way or another.

****

It is 9:10 a.m. Lazarus is late. Most people would forgive someone if they were 10 minutes late, but Lazarus has appeared for work at precisely 9:00 a.m. the first day and only three minutes later the second day. His work ethic is strong; he was raised during an era where being on time for a job was the difference between whether you ate or didn't. Of course, there are always unforeseen obstacles that can make people late, but three miles or a five-minute drive, is not typically a distance where a lot can happen.

I'm worried that yesterday's events have taken a bigger toll on Lazarus's health than I thought. Just when I was about to get my car keys and drive out to check up on him, I hear the loud chugging of his pickup coming up the driveway. Part of me is relieved he's all right. Part of me wishes he had stayed home, too ill to come. I meet him at the door as he walks up the stone pathway, something with weight protruding from his satchel.

"Morning, Griffin, sorry I'm late, but I had to go near Portland to get those vintage sink fixtures I had told your mother I had a lead on. The dealer called me after you left yesterday, and so I got up early this morning to purchase them. I have the receipt for your mother," Lazarus explains as he hands me the receipt, showing me the porcelain and silver knobs for the bathroom sink.

"Sure, I'm glad to see you. I was concerned after our talk yesterday," I say as I pocket the receipt. "Oh, before I forget, Mom wants to invite you for dinner tonight."

"What time?"

"Let me ask her now. I'll meet you in the bathroom in a few minutes." I watch Lazarus carefully mount the grand staircase.

Walking into the kitchen I ask Mary, "So, I want to ask Lazarus to come to dinner tonight, is that okay?"

"Sure, I wasn't planning anything fancy, just Italian sausage lasagna, garlic bread and Caesar salad," she responds with a slight trepidation in her voice. "You certainly have taken a shine to Lazarus."

"Yeah, I mean, 'Ayuh.' I still can't get use to that…I think he's lonely. I'm sure he would love to share a home cooked meal with a family. What time should I tell him?" I ask.

"Let's have cocktails at six and dinner at six-thirty."

"All right, I'll tell him," I shout as I bound through the foyer to the grand staircase. I relay the news to Lazarus.

"I'm not sure if I will be done with my jobs much before six," Lazarus informs me.

"If you don't, you can wash up here and wouldn't have to go home."

"Okay, but I'm coming empty handed. If I finish early, I want to get a bottle of wine. What are we having for dinner?"

****

Lazarus finishes working in the bathroom around 3:30 p.m. and decides to go home to shower and change into "dinner attire" as he puts it, and to presumably retrieve his bottle of wine. As I escort him out to his truck, I notice that the eagle isn't anywhere to be seen. This was the second day that I hadn't seen it on the grounds of Antioch.

When I return to the house, I call Christian's room to learn the results of his examination.

"Hello, Mrs. Gutmann, this is Griffin Meade. I'm not able to come in today to see Christian, but I wanted to know how his examination went today."

"Very well. They're going to release him tomorrow. We have many instructions, including recipes for his liquid diet, which he will be on for a few more weeks. He'll require some help with bathing and a few other things that I don't think he would like his mother to be helping with...He's waving his hands at me, writing something down...Oh, Christian! He told me to stop embarrassing him. I'm sure he would like to see you soon...why don't you come over on Sunday for lunch after church? He's nodding his head 'yes.' Are you free?" Mrs. Gutmann asks.

"Yes, I'm free, and yes, I would like to come over."

"Good, we usually get home from church by noon, so let's say one o'clock?"

"One o'clock sounds great, thank you."

"Well, I think it's about time we get to know Christian's boyfriend...Christian, now stop it, I'm not embarrassing you..." she says to me, fielding interference from Christian.

"Okay. See you on Sunday," I say with a lump in my throat.

Christian told his parents about us. I guess it's my turn. I was sure that my liberal parents will be fine with it; Jack already was. Acceptance in a small town. Are we becoming Bart's Bay newest version of Lazarus and Zack? Sunday seemed like a lifetime away from what was going to happen tonight. Angelus had not made an appearance yet.

****

Lazarus is prompt as usual, showing up at our doorstep at exactly 6:00 p.m., with a bottle of red table wine and a bottle of Chianti. He looks spiffy wearing a nice dark blue suit, starched white collared shirt, thin black tie, and black lace dress shoes. Classic and old school.

"Wow, you look handsome," I say, immediately hugging him. (I don't know why I hugged him but I don't know why I do many things lately).

I reconsider what I'm wearing. Is my aqua blue polo style shirt, madras shorts, and docksiders formal enough? After a moment of doubt, I decide this is the uniform of my generation and his suit and tie was his. Lazarus offers the bottles, and we walk together to the kitchen where Mom is busy with her food preparations and Dad and Jack are acting as sous chefs.

Mom is equally as impressed with Lazarus's clothing choice. "Well, well, well, don't you look handsome," she says, parroting my choice of words.

Lazarus has this Cheshire cat-like grin on his face. Mary's a striking woman, and I'm sure Lazarus has been complimented his whole life by pretty ladies, especially when he was the young Adonis I saw in

Angelus's flashback dreams. I present Lazarus's choice of wines.

Dad, not missing a beat, retrieves the corkscrew and asks, "What would everyone like to start with, one of the reds, a mixed drink…?"

"I would like a glass of the Chianti," Lazarus declares. Dad then opens the bottle, spilling a healthy pour into one of the wide mouthed goblets and hands it to Lazarus.

"Mary, boys?" Dad inquires.

Unlike most typical American households in 1983, Mary and Jack had allowed us to drink in our home when we turned 16-years-old. "Very European" a friend commented once, but my parents believed that if you learn how to drink responsibly then you wouldn't make the same tragic mistakes that can come with inexperienced teenage drinking. I opt for a glass of the Chianti as well. Mary asks for a vodka and tonic, which Dad joins her in drinking, and Jack grabs a Lowenbrau. That is so Jack.

Mary had prepared an appetizer of assorted cheeses including Vermont Cheddar, Blue Roquefort, and Gouda, with an assortment of stone wheat and multi-grain crackers. We all sample the cheese tray as we drink our cocktails, engaging in typical conversation.

Mary outdid herself with the meal. Everything was delicious. We ate, drank, and talked at the dinner table for what seemed like hours. I notice that it is getting dark outside and look at my watch. It is 8:45 p.m.

Mary makes an announcement. "The weather is so nice tonight, why don't we have our dessert on the porch? I have a cherry pie and vanilla ice cream. Boys, can you clear the table?"

With that instruction, everyone picks up their plate and hands it to Jack. I collect the silverware and place it on top of the Jack's stacked plates so he can bring it all into the kitchen. I'm clearing the table of the salad bowl and basket of garlic bread when I hear the unmistakable sound of dishes crashing onto the floor. Immediately, I run into the kitchen to see what has happened, and their lay Jack on the floor, unconscious amid a pile of broken dishes. I rush over to check him out. His pulse is fine, and he's breathing.

I try to wake him by shaking his shoulders. "Jack! Jack! Wake up. Hey, dude ,wake up!"

He's asleep. I then wonder why no one else has noticed the sound of so many dishes breaking, why no one else is rushing into the kitchen to investigate?

I call out from the kitchen as I kneel on the floor next to him. "Hey! Hey! Jack is unconscious, can somebody come in here!"

Nobody answers. Nobody is coming. I know I'm yelling loud enough for someone to hear me on the porch. But still no answer.

Finally, I stand up and leave Jack on the floor in the kitchen to find out where everyone is. Why no one has responded to my calls for help. Walking through the living room to the porch entrance, I see the silhouette of my parents' heads above the rims of the backs of the Adirondack chairs, with their rock glasses full of vodka tonics resting on the arms of the chairs.

Walking over to confront them, I angrily bark, "Hey! didn't you hear me? Jack passed out…"

I stop talking when I reach the front of the chairs, turning to look at them in the eyes. However, their eyes are not open. Mom and Dad are both unconscious as well, asleep in their chairs, heads slumped to the side. I start to panic. Then I notice that it's completely dark, except for the light coming from inside the house. I realize the longest daytime of the year is over. Now it starts.

I rush into the house to look for Lazarus. He's the only person that I have not found yet. Running into the living room, through the kitchen and the dining room, I cannot find him. I run through the foyer into the library. No Lazarus. I walk back into the foyer and look up to the top of the staircase, and I'm about to mount the stairs when I hear a Lazarus' voice.

"Griffin, why are you running? I was in the bathroom when I heard the sound of running."

"Where were you?" I ask.

Lazarus points to the restroom adjacent and only accessible through the library. It's not a bathroom that you would know about unless you were familiar with the floor plan of Antioch. I reason that its hidden location is why Lazarus didn't hear me yelling in the kitchen. Then it dawns on me, Lazarus and I are the only people awake in the house. This must be Angelus.

"Lazarus, Jack, Mom, and Dad are unconscious...sleeping, I don't know how to tell you this but."

Suddenly, I feel cold and dizzy, like I'm losing my balance and feeling like I'm going to black out. A thought crosses my mind: "Is this food poisoning? Are we all infected with a parasite or a virus?" I lose consciousness.

However, I'm awake at the same time. A perpetual cold chill moves through my vertebral column. I'm looking at the foyer and Lazarus, but I have no power to move. It's as if I'm watching a movie and cannot control what's happening. An observer. Like a puppet, I'm moving automatically. My body rises and walks toward the stairs. Mounting the first stair, I climb the staircase and look at Lazarus, motioning with my right hand for him to follow me.

As he slowly follows me, Lazarus is asking me a barrage of questions I cannot answer. "Griffin, where is everybody? Are they upstairs, is that why we're going upstairs? Why is it so cold in this house?"

My body is now at the top of the stairs, and I'm walking down the hallway, passing the guest bedroom, the bathroom, and turning left into my bedroom. My body walks toward the French doors and stands. I then hear a voice, a voice in my head that I have heard before in my dreams. It's Angelus's voice.

"Griffin...you will be able to see and hear what I want you to...but you will not be able to control anything...I have taken over your body, possessed it. Before you ask me, I have placed the rest of your family in a state of sleep while we complete the transformation. I don't want any interference, distractions, or interruptions. They will remain asleep until Lazarus's soul has been re-united with me for eternity. Only after this is completed, will I wake them up."

The sound of light footfalls is heard entering the bedroom. I then hear my voice speaking aloud, but it's not me choosing the words. "Lazarus," I say, a loud whisper, as my body turns to face him. He has a quizzical expression. Angelus continues to speak through me.

"Lazarus, I appear to be the young man Griffin

Meade, but he's not speaking now. I have possessed his body to communicate with you directly. It is I, Angelus. Your first love. The night I died, the night I leapt from the widow's walk, my soul, my spirit was condemned to the grounds of Antioch. I don't know why. The day I died was the longest day of the year, the summer solstice. Today is the longest day of the year. I contacted Griffin Meade when he moved into Antioch and have revealed our story through visions. I realized he, like us, would understand the kind of love we had, the love between men that transcends the physical. The love that is spiritual. He was instructed to bring you here so we can be re-united. Forever."

I hear Lazarus respond, "I don't understand. Griffin, what are you telling me? Where's the rest of your family?"

Angelus continues. "Lazarus, it is not Griffin. I am Angelus Bartholomew III, your first love."

"This is impossible, Griffin. Why are you doing this, have you gone insane?" Lazarus asks, his voice laced with concern.

"I see you're still not convinced. I will have to show you," Angelus states.

Moving closer to Lazarus, Angelus raises my hand toward his head. Lazarus pulls away slightly, but I grab his shoulder quickly and the palm of my hand lands on his forehead. Inside, I feel the same sensation when Angelus places his hand on my forehead, when we went on one of his journeys into his past. Lazarus's body gradually goes limp as my hand continues to hold onto his forehead. Gently, my free arm supports him, cushioning his fall. I kneel next to Lazarus's body, my hand maintaining contact with his face. A light begins to flash brightly and intermittently, and then an intense flash of light blocks out everything from sight. Angelus is taking both of us on a journey.

As if watching clips from the trailer of a movie, Angelus takes us through the scenes of Angelus and Lazarus's life together which I had witnessed in the ethereal voyages of the past weeks.

****

The first time Angelus views the magnificent body of Lazarus in the outdoor shower of the lighthouse. Then the proposal by Angelus to Lazarus to draw him.

The scene then shifts to the rocky cliff where the portrait is created. The sound of thunder interrupts the setting. We transport into Angelus' bedroom where the seduction scene with the sunburn salve takes place. The sound of Angelus's orgasm dissolves and I see Lazarus riding on the handlebars of the bike I'm pedaling.

We're gliding down the hill with Antioch in the background and then the bleat of the lamb, and we're lying in the field laughing at each other. The path to Antioch beach is seen, then the water of the bay, followed by the view of Lazarus running toward the water, stripping off his pants and throwing them on the beach. Shrieking is heard and then Lazarus states, "I think my cock and balls disappeared!" Lazarus is now riding waves lying flat on his stomach, his taunt nude body gleaming in the sun.

The focus shifts to the front porch of Antioch. A voice speaks. "Master Angelus is not available today." The point of view moves closer to the front door and Angelus's voice says from behind the door, "I'll come to the lighthouse in a few days when I'm feeling better." The view through the door closes, and

Lazarus's sad, handsome face disappears.

The rocky bluff with the lighthouse and the point in the distance come into focus. I see Lazarus's face hovering with a look of concern. "Angelus, it's all right, it's all right," he says with a comforting tone.

Angelus's voice echoes, "I almost forgot, I brought a surprise for you, for us," and a bright red kite is seen. Lazarus is holding the spool, a swift wind rattles the paper in the kite, and the kite ascends into the sky, the bold red color of the kite reflecting the sunlight, making it look as if it were on fire. Then a rumbling in the distance. Dark clouds gather toward the lighthouse and the point of the bay, the whole meadow is now cast in shadow.

Angelus's voice is shouting above the sound of the wind. "We need to run toward the woods along the path on the cliffside. Once in the woods, then we need to run though the backyard to the back door of the house. Follow me."

The call of a bird of prey is heard and then a bald eagle comes into view. Jagged bolts of lightning illuminate the sky. Antioch can be seen, illuminated by the lightning.

Lazarus is soaking wet; he's removing his clothing slowly and wringing out the extra water. Water is seen filling the large ball and claw tub, steam emanates from the water.

"Come on in, there is plenty room for the both of us," Angelus's voice beckons.

Lazarus' naked body sits in the tub, with bent knees, his thighs resting next to his legs. Lazarus's face is closer now, his lips are seen in close-up. A pale hand moves toward a tanned belly and Lazarus moans loudly. Close up to his face, darkness, sounds of kissing and soft moaning. The kissing stops. Lazarus's face is seen again. Then Lazarus's thighs and legs come out of the water, fully apart from each other. His face gets closer, darkness and the sounds of kissing and moans of pleasure. "Let's get in my bed."

The view is now of the frame of the four-poster bed. Lazarus's face is hovering above. Lazarus is lying on his back. Angelus whispers, "Ready?" Lazarus yells with a pained expression on his face. Then the sounds of moaning are heard.

A door in the bedroom slams against the wall. Our point of view quickly changes to a view of the floor. An older man with squinty eyes comes into focus. Fists move in rapid succession as the sound of flesh being pulverized is heard. The deeper voice yells "Perversion! How dare you bring this filth into my house! Blood is trickling down and pooling on the floor.

The view switches to a wet wooden surface and the sound of rain pelting the surface. Hands reach into the darkness, grasping pointed iron structures atop an iron rail of a short fence. The roof of a large house and the stone patio below are seen in flashes of light followed by explosions of thunder. A bloody pale white naked body is seen from the chest down, pelted with rain, and leaning against the iron railing. Then the view gradually edges over the iron railing and to the patio and the roof of the porch comes closer and closer until darkness.

Angelus's naked, broken body is seen lying in a pool of blood as a white light glows from the corpse. Above the corpse, an arm is forming, but it is translucent, ghostly. Bursts of light emanate from the corpse, move toward our view, and become ethereal body parts that resemble human anatomy assembling into a torso and limbs. A naked ethereal corpse without any wounds. Translucent and glowing a pale white light.

Our view is now rising very fast from the ground, and Angelus's broken body becomes smaller and smaller. We are back on a wet surface. The structure of the widow's walk is seen. Looking over its edge, we view the corpse of Angelus lying on the stone patio, blood pouring onto the patio from the head as lightning flashes illuminate the gruesome scene.

****

I'm back from the journey through the past that Angelus and Lazarus share. I'm still unable to move or speak my own thoughts. Angelus is still possessing me. I feel the strange cold sensation throughout my body. I'm standing, looking to the floor to see if Lazarus has moved from his position. He's still lying on the floor, unconscious, where Angelus touched Lazarus's forehead.

I thought we were travelling through the dreams of their past together, but now I wonder if Lazarus is still moving through the flashbacks. Visions from the past that I was not privy to. Visions that Angelus is using to show Lazarus how special and rare their love was for each other for his ultimate purpose. I start to think about all the scenes I saw through Angelus's eyes, specifically focusing on Lazarus: from the beginning of their relationship, through all the times they gave each other pleasure, to the last time they saw each other on that fateful night.

In his youth, Lazarus was an exceptionally handsome man, but he was also beautiful on the inside, a beautiful soul. He still is. Looking at Lazarus's humble life as the son of a lighthouse keeper, when compared to the lavish life into Angelus was born, most of the people of their time would have thought the only trait they shared was their uncommon beauty.

Lazarus and Angelus shared much more in common. They both lost their mothers when they were young children, a devastating loss for anyone at any age, but a mother's love is essential to shape a child's psyche for the challenges of the world. Without it, it leaves that child vulnerable to the forces that exist.

Both were seeking love from their fathers after their mothers had died. They both had unfeeling fathers that did not want to raise their sons. Erasmus Benedictine did not want to raise Lazarus at all, leaving him with his mother's siblings, much less raise him in a loving, nurturing home. Whereas, Angus was given the means and the expectation to raise his son in a privileged environment, but his physical, emotional, and mental abuse warped Angelus's concept of what a father was meant to be. Both he and Lazarus sought love from the men who were to be their principal role models from whom to learn how men function in the family and in society. They didn't receive that love, support, or guidance from the most important men in their lives.

They also yearned for male companionship of a different sort. Romantic love. Physical love. Sexual love. Emotional love. Love between men that was forbidden by society as it was inconsistent with the love of procreation, and therefore, perceived as being perverse, an abomination in the Judeo-Christian religion. Both were denied the love from men or between men. When they found each other and realized that there was a man in the universe that could fulfill those desires, what a revelation and joy that must have been, albeit short-lived. Is it any wonder that Angelus would go to these extreme measures to have that again?

They also shared an artistic, sensitive soul. Lazarus's talent was evident in the portrait he rendered of Angelus. It was more than a drawing. He captured Angelus's essence of what he saw Angelus to be: his Greco-Roman god that would be his savior from the cruel world who would rescue him from his misery on this earth. Who ultimately sacrificed himself like another savior he knew so that he would be safe from the tyrannical forces of men like Angus Bartholomew? Angelus's acting was more than a medium to show his natural, theatrical talent…it was an escape from his miserable reality. A chance to become another person in another existence, far from the cruel, secret life of abuse a youth of privilege lives. Lazarus was the missing character who he was seeking in the play he hoped his life could become, the romantic lead, the Romeo, the Horatio to his Hamlet. Together, their artistic souls found refuge.

Suddenly, Lazarus's eyes open. He awakens from his dream state. Trying to hoist himself off the floor to stand, disoriented, he falls to his knees. Wearing his suit trousers, white shirt, and tie, he looks like he's praying in church. It is in this position of submission, of prayer, that he speaks to Angelus through me.

"Angelus…why have you shown me these visions of a life long ago? Why have you made me re-live this love, this loss, and this pain again? Why have you brought me here?"

Angelus answers him using my voice. "Lazarus, my love, I have taken you on this journey into my soul to remind you of the love that we share, the physical and emotional love that we found in each other. The love I have for you that transcends death."

Lazarus responds sympathetically. "Angelus, I will always love you. No one ever forgets their first love. I have memories from our short time together that I cherish. There has not been a day when I was not reminded of you... or that you and our love did not inspire me through my art. But that was a long time ago. A lifetime ago."

"Lazarus, we can have that life again."

"How? I'm alive and you are dead."

"We can be together in the afterlife."

I could see Lazarus's confusion, having trouble finding the words to ask what he wanted. "When I die, I don't know if I would be ...a spirit like you. And if I was to become a spirit, how would I find you?"

"Lazarus, that is why I have brought you here. If you die in this house, if you die in Antioch, your soul will stay here with me for eternity."

I can see the fear in Lazarus's eyes and that he's hesitant to respond to Angelus. "But I don't live here. I don't know when I will die."

Like a puppet, Angelus is moving me. I'm now walking closer to Lazarus. I stop in front of him. My hand moves to rest on his shoulder as he continues to kneel, and then Angelus speaks ominously, "You will die here tonight."

Hearing this revelation, Lazarus speaks to Angelus with tears in his eyes. "Do spirits have the ability to see when people are to die?"

"No."

"Are you going to kill me?" Lazarus says quietly and with a quiver in his voice.

"No."

"Then how am I to die?"

"You will take your own life."

Lazarus looks as if he's going to lose consciousness. He swallows hard and then speaks, "But if I take my own life, that is a mortal sin. I won't be able to go to Heaven."

"But you will be with me...forever."

Lazarus cannot speak. Tears stream down his face as he learns his fate. Abruptly, he clasps his hands together so that the palms are touching and then interlaces his fingers in prayer.

"Please...Angelus, please...I cannot do this. I want to go to Heaven. I want to be with...Zachariah."

I can feel the anger building inside Angelus. I fear what will happen next. My arms then move closer to Lazarus, my hands grasp his wrists. I force his praying hands apart violently. Angelus speaks to Lazarus loudly, forcefully and with a demonic anger in his voice. "No. Lazarus, you will be with me here in Antioch forever! I have been alone since the day I died sixty-four years ago this night. Denied the love I am due, that I deserve. I will not be alone anymore!"

With that last statement, my hand points toward the French doors of the balcony, and as if commanded, both doors fly open. The cool night air rushes into the bedroom from the balcony contributing to the chill in the room that is already present. The cold wind blows the thin white sheer curtains into the bedroom, looking like specters themselves. The breeze on my face, my arms, the goose flesh rising across my body from the change in temperature.

Pointing toward the balcony, Angelus then commands Lazarus in that same demonic tone, "You will leap to your death! We will be together forever!"

With fear in his eyes, Lazarus turns his head toward the balcony. Raising himself from the kneeling position on the floor using his hands, he unexpectedly collapses, the left side of his body hitting the floor with a thud. Lazarus then grabs the left side of his chest with his hands, grasping the white dress shirt and the flesh beneath. His face contorts; his eyes closed tightly in an expression of extreme pain; mouth open as if he's trying to cry out. Only short gasps of air as if an unknown force is halting his breathing.

Helplessly, I watch him suffer. Angelus has imprisoned me in my body. I know that Lazarus is having a heart attack but I cannot help him get his medication. Angelus hears my thoughts. "Save him!"

Instantly, I have control over my body. Kneeling beside Lazarus, I frantically search his pants for his pills. Abruptly, the painful expression on Lazarus's face relaxes. With his eyes closed, his hands release his shirt and drop from his chest to the floor. His body goes completely limp. His chest remains still. He's not breathing. Lazarus is dead.

Trying to resuscitate him, I immediately punch Lazarus in his chest a couple of times with my fist to try to jumpstart his heart. There's no movement. I then try to give him mouth-to-mouth resuscitation to fill his lungs with my air. There's no response. Compressing his chest with my hands, palms stacked upon each other, fixed on the space to the left of his sternum, I count four compressions and then stop to wait for his reaction. There's no response. I punch his chest again. There is no response. Lazarus is dead.

Angelus materializes next to me, floating above the floor with a distraught expression on his face, as I look at Lazarus's body. Sitting down next to Lazarus's head, I begin to stroke his handsome, weathered face with my fingers, from his forehead to his cheeks and along his jawline. I have lost another friend. I begin to cry.

Unexpectedly, Angelus disappears. I can feel the cold sensation travel along my spine. He's possessing me again. My head moves closer to Lazarus's face as I continue to stroke the contour of his face. My lips gently touch Lazarus's lips. The kiss lingers for a moment. The last kiss that Angelus would ever feel from his first and only love.

Suddenly, a mist develops above Lazarus's body. My first thought is that it's the heat escaping from his body into the cold air, the air condensing into a cloud. But it's taking a shape I have never seen mist or fog form.

Then Angelus speaks to me. "That is not mist, it is Lazarus's soul leaving his body. Spirits can see other spirits as they leave their human bodies. You can see this because I'm possessing you. You're part of me, and I'm part of you."

The white translucent ectoplasm of Lazarus's soul increases in density, gathering into a more solid shape, forming into a facsimile of his present body, naked and floating horizontally above the corpse. The head of Lazarus's spirit turns toward me. His soul's face smiles at me, a joyful, sweet smile, and then the head turns away from me. The soul floats higher toward the ceiling when it rotates so that its feet are just above the corpse. It is now hovering vertically. I admire how beautiful and natural the facsimile of Lazarus's aged naked body looks.

Then, unexpectedly, a bright light illuminates the entire balcony and the night sky around it. The beam of light quickly becomes more intense, focusing on the space behind Lazarus's soul. His soul gradually moves closer toward the beam of light. Then in a flash, the beam of light consumes Lazarus's soul and disappears. It is beautiful.

I assume that Lazarus's soul is being accepted into the afterlife…to Heaven. Knowing that Angelus can read my thoughts, I resist thinking about whether it is Heaven or not. Angelus continues to stroke the face of Lazarus's corpse. He's quiet for a long time as he touches the face of his dead lover. Then abruptly, he violently and painfully leaves my body. His possession of me had been a cold sensation that was disorienting, but his exit from my body hurt!

In between the French doors, his spirit materializes standing upright, boldly illuminating as it floats above the floor. I had never seen this brilliance before. He's angry. His eyes are blank and menacing, the anger in them accentuated by his eyebrows forming a triangle above the bridge of his nose. His mouth is curled downward into a cruel scowl. I have only seen this facial expression once: when he threatened my loved ones if I didn't accept my part in his plan for Lazarus. I fear that this is the case this time as well.

Opening that cruel mouth, he emits a blood-curdling scream that pierces my brain, so painful is his banshee call that I cover my ears. I cower in front of him not knowing what is to come next.

He finally speaks, an earth-shattering volume; the hatred in his voice is palpable.

"LAZARUS! I HAVE BEEN DENIED LOVE AGAIN!

I AM CURSED FOR ETERNITY!"

Another wail comes from his mouth, shaking the room and the foundation of Antioch. A chunk of plaster on the ceiling cracks, crumbling to the floor. Bellowing, he directs his head and his gaze toward me.

"VENGEANCE IS MINE! YOU DID NOT SAVE LAZARUS! HE WOULD HAVE TAKEN HIS LIFE!

HE WOULD BE WITH ME!"

Angelus can see the fear in my eyes, I shield my face from his evil countenance with my arm.

"YOU MUST SUFFER! YOUR FAMILY WILL NEVER WAKE!"

Pleading on my knees, I pray to Angelus for mercy, "NO! Please, Angelus! I beg you! Do not kill them!"

"NO! I WILL HAVE MY VENGEANCE!" The earth shakes again as he dictates his evil sentence to my family.

The angry, illuminated spirit moves toward me, leaning down to my face. I hide my face to escape his wrath, but he does not harm me. Instead, Angelus whispers into my ear. Suddenly, it becomes clear what I must do.

Shaking, I gradually raise my entire torso until I'm standing. I then grasp the back of my polo shirt and pull it over my head. Unfastening my belt, I slip it through the belt loops and drop it to the floor. Using the side of my foot, I pull down on the heel of the docksider on my other foot to remove my shoe. I repeat the same

maneuver with the other foot to remove my other shoe.
Undoing the clasp at the waist of my pants, I unzip and
pull my shorts off one leg at a time. Standing there in
my boxers, looking at Angelus, I solemnly state the
most important words of my life.

"You will not be alone anymore."

I have Angelus's attention. Pulling my boxers
down, I let them drop to the floor. I'm standing
completely naked in front of this luminescent entity.
The light emanating from Angelus's presence reflects
eerily on my naked skin. My body looks like it is
cnvclopcd in a sheen of light. I'm glowing.

Standing naked on the balcony is exhilarating, the
sensation of the cold wind from the bay stimulating
every inch of my exposed skin. The skin dimpling all
over body, my nipples fully erect, and with my scrotum
shrivcled, my flaccid penis looks more prominent. I
take a deep breath and exhale forcefully.

I then walk, slowly and deliberately, through the
French doors, passing Angelus's presence and onto the
balcony. The cold and the wind are more intense on the
balcony. Walking toward the railing around the
balcony, I stop just before I reach it. Gripping the
railing in my hands, I lift my thigh, bending my leg at
the knee, and plant my foot on the railing. Using that
foot as leverage, I straighten my leg and lift my body
until my other leg and the side of my other foot can
slide underneath and rest on the ledge. Using both of
my legs, I carefully push down on my hands and
gradually stand on the railing, the bottom of my feet
gripping it with my toes. I steady myself until I no
longer feel like I'm unbalanced.

Looking at the night sky, I focus on the corona

surrounding the full moon. The hundreds of stars glimmering in the sky remind me of how small our world is, and that the Heaven that I saw Lazarus ascend to is up there somewhere.

I look at the stone pavement below. If I land on my feet, I will probably break my leg or legs; but if I land on my head, then I would most likely break my neck or smash my skull on the rock, like Angelus did when he jumped from the widow's walk. Either way, I would most likely end up dead.

I turn my head to look at Angelus, who has turned his spirit body toward the balcony, watching me stand on the balcony railing. He's staring at me with those menacing eyes. I turn around and look at the pavement below once gain. Lifting my foot an inch above the railing, my other foot is poised to push away from the railing, so that I will be clear of the railing and descend to the pavement below.

With determination, I push away from the railing and begin to fall when, suddenly, a large black shape flies into me and pushes me back onto the railing, my feet and toes desperately contorting to find my balance. Focusing my eyes in the moonlight on the creature that has pushed me back toward the railing, I see that it has large, outstretched wings like an angel.

But it is not an angel; it is the bald eagle that is stalking Antioch!

Its wings are enormous, able to cradle me completely in its feathered appendages. Its threatening talons are sharp and poised to grasp. I'm in awe of the size and the strength of the beast. Wings beating furiously, the creature hovers above the balcony while a strong draft of air wafts across the balcony and across the railing. The rush of air against my legs and feet increases the struggle for my lower body to keep me balanced, thrusting me toward the edge of the railing. This narrow wooden railing is the only surface I can balance myself upon, and I'm losing my equilibrium quickly. Sensing this, the eagle's talons move toward my shoulders and pierces the surface of my flesh as it grasps my shoulder. Flinching from the pain, my foot slips, pulling me away from the tentative grasp of the talons and I plunge head-first into the darkness of the night onto the pavement below.

I feel myself rising from the pavement, but it's not the weight of my body that's moving. It is "me," but it is not the "me" I am accustomed to. I feel extremely light. Like smoke or vapor. Developing more mass as I hover above my broken corpse, my form is increasing in density and in surface area. Then the vapor molds itself into replications of parts of my body, assembling into a shape that is identical to my naked corporeal body, only made of this vaporous mist, instead of flesh and blood. My soul is forming. Rising further, floating above my corpse until I'm vertical, standing above my body with my feet dangling.

My new spirit eyes can see my soul. It is my body in an ethereal form. The translucent essence captures every detail of my nude body, exactly the way it looked when I died, except for the shattered skull and spine. Floating toward the balcony and over the railing, there is no sign of the eagle, but Angelus' spirit is waiting for me.

He smiles at me, holding out his ethereal hand. I grasp it. It feels like a hand, but I know it is not a physical hand. When we touch, our spirit hands feel like flesh and blood. I look at him for an explanation, but he doesn't say anything. He only continues to smile. Angelus then moves his head toward mine and kisses me on the lips. It feels like a physical kiss. With our hands clasped together, our spirit bodies fade until we are gone from the balcony.

Chapter 33

Antioch
R.I.P. Griffin Andrew Meade—1965-1983
June 24, 1983

So…the secret is out: I am dead, and I have been telling this story from the grave.

I love to say it like that…it's so, Edgar Allen Poe…so, Vincent Price…so, *Creature Feature.*

And not like a Theater Queen, right? Yes, I said it, Theater Queen, not theater major, not theater aficionado…I'm dead, and who the fuck cares? Me? Own it.

I'm telling the last chapter of my story three days after the discovery of my body and of Lazarus Benedictine's death for many reasons. First, I can tell it like this because there's no great mystery left to uncover, well maybe a few small ones, and I'm dead. Secondly, some important events happened within those three days. Thirdly, it has more of a dramatic effect than simply reporting the grisly details of the discovery of our bodies See note above about Theater Queen.

So, many of you are wondering what is it like to be a ghost? A specter? A spirit? I'm still learning what I can and cannot do on this plane of existence. Angelus has been very helpful about what he knows, but I was surprised to learn that he does not have all the answers, and he has been dead for 64 years now. It's like that question that surrounds God that every child asks: If God created the universe, then who created God? Stock answer: He/she has always been here.

As a ghost (I like that term better than spirit or soul) I can move about the grounds of Antioch anytime of the day, but our power to materialize and manipulate objects physically is stronger during the nighttime. We don't know why. It's like we have a battery which we charge at night and use that energy either during the night or day until we can re-charge again at night. That is why most sightings of ghosts are during the night. That and the fact that our translucence is easier to see in the dark. This is contrary to what some believe: that all ghosts are evil spirits, and they have more dominion during the darkest hours of the day. We can be seen during the day, and we can move stuff around during the day—we are just limited by our energy capacity.

It's cool to be able to walk/fly/float through doors and walls and floors and fly in general. It's also fun to move objects in front of people when you don't let them see your ghost hand. Every time I do it, I can't help but think of the Abbott and Costello movies of the late 1940s or the Three Stooges shorts where they encountered ghosts in haunted houses that could levitate objects like candles.

The decrease in temperature that occurs when we are present is also interesting. For us to materialize or move objects or physically manipulate anything, we draw energy from the space around us and that is what causes the decrease in temperature. We absorb heat energy: and therefore we appear to be cold when we are touched or when we touch. Nevertheless, enough about being a ghost. Let me tell the end of my story.

I don't want to be maudlin about the discovery of our bodies. Of course, it was a shock, and it was very sad, but I don't want to dwell on this too long. I want to report the facts.

When my family woke and found my body on the pavement and Lazarus's body in the bedroom next to the opened French doors, everyone was obviously hysterical, and my family desperately searched for answers as to what could have happened that could have caused this tragedy. The authorities were called, of course, and there were all kinds of theories.

Sherriff Roberts, Sherriff's Deputy Hill, and the coroner, among others in the media, proposed theories as to what happened that night, and not surprisingly, some of them were linked to Trista and Anvil's deaths and Christian's accident. Most of them surrounded me. The most popular was that I was a serial killer that used a buzz saw to slice Anvil in two, push Trista down the stairs, rig Christian's car to swerve into the tree. Then in my remorse for what I had done, I committed suicide by jumping from the balcony, headfirst. It sounded like the bad script for one of the dozens of low budget slasher movies made in the 1980s. I can see the title "The New Kid in Town," or "Deadly Summer."

Of course, there was no physical proof of this. It was all theoretical, and the main suspect was dead, so there was no arrest or trial. Most of the theories did not include Lazarus's death. After the autopsy, the coroner classified Lazarus's death as dying from natural causes, a heart attack. Which it was. However, there were some that tried to pin that one on me as well. That I knew of his heart condition and purposely provoked him to have a heart attack by frightening him somehow or prevented him from taking his medication when he needed it.

There were also theories about why I committed suicide naked. Most of them concluded I was trying to wash myself of all the sins I had committed, like I took a shower or bath and then jumped to my death right after I had cleansed myself. Psych 101 anybody?

In the months after my death, more salacious stories in supermarket rags insinuated I killed these people in the nude so that I could wash the blood off in my "cleansing routine" after each murder. One of the theories stated that I was obsessed with Angelus Bartholomew III's death. That I slept with a drawing of him, using it in a sexual way, and that I was seeking revenge for his murder. That I wanted to die like he did in the nude, as a tribute, or something like that. I didn't care about any of these stories or theories, as I knew the truth, but I did care about how they could affect my family, especially Mary. But they knew the truth also.

Soon after my death, I needed to tell my family that I was in Antioch and the truth behind my death. Angelus warned me not to reveal too much too quickly to my family as the shock could harm their human body. I found this a bit disingenuous coming from him. But he had a point. I would have to reveal things slowly. But how?

When the authorities had finished their preliminary investigation, collected their evidence, cleaned the "crime" scene, and identified the bodies before the autopsies could be conducted, my family had the sad and difficult task of arranging for my funeral and burial. Being the extremely kind-hearted people they are, when my family learned that Lazarus had no relatives or family to take care of his arrangements, they accepted the responsibility and arranged for his funeral and burial as well.

As per usual, Mary took on most of the burden and orchestrated both services and burials. No one would ever have doubted her tremendous organizational skills, but I think my mother needed to stay busy so that she wouldn't constantly think about my passing and cry. She did her share of crying, in private or with my family, but to be bawling constantly in public or otherwise is not how a WASP conducts herself, especially not one from a family that belongs to New England royalty. That characterization may be a bit severe, I must admit, but it is the truth, nonetheless.

By the end of the third day after my death, Mary is exhausted from her preparations and fielding phone calls from relatives and friends giving their condolences. That night, after she has a light meal with the rest of the family, she retires alone to my parent's bedroom, at her request. I watch her cry herself to sleep. Dad sleeps in the guest bedroom as my bedroom is still off limits and under investigation. This is the perfect opportunity for me to comfort my mother by revealing that I, my soul, am still here.

When Mary wakes in the morning, in her clothes from the day before, she discovers a piece of paper lying on the pillow next to her. It is also uncharacteristically chilly in the room, even for Maine in the summer. Pulling the covers closer to her neck, she stares in wonderment at the crinkling paper next to her head. Lifting her head, she surveys the room to see if anyone is there who could have put this on the pillow.

I watch her face, observing her thought process. Reading her thoughts, it went something like this. No one was in the bedroom. No one could have come in last night as she locked the door to be by herself. Where did it come from? If it was here the whole time, how did I not notice it before? Did someone come in from the balcony and place this here?

Finally, she picks it up, sits up in bed, retrieves her glasses from the night table, and begins to examine the piece of paper.

Bart's Bay Players
Auditions for *Blithe Spirit*
a comedy by Noel Coward
Audition dates: June 23-24, 7pm
Script readings only
Bartholomew Bay Community Center
Show dates: July 27, 28 August 3, 4

At first, I can tell by her expression that she does not understand what this flyer means. However, a few moments later, her expression changes from confusion to joy. She begins to smile, and then my mother cries. Happy tears. She recognizes what this is and its significance. She knew this was the show for which I had talked about auditioning.

She looks around the room again, I get the cue. I wave my hand several times near her hand holding the flyer, and the flyer flutters in the phantom breeze. Amazed, she quickly looks at the windows and balcony to see if all are closed. No wind is coming from the windows or balcony. She looks at the ceiling, but there are no cracks that might create a draft. She laughs quietly while smiling.

She looks at the flyer again and her smile gets

more exaggerated. Obviously, the irony that the flyer is advertising a show about a ghost that comes back from the dead to contact her family, albeit to kill them so that they could be re-united, is not lost on her. She is now giggling, an atypical trait from a woman of her breeding that I had always admired. Then she speaks, "Andy, are you here, son?"

I would be crying if I were able. I have successfully contacted my mother. At that moment, I decide to partially materialize, as I didn't want her to see me naked. Whether I was a ghost or not, I'm still her teenage son and there are boundaries.

At my request, the upper half of my ethereal body slowly develops next to the bed. Seeing my gradual materialization for the first time, Mom lurches back from the side of the bed, gasping aloud and grasping a pillow, (For what purpose I don't know? To protect herself or hit me?) focusing her attention on my development. I make sure that my translucent face is fully formed first so that she will recognize me. When she recognizes her firstborn's face, she cries out, "Andy!" I'm not sure if her exclamation is from shock or joy or both.

I'm smiling while I look at her beautiful, tear-stained face. She continues to smile back at me. My neck, shoulders, upper arms, and chest have fully materialized. Expectedly, she extends her hand toward me to touch my ethereal arm, hoping to feel it, but her hand passes through the filmy air. She pulls back as she feels the chill.

"Andy, what…what happened to you?" she manages to ask through her tears.

As I approach her in the bed, she instinctively pulls

back from me. Placing my hand in the air to make a calming gesture, she stops recoiling. She watches my ghostly hand as I place it on her forehead. She falls asleep immediately.

Sharing visions is the second trick I have learned from Angelus after learning how to materialize. Through carefully selected flashbacks, I share the entire story of what happened to me from the day I stepped in Antioch to the fateful day of my death. I don't share the sexy stuff… again, boundaries. When she wakes, she has many questions, and she's extremely angry with Angelus.

"I hate him for what he has done to you and to our family," she spouts in a venomous tone.

I had never heard Mary ever say that she hated anyone. I answer her myriad questions with appropriate visions, but I also warn her about Angelus and his malevolent nature. Before I leave her that morning, as my "battery" is wearing down, Mary asks me one more question.

"Should I tell your father and Jack Jr. all that I know?"

Placing my hand on her forehead, I communicate to her that I will be contacting them soon, that I had an idea about what I wanted to share with each member of our family, and that it wasn't necessarily everything I had shared with her. I kiss her on her forehead. The icy chill makes her recoil at first, but then she relaxes and enjoys the gesture. Disintegrating into the morning sunlight, I innocently wave goodbye. She waves back as she did when I was a child. I contact Dad that night and Jack the next morning.

****

I learn from reading Mary's mind, the third ghostly ability that Angelus has taught me, that my funeral service is to be held in Boston at the end of the week. Apparently, the repair work to my skull is extensive. My body is to be buried in the Griffin family plot in a famous Boston cemetery (still no name dropping... not even in death). Lazarus's service is to be held in two days, June 27, at the Bartholomew Bay Church of Christ with a burial in the Bartholomew Bay Cemetery.

Chapter 34

Antioch
June 26, 1983

On the morning of Wednesday, June 26, Mary Meade makes a special breakfast for her husband Jack Meade and her only living son, Jack Meade Jr. After they eat, they share what they have learned from the ghost of their son/brother and then cry together at the table. It is a good, joyous cry. After that morning, it does not matter to Mary, Jack, and Jack Jr. what anyone else thinks about the deceased young man Griffin Andrew Meade or the Meade family of Bartholomew Bay, Maine. They knew the truth about what had happened to me and the sacrifice I made.

Chapter 35

Bartholomew Bay Church of Christ
Lazarus Benedictine's Funeral
June 27, 1983

Journal of Mary Griffin Meade
June 27, 1983 9:00 pm
Today was the funeral of Lazarus Benedictine, a
new friend to the Meade family, especially to my late
son Andy. He was a lovely older man who lived an
amazing life. Because Lazarus did not have any natural
family we could find in the short time from his death
until today's service, we took on the responsibility for
the service and his burial. The service was held at the
Bartholomew Bay Church of Christ, the church that the
Bartholomew family built but was not attended by the
last member of the Bartholomew family, Angus.

It is a beautiful church that has been maintained
extremely well. The stained-glass windows designed by
Tiffany and Co. are exquisite, the colored glass is still
clear, the strips of lead in between the glass pieces are
not chipped, and the frame is maintaining its integrity.
The dark mahogany nautical-themed woodwork of the
pulpit, the baptismal of the vestibule, the pews, the
choir loft, the molding in the nave, sanctuary, and
narthex is intact or filled and polished with the proper
oil-based products.

Many members of the church congregation attended the service. Lazarus and his late partner, a fisherman named Zachariah Kingston, were pillars of this church community. After listening to the parishioners' eulogies and talking to the attendees, I learned that Lazarus and Zachariah were not only accepted into this church community but were revered. Lazarus was the pro-temp repairman for all the maintenance issues in the church that included electrical, plumbing, structural, fixtures and the woodwork that I commented about previously.

Lazarus's artistic ability was also spoken of highly. Many attendees bragged about his sculptures, chimes and mobiles that decorate his home, which were always a treat to see during their Christmas Open House. I was told by more than one person that Zachariah had one of the most magnificent baritone voices you would ever hear outside of Carnegie Hall. Not only was he an anchor for the choir, but he also sang baritone solos in choral compositions and solo repertoire during Advent, Christmas, and Easter services. Eulogies also mentioned that Lazarus or Zachariah would play Santa Claus for children in the congregation and for the local children receiving social services including the orphanage in Brunswick. It was heartening to see a small-town community like Bartholomew Bay embrace a same sex couple for the people they were instead of being judged based on a flawed and narrow-minded interpretation of Bible scripture.

I also talked extensively with the Gutmanns, Andy's boyfriend's parents and members of the church. It was the first time I saw Christian since my son's tragic death. He fell into my arms when I saw him, and he cried on my shoulder. I started to cry as well. I told him that I needed to talk to him after the service, but that this was the time for remembering Lazarus. He looked good even though his jaw is still wired shut and he was wearing a cervical collar from the car accident that I commented on in this journal (June 13, 1983).

Because his shoulder joint had healed well enough, he was able to pay tribute to Lazarus by playing a selection on the pipe organ, apparently one of Lazarus's favorite compositions: Johann Sebastian Bach's "Jesu O Joy of Man's Desiring." He played it masterfully. There were tears in his eyes when he finished. Andy had told me that Christian played keyboards in a local band, but I had no idea that he was that talented or that he substituted for the organist in this church.

After the service, there was a reception in the manse, which was basically a potluck dinner. I told Jack and Jack Jr. that I needed to speak with Christian alone. We spoke in one of the pews as people filed into the manse. I talked candidly about the circumstances of Andy's death, clearing up some of the rumors that had been swirling in BB. It was a difficult conversation, as I had to confirm that Andy did commit suicide. Christian began to cry when I told him this, but I informed him that it was for a noble reason, a reason that I could not elaborate, but that it involved all of us. I hugged him again as he buried his head into my shoulder.

I then told Christian that I knew that he and Andy were more than just friends, that Andy considered Christian to be his first boyfriend, his first love, and glad he had someone like him in his life before he passed away. I also revealed to Christian that I did not know Andy was gay until he told me about how much he loved Christian.

Finally, it was time for me to tell Christian what Andy had told me to tell him: that he must never go to Antioch for any reason, for his safety. Christian nodded his head as I repeated Andy's warning. I gathered Andy had said this to him before. We both wiped the tears from our eyes and finished our conversation while walking to the manse. I told Christian that even though he was not to come to Antioch, I would still like to stay in touch and have coffee or lunch occasionally. He managed to smile when I made this suggestion. Christian is a very sweet boy; he would have made a wonderful son-in-law.

End of entry 9:30 p.m.

Chapter 36

Boston
Griffin Andrew Meade's Funeral
June 28, 1983

Journal of Mary Griffin Meade
June 28, 1983—7:00 p.m.
This will be a short entry tonight, as I don't have the stamina to write. My son's funeral was today. I buried my son today. He was only 18 years old. He made the ultimate sacrifice to save his family. My heart is broken. I'm deeply saddened that his family, friends, and boyfriend will never see him again, but I'm more saddened that so many people will never get to meet the exceptional man that my Andy was.

End of entry 7:15 p.m.

Epilogue

Antioch

First, before we go any further, let's talk about the elephant in the room.

Question: Did the Meade family continue to live at Antioch? The answer: yes.

Readers are probably wondering, after all that had happened to my family and me, why they remained. It's a good question.

I can confirm that my family primarily remains for one reason: me. After I contacted the members of my family and explained the circumstances of my death, and that I would dwell in this house for presumably eternity, they made the unanimous decision to stay at Antioch to be near my soul. Once this was decided, my family continued to live their lives as normally as possible. As a result, I made some decisions myself.

I decided not to interfere with any aspect of their lives unless they requested my involvement. I also warned Angelus not to do the same unless he was requested as well. Angelus agreed. This rule would be difficult for both of us. Angelus and I can read the mind of any human being who enters Antioch. So, no matter what we learn by reading anyone's mind, we cannot interfere, whether it is beneficial or harmful, unless we are asked. All the members of my family are aware of this power, and yet, still agreed to live in Antioch. Okay, now all the serious stuff has been discussed.

My family is generally "happy," and they have enjoyed our living arrangement. Mary finished her restoration of Antioch, and according to Angelus, it looked exactly like it did when he was a boy in the early 1900s, which is the era she was recreating. Dad is still a professor in medical school, obtaining tenure on schedule, which meant he could continue to teach his courses at this institution until his desired retirement. Mary and Jack seem to be living their lives without change. Jack Jr., on the other hand, has changed significantly in one aspect of his life.

Obviously, teenage boys experience major changes both physically and mentally, and no one should be surprised to see typical changes, including exploration of sexuality. However, it did surprise me to learn that Jack Jr. began to engage in same sex activity. He became close friends with a fellow football player named Derek during his first season for the Bart's Bay Buccaneers. Friendship became more by the end of the school year, about a month after Jack's 18th birthday (Interestingly, Derek and Jack had the same birthday; so, they lost their same sex virginity at the same age).

When Jack confided to me about the sex he had with Derek, which I already knew through my ability to read his mind, he told me he thought he was bisexual, as he still felt sexually attracted to girls. He wanted me to know this as he anticipated that it might happen when he and Derek were staying in Antioch. Jack had surmised that he and Derek did not have romantic feelings for each other, but Jack Jr. appreciated Derek's body and enjoyed the sex that they had. In Jack Jr.'s words, "a guy knows what a guy likes and knows how to deliver." Essentially, they were "friends with benefits."

Jack Jr. continues to amaze me. He asked me once if I would like to possess his body while he is having sex with Derek so that I could feel the pleasure Derek could deliver. I declined but told him I appreciated the gesture. It would have been too weird.

After Jack graduated high school, he left for college, and although he came to Antioch for holidays, he did not live at Antioch during the summer. I understood that he needed to live his own life, but I missed watching my kid brother become a man. He had girlfriends and boyfriends throughout his life, but he never brought any of them to Antioch for very long, using the excuse that "Antioch made him feel uneasy." He had every right to stay away, but it hurt me not to be able to share his life.

Mary and Jack Meade stayed at Antioch for the rest of their natural lives, and each died in the house from natural causes: Mary was 87 years old; and Jack was 91 years old. I witnessed their deaths, the formation of their souls, and their ascension into the afterlife. Antioch to this day remains unoccupied, but it is still owned by the Meade-Griffin family. In Jack Meade's will it states that Antioch will never be sold but will be maintained by a caretaker, to be paid from a trust until the money expires.

Presumably, forever.

July 24, 2019. Lackawaxen, Pennsylvania.

A word about the author…

The author has a Ph.D. in Anatomical Sciences and Neuroscience and this knowledge informs his writing, a unique blend of scientific knowledge with supernatural storytelling.